W9-AHH-088

MAYHEM IN PARVA

Also by Nancy Livingston:

MAYHEM IN PARVA

by

Nancy Livingston

St. Martin's Press
New York

MAYHEM IN PARVA. Copyright © 1990 by Nancy Livingston. All rights
reserved. Printed in the United States of America. No part of this book
may be used or reproduced in any manner whatsoever without written
permission except in the case of brief quotations embodied in critical
articles or reviews. For information, address St. Martin's Press,
175 Fifth Avenue, New York, N.Y. 10010.

Library of Congress Cataloging-in-Publication Data

Livingston, Nancy.
    Mayhem in Parva / Nancy Livingston.
        p.   cm.
    ISBN 0-312-06410-1
    I. Title.
PR6062.I915M38   1991
823'.914—dc20   91-20911
                                                                         CIP

First published in Great Britain by Victor Gollancz Limited.

First U.S. Edition: September 1991
10 9 8 7 6 5 4 3 2 1

This book is dedicated to
John Baty, badger lover

Chapter One

The atmosphere in the Well-Man clinic was deteriorating fast. Mr Pringle had risen to the challenge. He'd come at the appointed hour, not with a jamjar furtively wrapped in the *Sun*, but a full-bodied sample emerging from the *Guardian*, clear and golden. The nurse assessed the quantity.

"Cold out today is it? Age?"

"Sixty-six."

"Height?"

He couldn't remember. She insisted on weighing him, too, before giving him yet another tetanus jab.

Why was it, Mr Pringle wondered, that the only form of treatment he'd been offered in the last ten years had been protection against lockjaw?

When it was his turn, the doctor refused to look up, which wasn't encouraging.

"Any bladder problems?"

"No."

"Bowels satisfactory?"

"Yes."

"Count yourself lucky. At your age. What about exercise?"

"Oh, yes." Mr Pringle gave an inward, smug smile. Too much, according to his friend, Mrs Bignell. The doctor peered over half-rims.

"What, then? Squash? Badminton? Jogging?"

"Dear me, no!" A man could damage himself doing those. There was the brisk walk to the library twice a week, Mr Pringle explained, and then there was Mavis. She had always refused to marry him, believing instead in romance. Her reasoning had proved sound and their relationship stimulating. The doctor pursed his lips and narrowed his eyes.

"I wouldn't overdo it if I were you, Mr Dingle, not with the NHS in its present state. Cardiac arrest—at sixty-six you're more likely to end up in a hospice rather than casualty. No, take my advice . . ." He was already scribbling on his prescrip-

7

tion pad. "Next time you feel the urge, take two of these. Tell the next one to come in, will you?"

"It says 'sedative' on the label," said Mavis, handing back the bottle. "He was probably jealous. All the same—"

"All the same, nothing." Mr Pringle was uncharacteristically terse. She prepared to humour him.

"And your cholesterol level was too high, they said. That sounds nasty. Same again, dear?"

"I'll have a scotch."

"On top of sherry?" Behind the bar of the Bricklayers, Mrs Bignell's auburn eyebrows rose in eloquent disapproval.

"A large one."

Her magnificent bosom lifted fractionally, the merest hint was usually sufficient. "Someone's going to have a wicked head tomorrow."

Not where he was going he wouldn't, not with all that pure country air.

"Where?" she asked when he told her. "Wuffinge Parva? Where's that?" He had a large-scale road map open in front of him and indicated the counties of East Anglia.

"It's somewhere near here unless they've moved it. The village was listed in the Domesday Book. Ah, there's a word ending in Parva under this thick blue line, see."

"That's a motorway," said Mavis. "Why are the places you want always on the join? But what do you want to go gallivanting all that way for, nearly as far as Norfolk? That's the country, that is." Mavis Bignell had firm views on the dangers of straying from London.

"Suffolk, not Norfolk. I'm going back to my roots before it's too late." Mr Pringle tossed back his whisky defiantly. "Cheers."

"Roots? You haven't got any roots. You live round the corner."

"My ancestors came from Wuffinge Parva," he said grandiloquently.

"What ancestors?" She'd deflated him.

"My granny's buried in the churchyard. Enid and I stayed with her after our house was bombed."

"We all had to make sacrifices during the blitz. That's no reason you should go visiting graves when you're feeling depressed, not in the country. It's bad for your morale as well as your cholesterol."

But Mr Pringle had had intimations of mortality. So far he had left no footprint on Time's immortal sands. Until today Time itself had appeared infinite; now he knew for a fact this wasn't so. Moreover, as a retired member of Her Majesty's Inland Revenue Inspectorate he could disappear from the surface of the planet without a single murmur of regret. Indeed, in his despondent state he could only visualize one small bouquet on his coffin: "In memory of a dear friend, Mavis Bignell."

The Japanese communed with their ancestors, so why shouldn't G. D. H. Pringle? You never knew. Something reassuring might come of it.

It wasn't an error on the map. Driving north he saw the English Heritage sign: WUFFINGE PARVA CHURCH (SAXON) ANCIENT MONUMENT pointing to the left of the motorway with no indication of an exit. Twenty miles further on there was an exit. Mr Pringle took it, rejoined and headed back south. This time the rest of the village passed by on the other side. By now his Allegro was in need of a rest and so was he.

The waitress in the Happi-Cuppa said, "You've been there before?"

"During the war, yes."

"Why not try and go the same way this time?"

Down narrow winding lanes with passing places, Mr Pringle followed his nose. He drove over a humpbacked bridge beneath which the River Wuffen meandered, round the final bend and pulled up abruptly; there in front of him was the village, spread out like a child's illustration.

He recalled with swelling breast the great man of history who passed through Wuffinge over two hundred years ago. "An ugly place," Dr Johnson had written to Boswell, "with nothing pleasing to recommend it."

"It hasn't changed," Mr Pringle murmured in deep contentment. But in that he was mistaken.

The Wuffen marked the southern boundary, separating the glebe lands from those of Wuffinge Magna. That community had crumbled following the failure of the weaving industry during the fifteenth century. Any remaining inhabitants had

9

then been evicted in favour of the sheep enclosures in the nineteenth, and by way of commemoration a vast white pumping and sewerage works had been built on the site in 1971, in the path of prevailing westerly winds.

"Whence is that goodly fragrance flow-ow-ing," the choir carolled in Wuffinge Parva church and the answer, borne on the breeze, was always the same.

For Mr Pringle, with the windows of his car firmly closed, it was enough to savour the remembered triangular shape of Wuffinge Parva green. The road he'd driven in on continued northwards along one side of it, forming the one village street. At right-angles, along an ancient path, was a line of thatched cottages, their damp foundations embedded in old water meadows, with rear gardens stretching down to the river. These were the oldest houses in the village. During the war they had been condemned as tumble-down and insanitary. All that had changed. Now, coloured washed lemon, pink and cream, as succulent as fruit drops, these were residences of a most desirable kind.

Mr Pringle gazed at them in wonder. In his day, they'd been occupied by a succession of old biddies fighting a losing battle against rheumatism, damp and dirt. Torn, filthy curtains were what he recalled; broken panes stuffed with newspaper and smelly cats. Now there were leaded casements with elegant drapery. Outside, beyond trim white fences, BMWs were parked. Shining front doors had single bay trees in pots. The cottages had lost their numbers, too. They had strange new names: Wisteria, Woodbine, Sweet-Pea and Fuchsia, and oddest of all, Macavity's Pastures. All except one.

In the middle of the row, thatch toppling from it in gobbets, was a thoroughly neglected cottage. Window frame and door were bare of paint, the dingy plaster walls were stained and the hedge had turned itself into a wilderness of privet. A row of washing hung across the front garden in deliberate defiance of the new gentility.

Something tugged at Mr Pringle's memory, some long distant unpleasant experience. He had been inside that cottage once and he hadn't enjoyed it; he was blessed if he could remember why.

The Victorians had left their mark on Wuffinge. The next leg of the triangle was a mixture of villas with the occasional

Georgian refugee cowering between. The post office was housed in one of these, a perfectly proportioned, simple red-brick house before the planners had been let loose. Now thick bullseye glass in the false bay window plus a pair of carriage lamps made a frame for advertisements for supplementary benefits and television licence stamps. A permanent sign demanded SUPPORT YOUR VILLAGE SHOP and in front, amidst formal box and yew where once they had dug for victory and planted carrots, all was now paved for convenience.

His granny's cottage had gone, he noticed. Instead, on the third side of the green, along the village street, were semi-detached council houses, built not of cow plaster with bread ovens to accommodate dried flowers but to spacious 1961 Parker Morris standards, fit for people to live in. Here the gardens were full of prams and broken bikes. Old cars denuded of wheels were perched on piles of brick. Welcome notices were nailed to the gates: BEWARE ALSATION! These houses were occupied by the few remaining natives.

There was one small development since his last visit—Reynard's Covert—a cul-de-sac (or in-filling) occupying the gap between the last of the Victorian villas and the start of the council homes. Here were miniscule executive mansions decorated outside with plastic imitation beams. Ruched petticoat blinds hung at every window, blocking out the light, and beyond each patio door, barbecues fought a losing battle with the down-draught from the M13 overhead.

For the motorway soared in a concrete arch against a blue sky, deafening Wuffinge Parva with its constant surging roar. Concealed by it, out of sight at the further end of the village, were the Jacobean manor house and Saxon church. Mr Pringle was keen to renew acquaintance with them but was distracted by country sights and sounds he'd almost forgotten.

It was the time of year when all nature's creatures obey the life force and the eternal cycle begins anew. Mr Pringle watched with delight as a black bird with stripy white feathers mated with a much smaller brown bird already on the nest. That black bird was going at it hammer and tongs, nuzzling the little bird with his beak. Mr Pringle considered offering it one of his pills. He was disturbed when the magpie flew off to see that the small brown bird appeared so very . . . well, dead. And that almost immediately, a fieldmouse should venture forth and begin sniffing at it. A very large *grey* fieldmouse, with a long, long tail.

Mr Pringle tried to smother memories predicting an increase in the rat population due to the warming of the world's ozone layer. If that wasn't a fieldmouse, it was probably a water rat from the Wuffen. Like *Wind in the Willows*, with Mole, Mr Badger and Ratty. A friendly little creature, Ratty. But this animal was already *eating* that small defenceless brown bird . . . Mr Pringle felt his gorge rise but at the same time had to acknowledge his own need for nourishment.

There had once been a pub in Wuffinge Parva, surely that hadn't disappeared? A letter from Sir Walter Scott complaining of bed-bugs was its proud claim to fame and hung in the saloon. Mr Pringle planned to stay there for a few days, preferably in a different chamber.

At the outbreak of war, together with rest of the young men in the village, he had helped excavate a communal shelter in that same pub's back yard. It had been a comfortless hostelry in those days, the bar presided over by a landlady ever eager to impart the latest disaster—surely she must be dead by now? If Hitler hadn't managed it, one or two hapless fellow drinkers had sworn to carry out the deed. Wags amongst them suggested that the new air-raid shelter offered a greater degree of hospitality than the snug.

Ah, there was the pub! He'd missed it at first glance but in the midst of the council houses, set back from the road, Mr Pringle caught sight of the old sign: the Hope & Anchor. He leaned forward eagerly to peer through the windscreen.

There was a crash which lifted his car against the brakes and pushed it off the road into a wall. Mr Pringle ricocheted back and forth, bouncing off the steering wheel. Blood spurted from a split lip. The windscreen shattered, spraying him with glass, and through it all he heard the peremptory noise of a horn. In his rear view mirror he was shocked to see a fully laden hearse embedded in his boot. A roar of indignation from the undertaker reached his dazed ears. "That's a bloody silly place to park a car!"

Black-coated strangers helped drag him out of the driving seat. They struggled to free the two vehicles, watched by passive mourners in limousines. Men whose only prospect that morning had been to bear a quarter of the weight of one human being, plus casket, perched on a shoulder for the short walk up an aisle, now heaved and panted in futile exasperation.

"We're not going to pull it free . . . We're going to be late!" The spokesman glowered at Mr Pringle, now sitting on the kerb, a bloodied hanky pressed to his lip. He was, he realized, being held responsible for delaying a paying customer on his way to eternity.

"There was no yellow line," he countered feebly.

"Bugger yellow lines, this is a blind bend, always has been."

"It's not far, Jack. If we drove it a bit further and jerked the clutch, maybe we could shake it off."

Jack eased himself back into the hearse. Another colleague, still wearing his black top hat, climbed into Mr Pringle's car. Engines revved and the strange coupling bounced forward. The one called Jack wound down the window. "As soon as we've separated it, we'll leave yours in the pub car-park, all right?" Then, "I wouldn't care . . ." he jerked his thumb at the occupant behind. "He was once a magistrate."

The strange procession disappeared up the village street and Mr Pringle was alone once more, abandoned in the land of his forefathers. For a moment or two all was silence apart from wood pigeons cooing overhead. Then he heard a door open, a cough, and a voice called, "D'you want a cup of tea?"

It came from the neglected cottage, still sporting the number eight on the gatepost. In the doorway, a woman grinned at him. She wore bedroom slippers and an apron over a transparent blouse through which he could see her dingy vest. Her hair was tousled and her teeth, revealed by the grin, were an uneven henge, twisted and yellowing. Again, there was something faintly, disagreeably familiar. Mr Pringle rose unsteadily. His lip was throbbing and he dearly wanted somewhere to shelter. As he moved toward her, he searched the recesses of his memory.

She kicked open the rickety gate. As she did so, her knicker leg peeped below her skirt. Little Elsie! It came back in a flood of embarrassment. Little Elsie who'd exhibited her knickers to those who waited behind the bicycle shed and for half-a-crown much, much more besides. Oh, God! She was leering at him.

"I know you, don't I?"

"Pringle, G. D. H," he tried to make it sound cool and distant. She gave a disconcerting cackle and pushed the warped door another inch or two.

13

"Come on in." It was black as pitch. He stepped forward and cracked his forehead on something solid. "Ouch!"

"Mind the beam."

Instinctively, he put out his hand to save himself; the wall felt slimy to the touch. Opening his eyes he saw a blackened greasy patch beneath his hand.

"Folk are always banging their heads on that beam," Elsie explained reasonably. "When they do, they reach out to stop themselves falling over. They've been doing it ever since the place was built. Didn't seem worth while cleaning up. There's always someone new putting his hand in the same spot."

For three hundred years, slatterns had said as much to those they'd lured into number eight. Three hundred years of human sweat and grease embedded in flaking plaster. To hell with Aids! Why, he'd probably pressed up against the dirt of some Elizabethan peasant who'd died of the pox!

Mr Pringle took a few faltering steps and sank on to the sofa, squeezing in between the cat and her litter. Newspapers giving details of the Festival of Britain had been shredded for the kittens. Those of even earlier date lay undisturbed on the flagstones beneath his feet. He was surprised to see mouse-droppings but the cat's eyes were milky with cataract; perhaps that accounted for it.

Little Elsie had gone through to the lean-to kitchen and was heaving vigorously at the pump. She saw him watching her. "They're all modern next door. Both sides have got taps nowadays . . ."

"Oh, yes?"

"We sticks to what nature intended. No taps, no indoor lavvy, no pollution." A stream of discoloured water filled the kettle. "This is from the same old well grandfather used. Not a trace of chemicals in it." Nothing to disturb the bacteria in fact.

"A sad day to revisit Wuffinge," said Mr Pringle, casting about for a safe subject. "Was the deceased anyone I would remember?"

There was a minor explosion as Little Elsie lit the gas. The air cleared and she shuffled across to sit in front of him, legs splayed, revealing more of her erogenous zone. Mr Pringle kept his eyes resolutely above her waist.

"Major Petrie Coombe-Hamilton." Mr Pringle remembered the ancient family line, all of them inbred and mad as March hares.

14

"Wasn't he the idiot who marched us about the green the day war was declared?"

"That's the one." According to a swift calculation the Major must have been in his mid-eighties.

"Hardly an unexpected event?"

"T'wasn't natural causes. He died," and little Elsie leaned forward to emphasize the point, "because of the badger woman. Would you like something to put on your lip?" Would the tetanus jab prove efficacious? In this house, to apply salve was surely to invite gangrene.

"A tissue, perhaps?" Little Elsie disappeared down the garden path and returned with a supply of lavatory paper.

"We don't cut up newspaper no more," she announced proudly, "not since father died." Mr Pringle could've wished it had been less pink.

"Who's the badger woman, Elsie?" The kettle was boiling and she chattered as she made the tea.

"Miranda Kenny. I hates her. Always coming round, criticizing, bossy devil. She and her husband moved into the end cottage what used to belong to old Ma Parrot and started calling it Macavity's Pastures because of their disgusting tomcat. Stupid, I call it." Little Elsie indicated her own pet, now supine on the sofa. "Look at her, poor bloody animal, he never leaves her alone. I'm always having to drown her litters. Mr Kenny works in local government and drives one of those funny little French cars but *she's* the one responsible for the motorway being on top of us. T'wasn't planned like that. It was intended to go round the other side of the church and manor, outside the village altogether."

"Much more sensible, in fact."

"But when this Mrs Kenny come along to the enquiry and says 'What about the badgers?' we all thought she must know something we didn't."

"What badgers?"

"In Four-Mile Bottom, where the old setts are." He vaguely remembered a sloping piece of common land beyond the churchyard.

"Are there any left?"

"One or two the farmers hadn't managed to poison. But Mrs Kenny got a whole lot of people down from London, important people who talked about badgers. Then the BBC come. We were on the television."

Mr Pringle commiserated.

"Trouble was," little Elsie handed him his cup, "Mrs Kenny really didn't know anything at all. She thought by bossing everyone and make them sign petitions she was going to stop the motorway being built. She said even if it was, because of the fuss, they'd have to move it miles further on, only they didn't. They avoided the setts by building it right over the village instead. It shifted the badgers, though. Soon as the pile-drivers began, off they scarpered. The farmers was ever so pleased."

"I'm surprised Mrs Kenny didn't go after that."

"She said it was her duty to remain in order to protect the frogs." He stared. "Where they dug the foundations for the motorway was between some frogs and their breeding pond. Mrs Kenny got them to make a special little concrete under-pass. The kids try and block it up so she goes patrolling every day to see the frogs get through. It was the final straw for the Major."

"Was he fond of frogs?"

"Couldn't give a monkeys . . . No, he'd got high blood pressure and he lost his temper with her that night in the pub, that's what did for him. Heart attack. You'd hardly know the village nowadays. Dagger drawn because of that woman. Those who've been here all their lives claim she's trying to take over. But the newcomers say she's eco-logi-cally minded." Elsie pronounced it carefully.

"Ye-es." The lower the level of tea, sinister cracks were revealed inside his cup, deeply ingrained. "Whose side are you on?"

"I agree with Eddie," Elsie said firmly, "I think Mrs Kenny should be hit on the head with an 'ammer. He's willing to do it. He thought highly of the Major." Eddie? Another vague memory crystallized.

"That's your brother?"

"That's right. I've only got the one. He's got ever such a good job in Milton Keynes but he comes home every weekend. Last Sat'day, when he was in the Hope & Anchor, there was another row because of the flower festival." Mr Pringle confessed ignorance of the event. Little Elsie looked at him in surprise. "I thought that's why you must've come, because of the festival? It's been advertised. Don't you read the newspapers? We're raising money for the church. It's over a thousand years old and it needs rethatching."

He bought a bottle of disinfectant at the Georgian post office cum shop and retired to the Hope & Anchor to cleanse his wounds. In the car-park, his Allegro awaited surgery.

The pub-owner was sympathetic. "I won't charge more than a tenner a day till you get it fixed. Knew Major Petrie Coombe-Hamilton did you?"

"Briefly, before the war."

"Quite a character," the pub-owner knew how to steer a middle course through warring village factions. "The salt of the earth, in an old-fashioned sort of way. We were surprised when he dropped down dead like that. Here one minute, gone the next."

"I understand some sort of argument . . . ?"

"That happened every week. A regular exercise as far as the Major was concerned. He used to come in here, order a beer, pick a quarrel, make the other fella buy him a whisky by way of apology and then go home. Never failed. I used to enjoy watching him, like a fisherman landing a trout."

There was a large notice concerning the forthcoming flower festival. With war-time memories predominant, Mr Pringle suggested the event might prove to be a Good Thing and encourage the village to pull together. "Who knows, perhaps the festival will heal past differences?" The landlord smirked.

"I don't know about that but it's going to be good for business. It'll put Wuffinge Parva on the map. It's Tuesday, only three days to go and we've already got forty-two booked in for Saturday lunch. We're expecting several coach parties, in fact. The BBC hinted they might come back, especially when they heard about the wall-paintings. We've got to raise at least twenty thousand pounds because of them."

"How much?"

"Exactly. It's not just the church roof you see, it's paying for the restoration. It needed experts. The vicar organized it but those sort of people cost a lot of money. Nobody blames him because as Mrs Kenny said, the village could be on to a winner. The English Tourist Board are thinking of recommending us because of those pictures." Seeing his blank look, the landlord explained, "Maybe you don't remember the stories about the

17

church and the medieval wall-paintings underneath the old plaster."

"As I recall," another strand of memory returned, "they weren't medieval. They were much earlier. The first pictures in any church. Lord Wuffa's paintings, according to the legend, although it might have been fanciful. One tale claimed the building itself was originally a hall used by the Wuffinga tribe."

"Yes, I've been told all that," the landlord wasn't interested in history, "but the latest rumour confirms that they could be the earliest Christian paintings. The First Pictures is how they're being referred to now." Mr Pringle felt excitement well up inside.

"So they really do exist?"

"Definitely."

Those stories handed down from one generation to the next for over a thousand years. The interior of the church was decorated with paintings, his granny had told him, but priests decided they were a distraction and in the tenth century had had the walls replastered. From that day to this, no one could be sure what the paintings were, or indeed if they had survived.

What a treasure trove! Mr Pringle was elated. "I can't wait to see them."

"You'll have to, for a bit, like the rest of us. Screens went up as soon as the restoration began. That was because the work was so tricky. No one, but no one has had a peep since. And the two restorers have been staying at the vicarage so we couldn't ask them questions. None of us knows what to expect on Friday, not even Mrs Kenny and she's responsible for the fund raising."

"What time on Friday?"

"There's a grand opening to the public at half past two." He sighed, "That's been my only complaint. I wanted them to wait till closing time but Mrs Kenny was adamant. She says that way we'll be on the early television news and boost the crowds on Saturday and Sunday. The media are interested because there are experts coming from all over the world to verify them."

"I'm not surprised. Such early pictures must be unique. And just fancy, my own granny told me about them." He was full of pride. Perhaps his roots went right back and some Pringle ancestor would be revealed on the church wall! The landlord wiped away an imaginary splash.

"Everyone's granny had *heard* of them, but no one really knows if they were there or what they were like."

"Whose was the idea of combining the paintings with a flower festival?"

"Mrs Kenny," he said promptly, "which really caused a split. People were angry with her in the beginning because of the motorway but when she started talking about putting Wuffinge Parva on the map, that's when the younger ones started coming round. She's put a bit of sparkle into the place. The school was in danger of closure because of falling attendance, but Mrs Kenny organized the petition for Reynard's Covert to be built. That brought in young couples and now there are plenty of kids. Then when the vicar said he knew people who might restore the paintings and all it needed was cash, as well as for the new roof, Mrs Kenny went into action again. She said we must think big with plenty of attractions. As soon as she suggested a flower festival, the whole thing started to snowball."

"You don't think badly of the lady?"

"No I don't. This village was in danger of stagnating but she's livened it up a lot. There's even talk of a supermarket being built. Of course it's the older folk who don't like it, the ones who came here to retire; they think she's an upstart. But the younger ones think she's great."

"Yes," sighed Mr Pringle.

"If custom continues to improve, I'm seriously thinking of a Saturday night disco."

"How . . . enterprising."

"It all depends on the festival. Mrs Kenny's got the whole community involved. The WI are responsible for decorating the church with flowers. They've got a special dispensation to pick wild ones. Everything will be in keeping with the spirit of the paintings, you see. How things used to be when Wuffinge Parva first began. There's even going to be a Green Man on duty the whole weekend as well as the scouts and guides, to show the visitors round."

"Green Men are pagan, part of a spring fertility rite!" The pub-owner shrugged.

"Live and let live, that's what I say, especially if it's good for business. There's going to be a marquee on the green. That goes up tomorrow, Wednesday. Old English crafts as well as flowers. Corn dollies and copper bangles, you know the sort of thing."

Mr Pringle tried to recall if a single old biddy living down by the Wuffen had ever made a corn dolly in her life. None sprang to mind. One thing was certain; his visit to Wuffinge Parva wouldn't extend beyond Friday lunchtime. One quick glimpse of the paintings then back to London, he didn't relish being part of the massed hoards. He indicated his empty glass, suggested the landlord might like one himself and asked if there were any sandwiches.

"Thank you kindly, half of bitter for me. We do bar-snacks in here or you can have a proper meal in the Bunker."

"Pardon?"

"Out the back." Mr Pringle followed him to a window and stared at the fruit of his former labours. There was the old air-raid shelter, a gun emplacement on the roof and a camouflaged jeep containing sound equipment parked beside the entrance. With the window open he could hear the effects tape: first a siren, then a squadron being mobilized amid the distant firing of ack-ack guns. The landlord was expansive. "Really popular that is, especially with the yuppies. Would you like to see the menu?"

Brown Windsor soup, read Mr Pringle, a choice of Spam or Snoek with mushy peas and boiled potatoes, tapioca or junket to follow. £14.75 inc. Camp coffee essence. No coupons! The landlord waited.

"Most people ask me what Snoek is," he said eventually. But Mr Pringle already knew. His granny used to apologize each time the horrid oily fish appeared on the dining table.

"I'll have a roast beef sandwich with plenty of horseradish," he said firmly.

After lunch and a long phone conversation with one Gavin, who specialized in repairing wrecks, Mr Pringle set out for the other end of the village. He walked past a group of mothers waiting outside the revitalized school and continued on under the motorway. It was an odd sensation to stand and listen to powerful forces overhead. Down below rabbits bounded out of sight into the hedgerow. Flopsy and Mopsy on their way to visit Mrs Tiggywinkle, he thought sentimentally. To add to his delight, a moorhen gathered up her brood and dashed recklessly across the road in front of him.

This was still the narrow Lovers' Lane of his youth, thickly overgrown. Fifty years ago it had been the place where young conscripts brought their girls to demand eternal fidelity before leaving for overseas. Several centuries before that, other young men had asked for similar assurances before departing on crusades. One of them, Mr Pringle remembered, lay in eternal repose inside the church, his pet dog at his feet. And over there, it came back to him now, behind that very hedge, he'd once seen little Elsie lead Alf, the butcher's boy. Later he'd heard the squabble when Alf demanded a refund of his half-crown. Was that when Elsie's spell over them had finally been broken?

A pole bearing the notice: ECOLOGY FIRST! FROGS HAVE RIGHTS was propped up against a concrete pillar. On the back of it was an old SDP poster. There was no one about. The badger lady was presumably off duty.

Round the next curve he came across the war memorial set in a trim plot and beyond it, forming a semi-circle, three entrances.

In the centre, the lych gate led through to the churchyard. To the left of this, ornate wrought iron plus a gatehouse laden with security cameras protected the Jacobean manor hidden at the end of a drive of lime trees.

The manor had always been empty, not a house handed on from father to son. The first owner—a member of the nouveau riche during the reign of James I—had been forced to sell to meet his builder's costs which had escalated out of control. Afterwards the house had become bank collateral for three hundred years until the trustees finally relented and sold it to a minor Saudi royal family. They spent one night in it before decamping to a service flat near Harrods; the manor house had thus reverted to its normal uninhabited state.

The last of the three entrances, that leading to the vicarage, had a battered five-bar gate, permanently ajar. To this was tacked another poster for the flower festival.

The morning's accident was beginning to take its toll; Mr Pringle's neck was stiff and sore. It seemed prudent to find somewhere to sit. He entered the lych-gate and stared, memories of Sunday school flooding back.

The church was small, oblong, half hidden beneath the overhang of a heavy thatched roof, now in much need of repair. At the eastern end was the modern extension: a Norman apse.

Thick walls were clunch built, buff-coloured chalk, mottled with variegated grey and black flints. The building squatted, almost sulkily; a church which kept itself to itself rather than presenting a bold front, thought Mr Pringle whimsically.

The graveyard was small but the sexton had managed to accommodate the Major next to the tombs of his ancestors. On top of freshly turned earth were decorous floral tributes. The last of the Petrie Coombe-Hamilton line, according to little Elsie, apart from his unmarried daughter.

What had the Major achieved during his fourscore years and six? In the autumn of 1939 he'd made plenty of young men miserable. Mr Pringle remembered the square-bashing on the village green, the Major having taken it into his head to assume extraordinary military powers.

Granny Pringle's plot, when he remembered where it was, was overgrown. Mr Pringle dearly wanted to pull up the brambles but his back hurt too much. Another day he would return and do the job properly.

Inside the porch, he twisted the heavy iron handle. He put his shoulder to the thick oak door and shoved. It was locked. Frustrated, he sat down to wait.

The landlord had assured him the church would be open all afternoon. "The preparations start in earnest today. The WI women are due to set out the tables and vases, that kind of thing."

Mr Pringle guessed they wouldn't be long. He needed a rest before beginning the walk back. Despite the noise from the motorway he could hear bees humming, he would just close his eyes a minute or two.

He jerked awake and immediately regretted it. Sore muscles sent out a warning message, he sat very still. A noise came from beyond the porch, low down. A rasping and scraping of wood. Hidden by the porch Mr Pringle gazed out and saw the leper window set very low in the church wall, only a few feet above the ground. Closed since the sixteenth century, it was on the move! Someone was attempting to re-open it from the inside.

He saw the shape of a hand behind the thick rough glass. Simultaneously a Volvo pulled up beside the war memorial and disgorged a group of jolly ladies who began dashing about and unloading equipment. Immediately the window was pulled shut and the hand disappeared.

22

Mr Pringle rose to his feet as the first of the ladies detached herself from the group. She walked toward him determinedly, sunlight glinting on her glasses, a naturally bossy woman who was probably the mainstay of Wuffinge Parva Women's Institute. "Oh, good," she cried, accepting his presence without question, "another helper. All hands to the pump! There're six trestles to be brought in first, if you wouldn't mind." Obediently, Mr Pringle went to go to her car but he heard a bolt slide back and the church door finally opened.

The vicar stood there. At least he assumed it was a vicar. A tall man, who'd shed his cassock for a thick sailing jersey and battered-looking trousers. He appeared young because he was fair, but as he moved into the daylight, Mr Pringle judged him to be nearer fifty.

"I hope we haven't kept you waiting, vicar?" the organizing woman demanded. She would have been affronted had he said yes. Fortunately he shook his head.

"Not at all, Mrs Leveret. I'm in a bit of quandary, though. I took down one of the screens. I broke the rules but my sins have found me out. I can't get the confounded thing back up. It's too heavy."

"You mean you haven't seen the paintings before?" Mrs Leveret was obviously surprised. "We all assumed you've been watching the work throughout." He shook his head.

"I was strict with myself until today. I'm glad, too. Instead of being revealed piecemeal, it's been an absolute revelation, but I really must lift the screen back in place again."

"Can I help?" The vicar looked at Mr Pringle doubtfully. "You don't live in Wuffinge, do you?"

"I used to, years ago." The man was obviously torn.

"I need to be able to rely on your discretion. The rules of the festival committee are strict; no one to be allowed to see the paintings before two thirty on Friday afternoon."

"I shall not speak; my lips are sealed."

"You too, Mrs Leveret?"

"Naturally." She looked annoyed.

"Very well, then. Thanks." They followed him into the church. Back at the Volvo the other ladies continued to unload.

"I think you'll both agree," the vicar was saying, "just the one painting is stupendous. On Friday, when we see all of them and get the full effect, I'm sure we'll be even more delighted.

23

But on its own, this one is certainly remarkable. Oh, do mind the steps!"

In the nick of time, Mr Pringle remembered. This ancient building was at a lower level than the rest of the village. Four shallow blocks of stone, each with a deep depression in the centre due to centuries of shuffling feet, led to the floor of the church. Mr Pringle descended and looked about; it was just as he remembered.

Declared a "simple gem" in the guide books, it had the plainest interior of any religious building he'd ever visited. Not more than thirty foot long, divided equally by the nave, the construction of the thick walls could be clearly seen, with more glossy flints embedded in the plaster. A row of niches had been hewn at shoulder height to contain lamps. Latterly these had been fitted with electric lights but the circular iron candle-holder still hung from the central beam.

There were five windows. All had plain glass, so thick it was nearly opaque. Not a single piece of ornamentation marred the simple interior. The young crusader and his dog slept close to the wall up at the front, beneath the modest pulpit.

In the Norman apse a brass cross and candlesticks decorated the altar and a gold-embroidered cloth hung from the lectern, but these didn't detract from the simplicity.

Oak pews had been pushed to one side following the Major's funeral service, to allow for the entry of the festival ladies. Mr Pringle inhaled the musty smell of past centuries that had been disturbed. He looked up at the heavy wooden spandrils. In other churches these had been decorated; here they were plain with only the marks of the adze for a pattern.

A pair of wooden angels he didn't remember now hung above the arched entrance to the apse. This was at a higher level and there were three stone steps up to it. Below, low on the right-hand wall was the leper window.

Mr Pringle remembered the mysterious disembodied hand—hadn't it worn a ring? The vicar's fingers were bare. He now waited impatiently, supporting one end of a heavy wooden screen. Mr Pringle hurried to catch a glimpse of the forbidden fruit before helping cover it up again.

The panel was the one nearest the pulpit. Mrs Leveret, the flower organizer, also waited to see his reaction. Mr Pringle gave it, plain and simple, "Goodness me!" He was utterly astonished.

Protected by a sheet of Perspex, a medieval Adam and Eve stared round-eyed at a writhing serpent in an apple tree above. All about them, a bright primitive Eden was reminiscent of Suffolk with fields and hedgerows, trees and animals. Wild boar and woolly, horned cattle, rabbits and chickens, all of equal stature filled every square inch while in a corner, peering out from behind a wattle hut, a scarlet devil with a flat round face, spat his contempt. Mr Pringle became more fascinated with every detail. "I say, what a marvellous picture!" The vicar tried to subdue his own excitement.

"You think so?"

"I most certainly do. And what wonderful restoration, such vivid colours. Hardly any fading . . . and even here, where the plaster shows through, there's a clear translucence . . . Oh, such detail! Are the others as good?"

"I really have no idea," the vicar shrugged, palms upwards. "As for the fresh appearance, that's because elements in the limestone protected the pigments all these years, apparently. The chief restorer, Robert, assures me two are as good but this is the only one I've seen. Now, if you wouldn't mind giving me a hand."

Mr Pringle found the screen extremely heavy. It was also designed to fit snugly, excluding the daylight. A perfect security device, in fact.

Mrs Leveret said slowly, "I don't know much about art, but it's a very *lively* picture."

"More so even than a Brueghel," Mr Pringle was enthusiastic. "It seems like sacrilege, covering it up again."

"That will be their fate for most of the year, I'm afraid. I'm advised that sunlight will cause them to fade extremely quickly. The artist used very primitive materials, especially when executing the two over on that wall." The vicar indicated two screens on either side of the leper window. "I understand those are in a very poor state. Osmosis and salt penetration. It's doubtful whether we can even reveal them on Friday. They'll certainly have to be protected from photographic lights. They're under smoked glass which makes it even more difficult."

"It's our duty to protect them for the benefit of future generations," Mrs Leveret announced.

"Yes, indeed." But the vicar laughed boyishly. "I must say, now I've seen one, I'm looking forward to Friday enormously."

"So am I," said Mr Pringle, "I couldn't possibly return to London before I've seen the rest."

"You hinted at a connection with Wuffinge?"

"More than a connection, I think," Mrs Leveret stared at Mr Pringle. "I'm fairly sure this gentleman used to live in the village with his grandmother during the war." She addressed him directly. "One of De'ath's men recognized you this morning. You're the Pringle boy, aren't you? Your granny had a cottage where the council houses are now. I was in your sister Enid's class at school."

Boy! He could have hugged her.

"How is Enid?"

"Oh, er, well, I believe. We've . . . lost touch." Especially after Mr Pringle had brought Enid's son Matthew to justice for murder. "You know how it is," he finished lamely.

"What brings you to Wuffinge now?" she demanded. "You're a bit early for the festival."

"It certainly wasn't to bid Major Petrie Coombe-Hamilton farewell."

"No," she frowned, "they said you'd caused an accident."

"I've come back to my roots."

"Roots?" The vicar was curious. Mr Pringle gestured extravagantly at the paintings.

"My grandmother and great-grandmother are in the churchyard. There may be others, who knows? Perhaps one of my ancestors acted as a model for one of the figures." Mrs Leveret sniffed.

"I'm sure my family didn't. They were naked in that picture. I'm Doris, by the way, Doris Leveret by marriage. Remember me to Enid next time you're in contact. And now, we'd better make a start."

He followed her dutifully. If she was roughly Enid's age, that meant five or six years younger than himself. But she looked older, he thought cheerfully; fatter, too. Broad in the beam, narrow in the mind, with sensible expensive clothes. In his day there hadn't been any wealthy people in Wuffinge, which probably explained why Doris Leveret was so bossy. She was also a bully.

"The trestle supports first, Mr Pringle. Then the tops. One of my ladies will give you a hand, then Ruby can polish them. We can't begin our display until all eight tables are ready."

At four o'clock the vicar returned with a Thermos and

26

biscuits and announced a break. Mr Pringle sank into a pew. Sweat made his shirt damp and sticky. His arms felt loose in their sockets. He longed for a hot bath to ease the aches and pains. Even so he was able to watch with amusement the strict hierarchy applied to the simple tea ceremony.

By virtue of occupying the best remaining example of Georgian architecture, Doris Leveret was given a cup and saucer. Two thatched-cottage-owners came next, Lorna and Felicity, who merited mugs. Following them came breathless plump Joyce from a Victorian villa, Michelle and Tracey, young housewives from Reynard's Covert; lastly and definitely least in everyone's eyes came Ruby from the council house. She was only offered a plastic cup.

The ladies were kind to Ruby, Doris Leveret excessively so. It was perhaps inevitable that she should be the only one to take sugar and defend herself by saying, "Got to keep out the cold." Why was it, Mr Pringle wondered sadly, that women with enough blubber to see them through an arctic winter were always the ones to take too much sugar? Someone was speaking to him. He blinked.

"I beg your pardon?" It was Michelle.

"I wondered if you'd come across any old acquaintances in Wuffinge?"

"Only little Elsie. From number eight."

He'd dropped a clanger this time. The group froze in a burst of togetherness, their disapproval crackling like hoar frost. Mr Pringle could have sworn the vicar smothered a grin but it was Doris Leveret who picked up the challenge, through pursed lips.

"And how did you first come to know her, Mr Pringle?"

"At school, I think. I can't quite remember. However, this morning after my accident, she very kindly invited me in and gave me tea." He'd said the wrong thing again. They'd obviously all heard of little Elsie's habits.

"Invite you in? Yes," Doris Leveret said pointedly, "Elsie would."

They might be in the House of God but so far no one had managed a charitable word for one poor sinner. Mr Pringle decided to be hung for a sheep as a lamb.

"Wasn't she in your class, Mrs Leveret?"

"I went to the grammar school in Ely after I'd passed the scholarship, I've scarcely seen the woman since." Not in fifty

27

years. Perhaps, like himself, Mrs Leveret had moved away from the area.

He suggested gently, "If I was mistaken maybe Elsie was in your brother's class?"

Ruby laughed. "If she was, he'll probably deny it as well. Plenty do nowadays. Poor old Elsie, she can't help the way she's made, eh vicar?" Fortunately there was a diversion. Another woman stalked into the church and stood, arms akimbo. Mr Pringle didn't need anyone to tell him this must be Miranda Kenny. Woolly Aztec hat, sweater, mittens and jeans, she was attractive even if her hair was cut no-nonsense short and she sported granny spectacles.

As she entered, he became aware of another subtle change. There had been condescension toward Ruby, scorn over little Elsie but this time it was stronger: hostility. It emanated from Mrs Leveret. Other women watched the pair silently. If Miranda Kenny was aware, she gave no sign. Presumably because she had other matters on her mind. She addressed the vicar.

"There's been a massacre, Reg. Children using skate-boards. I need to dig a communal grave."

"Down by the hedge, Mrs Kenny, if you would," he replied. "The verger mowed the grass this morning and we want to keep everything shipshape for the festival."

"Thanks." Miranda Kenny spun round on her Hunters and exited. Tension evaporated.

"A massacre!" Tracey giggled. "Fancy talking about frogs like that." But Mr Pringle was impressed: who in London would be so caring for the environment? Talk about it, perhaps, but actually to protect such horrible moist-skinned amphibians . . .

"You've got to admit Miranda does have a point about ecology," Joyce Parsons pointed out. "If she didn't, I doubt if there'd be a single tadpole left in Wuffinge, never mind a colony."

"She's a pain in the arse," declared Ruby, "I hope she gets trampled to death by the damn things." As for Doris Leveret, she said nothing at all.

Chapter Two

The landlord explained the distance between bathroom and bedroom with more resentment than regret.

"It's always the same in these old places . . . We can't cut into that beam to fit a water tank because that's what's supporting the roof and the whole damn place would fall down. As it is, it can be quite exciting in your room if there's a wind. Take no notice of the dust, only a bit of woodworm, but my advice would be to keep the window shut. And it's not difficult to remember the way. Out of your room, turn right. Down the passage, mind the step and the sharp turn at the far end, turn right again, through the fire door—we leave the red light switched on all night, no expense spared—down three steps, along another passage and it's the second door on the right at the end. Not the first. That's a bedroom let to a honeymoon couple, unless I'm mistaken. I haven't even seen the wife yet, my barman signed them in and they won't want you blundering in during the night, ha-ha. Anyway, you can't miss it."

Mr Pringle hoped fervently that he couldn't.

"If only we'd been able to sink another earth pipe at this end of the building, we could've demanded a second star from the AA. As it is, I can only charge you £24.25 plus VAT. Full English Breakfast, £6.75, Continental £3.99. Sinful, isn't it?" Mr Pringle agreed that it was. He wondered if anyone in Wuffinge offered more modest accommodation. He'd make cautious enquiries tomorrow. His car had been towed away; it would be imprudent to offend mine host. The village was twenty miles from the nearest railway station and the only bus operated on a twice-weekly basis.

Despite the advice, Mr Pringle opened the casement and leaned out to enjoy the view. His room was at the front overlooking the green. He felt gratification at the knowledge his granny would have been delighted had she known he could afford to stay here, albeit briefly.

Next week however, all that would change. "Once the festival puts Wuffinge on the map, I can't promise to hold down

29

my prices," the landlord had warned. Mr Pringle had understood. In one way, he didn't mind; it would help concentrate his thoughts on whether he really wanted to move back to Wuffinge Parva, permanently. Today was Tuesday; by Friday he would have made up his mind.

Dusk was falling but he could still make out the charming roof and chimneys of houses opposite, on either side of the post office. He now knew that Doris Leveret lived two doors further along in the house with an eighteenth-century garden. A row of elegant standard roses led up to the delightfully proportioned front door. Ruby had whispered that old man Leveret had done well. Mr Pringle could see that he had. He wondered idly whether he should mention his former occupation as a member of the Inland Revenue? In the past, he'd occasionally enjoyed seeing strong men turn pale. Perhaps not. Especially if he planned to settle here.

Which had been the house of Doris Leveret's childhood, he wondered? She might remember him but he couldn't say the same about her. Girls, especially those in Enid's class, had been out of bounds. "You stick at your homework," his granny had insisted, "plenty of time for that sort of thing later," and being obedient, Mr Pringle had.

He was mildly interested in the tussle between Doris Leveret and Miranda Kenny, to become leader of Wuffinge Parva society; if he'd been a betting man, his money would be on the latter, he decided. Hers was a more steely personality.

He turned his back on social mores and gazed instead at the row of thatched cottages, coming to life as lights were switched on. At Macavity's Pastures, Mrs Kenny had genuine oil lamps, naturally. From his window, he could see her fight to control a smoking wick. In her living-room an ecologically acceptable wood burner blazed. Others were less scrupulous. A few doors along, at number eight, a bare bulb glowed and beneath it, in front of an electric fire, little Elsie sat watching television.

A lorry arrived on the green and men began unloading canvas, scaffolding and ropes. Yesterday, after the Well-Man clinic, Mr Pringle had felt extraordinarily depressed. Today, back where he belonged, it had taken only a little time for life to perk up. Even the simplest things pleased him. Fancy being excited at the prospect of a flower festival and craft fayre! Mavis would scoff. He sighed. Could he ever persuade the sophisticated Mrs Bignell to share the simple life? It was most unlikely. Which would mean Mr Pringle becoming one of those commuters he'd heard about, unable to afford season tickets as he fought his way through frustrated crowds to meet his beloved, courtesy of British Rail. He might end up needing those tranquillisers after all.

Down below the lorry drove away. Mr Pringle waited patiently for the next piece of excitement. A man appeared, walking his Rottweilers along the pavement in front of the pub forecourt. Both dogs with regular habits, he noticed. Their owner had a flat round face reminiscent of the devil in the wall-painting. As Mr Pringle wondered with increasing excitement if the man were indeed descended from the original, he leaned over the white chain-link fencing and spat a mouthful of phlegm on to the forecourt. On his face was the same expression of contempt—obviously there was a connection.

Mr Pringle inhaled a final lungful of nitrate-laden country air before closing the window. He shut out the sound of Dame Vera serenading diners in the Bunker. He wanted an early night. Tomorrow he was taking the first tentative step; he was going to view a house.

When Mr Pringle hinted to the WI ladies that he might be looking for a suitable property, Joyce Parsons had revealed her occupation: she was a sales person for the local estate agent and it just so happened there was one house remaining in Reynard's Covert. The show house, in fact. The group had become very excited. As a widower, Mr Pringle learned, he would be an extremely valuable member of society, and a former Wuffinge Parvian to boot, what could be more appropriate?

They'd promised him membership in the over-sixties, threatened him with the Conservative garden party and sold him a book of raffle tickets for the flower festival. Mr Pringle hoped he could avoid winning third prize: 5 cwt of compost. He had an uneasy notion of what Mrs Bignell's reaction might be if he returned to London with that. Banishing all such worries, Mr Pringle seized his towel and set off into the hinterland in search of a bath. Tomorrow morning at ten a.m. precisely, was his first appointment to view!

A short distance from Macavity's Pastures, Oliver Kenny pulled up in his 2CV and contemplated both his wife and his future. It had become a habit lately, a way of putting off the inevitable, for Oliver had come to loathe his existence. To be seen by the neighbours in this French joke of a car was to feel emasculated. He'd only bought the damn thing because Miranda had declared it ecologically viable. As he brooded he felt the familiar hatred building up inside.

There had been too many times when he'd given in over the years. He'd gone to university a robust, beer-drinking, rugby-playing Englishman and emerged in thrall to a domineering vegetarian who practised what she preached.

At first Oliver told himself none of it mattered because Miranda and he adored one another. But the end result now was an uncomfortable house, a poncy car and a disagreeable job to enable them to live in this village!

And now that dear wife of his was up to something. He hadn't been able to prove it yet but he was suspicious all right. One of the villagers had even hinted at it. Protecting frogs half the night! Only a fool would be deceived by that tale. He'd follow Miranda, it was the only way to discover the truth for himself.

He turned the key and drove the remaining distance to his front gate. Blast! Elsie Runkle was leaning over the gate of number eight. Oliver bounded down the path and slammed his front door. In his sensitive mood, he imagined he could hear her sniggering.

Very early on Wednesday morning a ground mist rose up from the Wuffen and covered the land. Through it, the old vixen made her way in a curve across the landscape. The tom from Macavity's Pastures spotted her. Fur bristled but the vixen was contemptuous of cats. She kept her distance nonetheless, pausing every so often to smell the air, every sense alert. She had an objective; she'd been there before and knew what she might find. Today she'd brought her two cubs, to train them in the ways of survival, as always using man as her benefactor.

The vixen had been brought up by her dam to raid hen-houses but those were a thing of the past. What mattered was learning to adapt. In Wuffinge, older villagers had gradually given up keeping chickens and newcomers preferred theirs freshly plucked from the supermarket. This no longer worried the vixen for she'd discovered a poultry supply. She gave a brief, sharp bark. Her young appeared noiselessly out of the mist. Padding close behind, they too began to circle the green.

In Reynard's Covert, Michelle was in a temper. Yesterday's brief encounter with Miranda Kenny in the church had upset her. Michelle had been reduced to assisting Doris Leveret; this caused great chagrin. Michelle wanted to be Miranda's lieutenant but hadn't been asked. It was so humiliating! And yesterday, not even a greeting. Michelle flounced about the kitchen in her sprigged apron.

Of course she didn't really *like* Miranda Kenny. In many ways, she detested her; in fact, Michelle had already determined that she and Gerry would beat the Kennys at their own game. Then she too would be able to patronize; that would put her on an equal footing with her dearest friend.

Last night Michelle had lain awake, re-enacting the scene in the church, coming out with spontaneous witty remarks so devastating, Miranda Kenny could only gasp. If only she'd thought of them at the time! But she'd never have had the courage to say them. It was always the same; other people were clever, Michelle Brazier was ordinary.

The thought drained her small self-confidence. Ambition had brought Michelle and Gerry to Reynard's Covert. Michelle had been so proud of her brand new home. She studied magazines and decorated every room within an inch of its life but then she'd met Mrs Kenny.

When she first accepted an invitation to tea, Michelle had been ecstatic. Mrs Kenny supported causes and read the *Independent*, she was Someone Who Mattered. Michelle set out her best embroidered tablecloth but as soon as Mrs Kenny spotted the label, she'd given Michelle a lecture on sweated labour in Taiwan.

They'd toured the house. At first Miranda Kenny appeared to marvel. As each door was opened, Michelle heard her say: "Amazing!" and preened. All those pretty pink frills, the pink carpet with roses, the daring purple in the bathroom to contrast with the avocado suite, it had all been worth it if Mrs Kenny was impressed.

But once downstairs, Miranda Kenny sank cross-legged on the sculptured, wall to wall, lounge/diner propylene, and enlightened her. It was nothing but *ersatz*.

Not knowing what this meant, Michelle smiled gratefully. It was only when the mobile library called and she learned the dreadful truth that she was mortified: Mrs Kenny actually despised her home!

Happiness disappeared. Overnight Michelle changed from a contented young wife into a termagant. She would show Mrs Kenny. How dare she patronize! Ignoring Gerry's protests, foam-filled comfort was jettisoned in favour of second-hand pine. Bunches of herbs hung in a row to conceal her now despised imitation marble-topped kitchen units. The next step was to sell up and buy a ruin. Highest scoring of all would be a barn; they would be socially impregnable once they lived in one of those.

Michelle gritted her teeth at the thought of the back-breaking work which lay ahead but there was no defying convention. If they were to beat the Kennys, a derelict barn it had to be. She'd already found one. For some reason it was full of farm machinery but no doubt the farmer could be persuaded to store his tractors elsewhere.

She hurried outside and put down the bowl of dogfood. Normally the small spaniel bounded out to greet her but this morning he remained inside. Hardly surprising with the vixen and her cubs watching unwaveringly from behind the toolshed.

The dog gave a terrified whimper but his mistress ignored him. Back at the sink she heard first a snarl then an agonized cry. Looking out, for the first time in her life, Michelle saw three real, live foxes. She immediately behaved as any other housewife in the Covert would have done: she began to scream.

The vixen wasn't fazed, a scream didn't hurt. There was still time for her sharp-eyed cubs to learn another lesson. They now knew that chicken meat was available, deliciously cooked and served on a dish. Now their mother stood on hindlegs to reach into the dustbin and demonstrated ripping open a plastic bag to gulp the contents. Having absorbed this, the cubs and their mother padded away under the motorway into the concealment of a copse.

The screams sounded near at hand: Mr Pringle found them disturbing. Was someone being murdered? But Joyce was working on commission so couldn't hear. "Because of our royal neighbours in Norfolk, we've named our houses to complement," she explained with a professional smile. "The semi-d's are either Sandringhams or Windsors, depending on whether or not they have a personalized ornamental cherry. This," she paused, "is the Balmoral." She waited expectantly. "So?

34

What's your first impression?" They were standing in a pencil-thin tube.

"Can we go inside?"

"We are inside, Mr Pringle. We came in through the garage, which I'm using as a temporary office. That's the front door on your left which leads out on to the driveway. This is the hall."

"Is it?" His house in London had a hall. It was a largeish area where people could move about, with a hallstand for coats. That reminded him he was too warm: the central heating must be going flat out. Perhaps he should remove his mac. "May I . . . ?"

"You can put that in the cloakroom. Through there." Joyce opened a door. It was a tiny room with one hook and yellow sanitary ware. "Sun King," she murmured.

"And a urinal," Mr Pringle said in surprise.

"That is a finger basin. It is a standard fitment in all our cloakrooms. Shall we proceed to the kitchen?"

How had he managed to live so long without a microwave? Joyce talked triumphantly of fan-assisted and halogen, of washing cycles and rpm, even an instant freeze button, but all the while Mr Pringle was wondering where he could put his galoshes.

"And through here, we have the lounge/diner."

"With a staircase?"

"That rises to the first floor." Well it would, wouldn't it, he thought a mite peevishly. Staircases seldom went anywhere else.

"Why is the dining table tucked under the stairwell?"

"For convenience," Joyce's tone was a shade more tight. "It can thus remain out of sight until it is required."

"Could you show me?" Joyce consulted her watch but Mr Pringle wouldn't be deterred. "When you want to eat, I suppose you have to pull it out—"

"Careful!" The round table had been carefully set with candles, silver, crystal and linen. Mr Pringle eased it from its concealment.

"Now if we set the chairs in position." They were the folding variety. He pushed the fourth in place and stood back. "Oh, now you can't get out to go to the kitchen."

"Your hostess would naturally sit over here with her back to the open door," Joyce demonstrated. "All she would then have to do is rise, and slip outside." But Mavis Bignell's hips were

35

generous to a fault, he adored wrapping himself round them, and that doorway was narrow. Full of doubt, Mr Pringle surveyed the lounge end.

"Why is the furniture in here so small?"

"Compact. For convenience. After all, you don't want to spend your life dusting and hoovering, do you?" Five minutes with a carpet sweeper would be more than sufficient in his estimation. And to open the french windows would mean moving the sofa each time. She saw the direction of his glance. "You've spotted the barbecue on the patio? That comes as part of the Balmoral package; with the Windsors or Sandringhams, it's an extra."

Why was there a piece of knitting on the armchair? It worried Mr Pringle because it was grubby and had obviously been there a long, long time.

He stared up at the ceiling in search of distraction; that looked as if a budgie had paddled bird lime all over it.

"Artexed," Joyce explained. His own was smooth with a nice big plaster rose in the centre.

He followed her up the shallow stairs. At the top, she produced her *pièce de résistance*. "The en-suite," she said simply.

"The what?"

"Off the master bedroom, naturally." Mr Pringle saw with dismay a tiled broom cupboard containing a lavatory barely three foot from the head of the double bed and separated from it by an arch with a folding plastic door. He and Mavis had once come across such an arrangement in a French hotel. Thrice during the night he'd had to pay a visit and she had leapt panic-stricken from her pillow at the sound of rushing water so close at hand. "Whisper Pink," Joyce confided, "and the family bathroom is in Libido Blue."

"Where's that?" If it was as far away as the one in the Hope & Anchor . . . ? But then no bathroom could be. She enumerated its finer points.

"As well as the pulsating shower we are also offering a jacuzzi and exercise bike this month." She assessed his potential and suggested kindly, "You could have a fireproof door through to the garage if you prefer, that's another of our alternatives."

They sat side by intimate side on the little sofa to drink the coffee that had been percolating throughout his visit. He couldn't drag his eyes from the ball of wool with the knitting needles protruding from it. "What's that doing there?"

"It's a Homely Touch. We have one in every room."

"I must've missed the rest." Joyce Parsons listed them.

"The plastic loaf in the kitchen. We used to have wholemeal but it kept going mouldy. The tennis racquet in the teenager's bedroom—you tripped over that."

"So I did."

"The floral shower cap and negligee—"

"I remembered those. I didn't realize what they were."

"And the cutout of the customized Ford Fiesta in the garage."

"Ah . . ."

"So what do you think?" He knew he was going to be a disappointment. He considered the upwardly mobile young man for whom this dwelling was intended, his slim-hipped wife and—of necessity—their two stunted children.

"I'm afraid I might not be able to adapt myself to the concept of the Balmoral," Mr Pringle replied; it was amazing how quickly one picked up the jargon. "I'm rather set in my ways. Do you have anything a little less fashionable perhaps?"

She didn't scold. To his surprise she immediately produced a handful of brochures. Half of Wuffinge Parva was up for sale, apparently. Top of the pile was a photograph he recognized. "Isn't that the Petrie Coombe-Hamilton house?"

"That's right. D'you know it?"

"I remember it from when I used to live here. I've never been inside."

Joyce's professional exterior slipped. "Do me a favour, go and have a look. None of the rest of us have seen inside, either. The Major never socialized, neither does his daughter. We're dying to know what it's like." Which wasn't surprising, Mr Pringle reflected. The Major had always considered himself a cut above Wuffinge Parvians, unwilling to mix with social inferiors.

"His daughter put the house on the market the day he died."

"She didn't waste much time!"

"That's what we all thought." Joyce was checking phone numbers. "I'll make an appointment for you now, shall I?"

"It's far too big a place for me," he protested.

"Just go and view," she begged. "Come back and tell us

about it. We'll be at the church. We're putting up the background greenery today."

Miss Petrie Coombe-Hamilton was at home and could spare a quarter of an hour.

"Be warned," Joyce said cheerfully, "she's difficult. If she doesn't like the look of you, she'll probably send you round to the tradesmen's entrance." Mr Pringle set off, brochure in hand.

On the green, a strong breeze was flapping the canvas of the marquee. Men were straining at the ropes. Issuing unnecessary orders in a penetrating voice, was Miranda Kenny.

"Good morning." Slightly startled, Mr Pringle raised his hat. It was one of Doris Leveret's WI ladies, from the thatched cottages. Joan? Felicity? She saved his embarrassment. "We met yesterday. I'm Felicity Brown."

"Of course. Good morning." She, too, had paused to watch Miranda Kenny.

"Doesn't that woman make you want to cringe! In her element, of course, bossing everyone around. The marquee is her department, Doris has the church. The vicar kept 'em apart, sensible man, otherwise there might have been civil war."

"Mrs Kenny seems to work very hard on the village's behalf."

"Huh!" Felicity snorted. "On her own account, you mean. She terrifies the weaker sort. Always flashing her degree and her so-called erudition. They're stupid enough to think her opinions gospel and follow like sheep."

"Whereas you . . . ?" he enquired.

Felicity laughed. "I can't stand either Miranda or Doris, to be honest. Ted and I go our own sweet way and try to avoid the arguments. How did you get on with Joyce and . . . the Balmoral?" Mrs Brown was big, and shiny and as wholesome as an apple, with an infectious laugh.

"It was a most . . . interesting house," Mr Pringle answered cautiously then, responding to her warmth, "you know, I haven't looked at any since Renée and I first chose ours, oh, must be over thirty years ago."

"Somehow I didn't think the estate—which is how we refer to Reynard's Covert—would be your cup of tea. Fit only for pygmies, in my opinion. So, where are you off to next?"

"The Petrie Coombe-Hamilton residence," he admitted bashfully.

38

"My, oh, my!"

"I know it's far too grand," Mr Pringle said hurriedly, "I really shouldn't be taking up the lady's time."

"I bet Joyce put you up to it, so that you can tell the rest of us about it?"

"Yes, she did."

"Mind you come straight round to the church. Here, you wouldn't fancy eating with Ted and me this evening? Take pot luck?"

"That's very kind."

"No it isn't. I'm on ivy detail this morning, I'll probably miss your description and I'm as curious as the rest. You can tell Ted and me all about it this evening. Sevenish, OK?"

"Perfect, thank you." She waved her secateurs.

"Bye."

He walked back over the humpbacked bridge and struck out another quarter of a mile. The For Sale notice confirmed he'd arrived. That and a large TRESPASSERS WILL BE DEALT WITH fastened to the Public Footpath sign pointing up the drive. Mr Pringle wondered uneasily if it were mined.

With the manor house permanently unoccupied, the Petrie Coombe-Hamilton family had stepped into the squirearchical breech. Their home was an old farmhouse resting comfortably on its foundations until the Major's grandfather had set about restoring it during the 1930s. Now a flat-roofed conservatory ran along the length of the southern flank and an inappropriate aluminium porch protected the front door.

Miss Petrie Coombe-Hamilton was already waiting. A brisk woman in her early sixties, wearing an ancient quilted weskit and headscarf, with an inherited attitude toward lower ranks.

"I've been clearing out old papers. Kindly carry those down to the gate before we start, would you. The binmen are due today."

"I'm afraid I can't." Each black plastic bag must weigh a ton and there were at least a dozen. The Major had already injured his neck, he'd no intention of allowing the daughter to break his back. "Perhaps one of your staff . . . ?"

"Staff! Where have you been for the last fifty years? Come back from abroad?"

"No. London." Mr Pringle followed sensible shoes at the end

of thick legs up the front steps and into a proper hall. "I've recently retired."

"What brings you to Wuffinge Parva?"

"I used to live here years ago." She peered more closely. "Oh, yes, you're the man who spoiled Daddy's funeral. Enid Pringle's brother."

"Were you in Enid's class at school by any chance?"

"Good lord, no. I had a governess. Mummy used to let Enid come up here and play. She was the right sort." Mr Pringle was unable to express any gratification on behalf of his sister. He maintained an aloof silence. "We'll start with the attics," Miss Petrie Coombe-Hamilton announced. "Did the agent mention the roof?"

"The brochure states . . ." he referred to it, "the roof is in need of attention." She gave an abrupt braying laugh.

"It's a bit more than that. One more flight. Come along, don't fall behind." It was steep, suitable only for servants. At the top she flung open the first attic door. Nesting pigeons squawked angrily at being disturbed. Mr Pringle observed the route of their fluttering exit, through long-established holes in the tiles.

"Daddy simply shut off the whole floor. Last year the estimate for repairing the roof was twenty thou and his weak heart nearly gave way. But he rallied," she sighed. "I had to stick it out another eight months. Have you got twenty thou?"

"I have not," Mr Pringle was utterly sincere.

"You'll have to shut the attics off as well then."

As she led the way through a series of ice-cold bedrooms on the first floor, he realized he'd been remiss.

"May I offer my condolences—"

"Please don't. Daddy was simply frightful to live with. This is his room. I'm so *thankful* he's gone." Mr Pringle found such honesty disconcerting.

It was a meticulously tidy chamber apart from gaping drawers, the contents of which, he guessed, must be in those black plastic bags downstairs.

"Have you had time to make any plans?"

"Oh, *yes!* I'm buying a mobile home near Beccles. Such a dear little place. It'll be small, clean—and *warm.*" Miss Petrie Coombe-Hamilton was enthusiastic as she opened another door. "This is my room, d'you see." It was large with badly warped sash windows and warmed by an inadequate paraffin

40

stove. She recollected she was trying to sell the property. "It's quite pretty though, isn't it. My mother chose the wallpaper before the war." The design was palely discernable beneath five decades of neglect.

"I think I ought to make it clear that your charming house is a little too large for my requirements," Mr Pringle began but she'd got the bit between her teeth.

"Do let me show you the rest of it. It'll be practice for when the right person turns up."

He followed her through a dining-room large enough to accommodate the entire Balmoral, en suite et al, through morning- and sitting-rooms, study, dairy, butler's pantry, still room and kitchen. Apart from the study, the house spoke eloquently of neglect. On the Major's desk an attempt had been made to sort business papers. On the arm of his easy chair beside the fireplace, a book lay open, just as its owner had left it. Mr Pringle leafed absently through pictures of rodents and small mammals.

"I have been told your late father died as the result of a quarrel," he ventured. The daughter shrugged.

"Something like that. He'd been to the pub to con a few drinks from someone and he certainly started to row with the Kenny female. No one remembers the details, it wasn't that important. Daddy was probably drunk by then. It didn't take much. Anyway he left the pub and everyone thought he'd gone home."

"But he hadn't?"

"No. They found him in the lane under the motorway the following morning. D'you want to see the verandah? It's where he kept his sports things but I'm afraid the roof leaks in there as well."

The Major had, over the years, played cricket, croquet, golf and bowls. The smell of decaying wood was unpleasant. His daughter surveyed the mess. "I shall be so thankful to send all this to the tip. The police brought Daddy back here, of course. I'd just come down to make breakfast when they arrived."

"How very distressing."

"Not really," Miss Petrie Coombe-Hamilton was frank. "I was a bit surprised, naturally, because I thought he was still asleep upstairs." Mr Pringle decided his curiosity was unlikely to cause her further sorrow.

"Did there have to be . . . Was there an inquest?"

"Oh, *no*. It was natural causes. Blood pressure and temper had brought on a heart attack. The doctor had been expecting him to go for years and frankly, I'd been praying for it. It was a shame he was out there all night, of course, but the rats hadn't had a nibble, thank God."

"Rats!"

"Oh, *yes*. This village is infested, didn't anyone tell you?"

Not dear old Ratty but real live horrible creatures, the sort that carried plague-infected fleas in their fur. As he left, Mr Pringle was tempted to tuck his trouser legs into his socks. He made his way back, keeping to the centre of the road and stepping carefully over a newly flattened hedgehog.

The marquee now buzzed with activity. Craft-workers were arriving to put up their stands and Miranda Kenny had taken command of a megaphone.

He was tired and his neck was beginning to ache once more. Nor were the ladies waiting for him at the church, as promised. He hadn't noticed it was lunchtime.

The indefatigable Mrs Leveret was there however, apparently brow-beating the vicar. "You must listen to what I say—"

"I'm sure there's very little risk . . . Ah, Pringle . . ." The interruption was obviously welcome. "Back from your house-hunting? How did it go?" But Mr Pringle was staring at the two solid lines of trestle tables.

"Won't those prevent visitors getting close to the paintings."

Mrs Leveret was officious. "That's the whole idea. You didn't think we would risk anyone *touching* them, did you? They're far too fragile."

"But I thought . . . The sheets of Perspex . . ." At this, the vicar shook his head.

"I'm afraid not. Have you any idea of the desecration that happens every day in churches that are left unlocked? The vandalism? We must guard these treasures. . ."

"We must," Doris Leveret interrupted emphatically. "These could be the oldest Christian paintings in existence."

"It's a marvellous thought." It made Mr Pringle happy.

"Provided the experts can confirm . . ." murmured the vicar. Mrs Leveret rounded on him.

"I've been told they are due here on Sunday? Has that been checked? What arrangements have been made?"

"I'm collecting them from the station. They'll examine the pictures after the evening service, please don't concern yourself," but she was shaking her head at the mess of boughs and ivy that littered the floor of the church.

"There's still so much to be done—"

"You cut along, Mrs Leveret," the vicar asserted himself. "It's time you had your lunch. You need a break, the other ladies will be back in less than an hour."

Mr Pringle watched, amused, as despite her reluctance, the vicar shooed the woman outside. When he returned, he let out a long, slow breath.

"Whew!"

"A little of Mrs Leveret can go a long way, I fancy."

"It can! Mustn't criticize, though. The church can't afford to offend tireless workers."

"Once the paintings are authenticated, perhaps financial stringency will be a thing of the past."

"D'you think so?" he asked guardedly.

"The glimpse I had . . . I thought looked delightful. I have a small collection myself, nothing so antique, but paintings are a hobby of mine."

"And in your opinion . . . ?" Without the careworn expression, the vicar's enthusiasm was almost boyish.

"In my opinion, and speaking as a complete amateur, I think Lord Wuffa has done the village proud." The vicar laughed.

"He has, bless him. Thanks, thanks very much indeed."

Mr Pringle's head ached as he made his way towards the Browns' cottage that evening. All afternoon, Mrs Kenny's voice had boomed in the marquee beyond his bedroom window. Joyce had telephoned to offer further appointments but he had declined. He needed to marshal his thoughts. Did he really want to leave familiar surroundings in London, shabby though they might be, in exchange for the virtually unknown Wuffinge Parva of 1990?

At considerable expense he'd armed himself with a contribution towards the evening's frivolity. The landlord's ideas of off-licence were lordly. "You'll find that red one has a lovely bouquet, cheap at half the price." His customer remained unconvinced.

He knocked at the Browns' front door. "Hello, there. Glad to see you again. Come on in." Ted Brown, rotund and jolly like his wife, was vaguely familiar. "Make yourself at home. Good God!" He'd seen the bottle. "You didn't pay greedy Syd's prices?"

"I'm without transport at present."

"Ah, yes. The Major's funeral. I heard you'd livened things up. Well done. The rest of us couldn't stand the fella. Sit ye down, we've got something to show you." He and Felicity were bursting with excitement and Ted flourished the album almost before Mr Pringle was in his chair. "How's that?"

It was an old school photograph. It was *his* old school photograph!

"You don't recognize me, do you, Pringle? You were three years ahead of me."

"Good heavens! Of course. E. L. Brown, form 3AX. You weren't *Ted* then though, you were Edward."

"And you were—"

"We think we've found you," Felicity chipped in. "In fact we know we have. Middle of the second row from the back, isn't that right?" Mr Pringle gazed at youthful anxious eyes behind steel spectacles, baggy knee length shorts and short mousy hair.

"Yes, that's me . . . Without the moustache, of course. Well, well, well."

"And this is me." Ted's chubby finger pointed to a sylph nearer the front.

"You should be ashamed," his wife scolded.

"Shouldn't I just? What'll you have, Pringle?"

"A sherry, if I may." He wasn't driving, he didn't need to be abstemious tonight.

Several sherries later they had relived their schooldays, mused over those who had lost out in life's lottery and expressed incredulity over those who'd won. Now they'd arrived at the present. "So, Wuffinge Parva revisited—how does it strike you?"

"A hotbed of intrigue." Mr Pringle was solemn. "Daggers drawn across the green. Factions. Social conflict. A body under the motorway. Goodness knows what the morrow will bring."

"If you're talking of conflict, you must be referring to Miranda Kenny. Funny how she affects everyone the same way."

"The younger ones think she's marvellous," Felicity protested. "Look how that stupid creature Michelle imitates her,

44

always quoting her opinions. Everything was 'ersatz' for a week or two. She'll try and sell you her house, by the way."

"Oh?"

"It's one of the semis on the new estate—"

"A Windsor, I believe," Ted grinned.

"She wants to trade it in for an old barn. I've warned her. That nice Gerry of hers will get fed-up and leave her high and dry. He doesn't want to spend the next five years of his life renovating a *ruin*." Mr Pringle thought he must have misheard.

"A barn? Is she about to become some kind of hippy?" Felicity smiled tolerantly.

"Have a peanut. Hippies went out with the sixties. Nowadays barn conversions are the in-thing."

"Are they really? I think . . ." he found his glass being refilled yet again. "Most hospitable, thank you. I think barns are better left to owls." He'd never been so funny. Ted Brown roared his appreciation.

"Come and eat," Felicity ordered, "before you two fall off your perches."

Over the soup, Ted returned to his theme. "The Kennys behave like typical newcomers. Now they're installed, everyone else has to fall into line with their opinions. First it was the idiotic Save the Badger campaign which misfired. Then it was Save Our Village School—"

"Which worked," Felicity pointed out, "thanks to Miranda's tireless efforts."

"Well, yes, and I agree it's good for the village to see new blood arriving. But they're always threatening Elsie and Eddie with preservation orders and that's absolutely futile. *They're* perfectly happy the way they are."

"Eddie has a solution to the problem of Mrs Kenny though." Mr Pringle told him what it was.

"Never mind an 'eavy 'ammer, I'm surprised he hasn't taken his shotgun to the woman. He's been patrolling at night for months, trying to shoot the old vixen."

"Little Elsie and Eddie must be among the oldest inhabitants." Ted thought about it.

"They're not that old but they've never moved away. Quite a few of the original families are still around. They've stayed while the rest of us have come and gone. We've been here, how long?"

"About eight years," Felicity set fresh plates in front of them.

"I must say, as an outsider, I like Wuffinge. And although we fondly imagine the village stays the same, there have been plenty of changes. The names you'd recognize though, are the De'aths and Runkles."

"Ah, yes."

"You met Elsie's cousin this morning, Ruby."

"I did, yes."

"They're both Runkles, of course," said Ted. "Among the newcomers, there's greedy Syd. He took over at the Hope & Anchor shortly after we came. Then the new vicar arrived. The village maidens had high hopes, there aren't many eligible bachelors around. So far though, he's resisted their blandishments."

"I'm not sure if he is available," Felicity said slowly. "When he first came there was talk of an estranged wife."

"The Kennys arrived fairly recently. It just feels as if they've been here for years. Miranda has been remarkably active in a short time."

"Because she doesn't go out to work," Felicity pointed out. "She told me Oliver insisted she should devote herself to good causes and leave the paltry business of earning money to him."

"A veritable altruist," murmured Mr Pringle.

"No, a determined female," Ted grinned. "Anyway, the Leverets came before the Kennys."

"Of course. I was forgetting."

"Mrs Leveret has the advantage," Mr Pringle confessed. "She remembers me but I'm afraid I can't return the compliment."

"Doris Winkle," Ted said promptly. "Snotty nosed. Mass of brothers and sisters. All of 'em lived in that one-up, one-down at the end of the street beyond the coal merchants."

"Doris Winkle! Good gracious me." Felicity laughed at his amazement.

"I've only known Doris since she returned with her wealthy old husband Cyril, who must be eighty if he's a day. There was no hint then of what her past had been."

"Doris is on that school photograph . . ." Despite her protests, Ted left the table to fetch it. "Here we are," he propped it against the vegetable dish. "Doris Winkle, her brother Fred, that's another of the tribe—can't remember his name. All of them have disappeared, she's the only one to come back." Mr Pringle angled the picture under the light. The narrow, tough little face stared at him belligerently.

"What a difference!" He forgot his manners. "She's so much fatter!"

"Comes of being comfortably off," Felicity laughed. "And living in that wonderful house. Can I tempt you to another helping?"

"Thank you, no," he replied hastily, "but it really was delicious." She continued to clear while Ted poured more wine.

"Doris Winkle went to train as a nurse," he said, concentrating. "She'd won a scholarship but gossip was her parents couldn't afford to send her."

"She gave me the impression she'd actually attended the grammar school." Ted shook his head.

"That's not as I recall it. Mind you, it is a long time ago. When she moved back—a very different woman from the one who'd left—she mentioned a first husband who'd 'passed away' and that when she'd met old Leveret it was quote 'a whirlwind romance' unquote. We all assumed he'd forgotten to clean his glasses—"

"Ted! Doris was—is—a marvellous hostess. He still entertained when they first came. Big cars came up from London for the weekend; she was in her element, caterers hired in, servants."

"Then it all went quiet," said Ted. "Some of us wondered if old Leveret had lost his money in the stock market crash."

"Surely it happened earlier than that?" Felicity was uncertain. "Before the Kennys arrived? But I'm sure Doris still believed her own position unassailable even after the advent of Miranda. The Major was unofficial squire of Wuffinge, Doris was lady bountiful, telling people what was best for them. Then everything changed. Sometimes the wrangles between them were so bitter, the Major had to act as arbiter."

"Not the vicar?"

"He prefers a quiet life. This wall-painting business surprised everyone, he's never bestirred himself so much before."

"Be fair, Flick," Ted protested, "there hasn't been the need to raise so much money before. When rumours began that the pictures really were unique, he was keen as the rest. He backed Miranda's idea of the craft fayre."

"Ye-es. Doris's role has certainly shrunk. The trouble is,

with the Major gone, there's no one to sort things out any more."

"Tell you what," Ted said with the air of a man who's just had a great idea, "why don't we open your bottle, old man?"

They were mellow by the time coffee came. Felicity demanded a description of the Petrie Coombe-Hamilton residence and Mr Pringle obliged, though discreetly. She nodded she'd understood.

"It doesn't surprise me. We always thought they must be living there on a shoe-string. The Major was the sort who would send a handsome contribution to the Conservatives and forget to pay the electricity bill. No wonder Guinevere is thankful he's dead."

"Guinevere?"

"Miss Petrie Coombe-Hamilton." Oh dear, oh dear, thought Mr Pringle. "The Major took it as a personal affront when the vicar and Doris started raising money for the church."

"Why?" he asked, surprised.

"He thought it was the moral responsibility of the village to keep the roof in good repair, not expect outsiders to contribute. He was against exhibiting the wall-paintings. He used to turn up during the restoration work and attempt to interfere, I believe. The vicar had to warn him off."

"What I can't quite understand is why on the night of his death, the Major should turn left instead of right when he left the Hope & Anchor," said Mr Pringle. "He must have done so to be found dead under the motorway."

"We all assumed he'd gone off to stamp on Mrs Kenny's bloody frogs," replied Ted. "He'd had a shouting match with her earlier."

"Do frogs hop about at night?" His hosts were uncertain.

"Perhaps he wanted to get hold of her pole and break it over his knee," Ted suggested, "'nother brandy?"

"Thank you but I really must be getting back. I suppose the count-down begins in earnest tomorrow?" He tried not to wobble. Those tumblers of Ted's were larger than he realized.

"Don't!" Felicity groaned, "I'm due to join the wildflower pickers at dawn. We're being supervised by some expert to make sure we don't damage the environment, and we're raiding every garden in Wuffinge to make the church look nice. At times like these though, I wish I'd never volunteered."

"I shall go and view another house," Mr Pringle decided, "it'll keep me out of the way of Doris and her constant need for helpers."

"Here . . ." They were already in the porch and Ted was nudging him. "Did you ever . . ." He winked heavily and jerked his head in the direction of number eight. "You know . . ."

"Did I what?"

"Pay your half-crown."

"Don't you dare answer that! Just 'cause this one was once a silly old fool."

"I wasn't old in those days, Flick. Anyway . . ." Ted glanced again at little Elsie's cottage. "Alf was right. It wasn't worth it."

"My pocket money was a florin," Mr Pringle said primly, "below the going rate."

"Hmph," said Ted but nothing more was vouchsafed him. Mr Pringle had had a lovely evening, he told his hostess emphatically and surprised himself by kissing her goodnight. Felicity Brown didn't object.

He was so happy, he decided to take a short cut across the green. He must remember to watch out for the marquee! Mr Pringle giggled at the idea. How could anyone miss a tent as big as that. But the further he went, the darker it became. He'd forgotten just how dark the country could be without a single street light.

The Hope & Anchor beckoned. Greedy Syd had put the Christmas lights back up in honour of the festival. These flickered like a lighthouse, enticing him on to the rocks. Judging himself clear of the marquee Mr Pringle swerved to alter course. He must be careful not to trip over the guy ropes. He suddenly remembered Eddie Runkle was on patrol somewhere in the darkness, carrying a gun.

Instinctively, Mr Pringle began a quavering carefree song, to warn everyone of his presence. Then he imagined he heard bats squeaking, and stopped. He'd certainly heard a shriek close at hand, a cry of absolute terror. Mr Pringle froze. Out of the darkness a shape streaked past, bearing something in its jaws. One of the foxcubs, already tired of his bland tinned diet was carrying Flopsy, Mopsy—it could've been Bobtail—back to his lair.

Chapter Three

It was his own fault. He woke with a thumping headache and no possibility of returning to sleep. His mouth was unpleasantly dry. The nearest source of water was out of his room, turn right, continue down the passage to the end, etc, etc. Pulling his dressing-gown close, Mr Pringle set off in a savage mood. Caring nothing for the susceptibilities of honeymooners, he ran the tap until the temperature was icy and splashed himself to try and cool his brains.

Back in his room, he opened the window and stared at the dark landscape. There was a thin moon but nothing stirred. Not a single light showed throughout Wuffinge Parva. On this, the final day before the flower festival, everyone was conserving their energy.

Mr Pringle had a puritanical need to exorcize his debauchery. He would go for a walk—there was just about sufficient daylight, it was increasing all the time. Provided he stuck to the road, there wouldn't be any danger. He would walk off his hangover and return cleansed and refreshed for a further hour in bed.

Guests at the Hope & Anchor were not permitted a front door key. He would have to leave the door on the latch—in this village it was safe enough. He borrowed a walking stick from the landlord's collection in the hallstand and set off in the silvery silence.

His own footsteps made him nervous at first, everything was so still. The night-time creatures had returned to their habitats, the dawn chorus had yet to begin, he was the only creature abroad. That thought cut through the alcoholic fug and enchanted him, making him walk more softly. "Four o'clock and all's well," he whispered to himself. As he walked out of the village he thought he heard a distant car engine. From the motorway, he decided. Always something nowadays to spoil the peace.

Across the humpbacked bridge, keeping to the verge, he arrived at the late Major's residence. The house was still in darkness. Miss Petrie Coombe-Hamilton must be dreaming of her Camelot at Beccles. Mr Pringle tramped a further half-mile before retracing his steps and setting out to complete the triangle of the green.

He walked along the path that bordered the thatched cottages listening to the chuckling of the Wuffen beyond, past number eight, past the Browns, then the Kennys at the end. All of a sudden, the old name for the houses came to him: Beggar's Row. That's what his granny had called them. Nothing less than Wuffen River Walk nowadays, he noticed. He must remember to jog Ted's memory when he rang to thank them.

He was at the angle where the path turned, widened into a proper road and continued on past the villas and post office. Outside the Leveret house, he paused to admire the symmetry of the eighteenth-century garden and the graceful tracery of the fanlight above the door.

The birds had begun now. From tree to tree, they called a greeting to the sun. There was enough light for him to walk back across the green instead of via Reynard's Covert and the street. The marquee looked most attractive now that the decorative awning was in position, pearly pink and white stripes. Mr Pringle stopped to admire that as he drew near.

A slight movement, a piece of canvas flapping lazily caught his eye. According to Felicity security guards were due this morning once the various craft stalls were dressed. Last night, with only empty stands, the entrances had simply been lashed shut. Mr Pringle had once been a scout and knew about knots. If one had come loose it would be a pleasure as well as a good deed to secure the rope.

He peered inside. It was amazing how high the bell-shaped dome appeared to be. What a quantity of stalls too, rising in tiers. Miranda Kenny had done her work well, something here for everybody. Mr Pringle read the signs: PATCHWORK QUILTS AND HAND-KNITTED ARAN SWEATERS; DRIED FLOWER ARRANGE-MENTS; EMBROIDER YOUR OWN SAMPLER; YOUR HOUSE SIGN IN POKERWORK; TAROT READING. My goodness, all this expertise in Wuffinge. It had been dull at jumble sales when he was a lad; nothing but knitted dishcloths, home-made marmalade and white elephant stalls.

He took one further step inside and peered round the stands to his left. There was a person lying face down on the grass.

She was extraordinarily still, as motionless as the inanimate objects surrounding her. Why didn't she get up?

Suddenly Mr Pringle couldn't breathe. He shivered. His heart was pounding and his glasses misted up as he stumbled towards her and sank to his knees.

"Hello . . . ?"

One eye was as glazed and dull as the small brown bird's had been after the magpie had done his worst. Mr Pringle reached out a shaking finger and gave a tentative prod—her clothes were soaking wet! "Hello? Wake up, please!"

She was wearing a woolly Aztec hat but not her glasses. Her face was squashed against the turf as if someone had shoved her hard. He pulled at her jacket and suddenly she rolled over on to her back.

A thin wailing noise emerged from Mr Pringle's throat, there was no doubting the situation now. He staggered to his feet and rushed outside, heading back towards the pub. It was almost dawn yet he was still the only person in sight. "Help!" cried Mr Pringle. Behind drawn curtains if anyone else was awake they gave no sign of it.

The front door wouldn't budge at first. For a moment he thought he'd locked himself out but it was only his fumbling. Once inside, he remembered there was a pay phone in the public bar but when he reached in his pocket for 10p he realized he'd left all his loose change in his room. Up the stairs—he didn't care how much noise he made this time—at the half-landing he came to his senses: you didn't need money for this sort of call. Back down again, heart still pounding, he slipped and took the final three steps in a rush, landing heavily. Was it still 999 or had they changed the code? He was so agitated he misdialled the first time.

"Emergency, which service do you require?"

"Police."

"Here, what d'you think you're doing!" Greedy Syd, his trousers pulled on over pyjamas, appeared from the door behind his bar. "What on earth's going on? Are you drunk?"

Not any more, thought Mr Pringle. He was terse.

"There's a woman out there in the marquee. She's dead." He didn't identify her but couldn't have said why. Syd crossed the floor rapidly.

"You had a bang on the head?"

"Certainly not—hush. Hello? Is that the police—"

"Listen . . ." Syd's reaction was instantaneous, "we don't want them coming down here—"

"Be quiet!" He was authoritative. Syd listened open-mouthed as Mr Pringle identified first himself, then the location. He described his find discreetly, as a middle-aged woman exhibiting no sign of life. Panic was almost under control now and he understood what he was being asked to do. "I'll wait outside the marquee, shall I? To prevent anyone else going in." He didn't want to have to gaze again on those empty sightless eyes.

The police would be there in a matter of minutes, he was assured.

Mr Pringle put back the receiver and felt his energy draining out through his toes. "I have to go outside again," he said trying to control the quaver, "when I come back, I'd like hot coffee."

"Can't do breakfast before seven a.m.—"

"Hot coffee," Mr Pringle repeated, suddenly loud. "A large pot and none of that instant stuff, d'you hear."

Dawn had melted into daylight as the sun rose higher. From where he stood on guard, he watched the village come to life. People were appearing everywhere now, driving off to work. All save one inhabitant who would never draw breath again.

The police car had a flashing blue light but no siren, for which he was thankful. He felt so shaky, any noise might have been too much. He flailed his arms unnecessarily. "Over here," Mr Pringle mouthed, unaware no sound was coming out. The white car drove on to the green and pulled up within inches of him. "She's inside," he gabbled as soon as the first policeman emerged. "I saw the flap open and went to fasten it, I didn't see her lying there at first—"

"All right, sir, thank you. We'll take a look. Just stay by the car, if you would." The two disappeared into the tent and Mr Pringle waited.

Disembodied voices spoke to one another over the open radio channel. He wanted to switch it off, it was too much to cope with on top of what he'd seen. The first officer re-emerged and stood there, holding open the flap.

"Excuse me, sir."

"Yes." Mr Pringle went forward reluctantly.

"Would you mind coming into the tent." He put out both hands.

"Oh, I don't think I could . . . really, I'd much rather not."

"It won't take a moment, sir," the officer insisted. Mr Pringle forced himself to enter. "If you could just show us precisely where you saw the body, sir?"

"But she's round here . . ." He stopped. He was already pointing but the patch of ground was empty. His feet were uncoordinated as he stumbled forward. "She was lying here, her head at this end, her feet nearest the bench. Her clothes were soaking wet. Ah!" He was kneeling in the same place before, scrabbling on the grass in front of him. "Here . . . feel for yourself," he begged. "You can see how wet it is. She was lying face down, not moving. I touched her . . . but she was quite definitely dead." The officer was stern.

"It's a very serious offence, bringing us out on a hoax call—"

"But I didn't!" Mr Pringle was back on his feet, grabbing the policeman's sleeve. He tugged him toward the opening, indicating one of the houses opposite. "She and her husband live over there, the one with the ornamental gateposts. Go and knock at the door—she won't be in, he'll tell you. God knows what happened here . . ." He looked round wildly, helplessly. How could a dead body levitate itself and disappear? "But when I came inside—just as it was getting light—minutes before I telephoned you in fact, she was lying there and she was dead. For some reason she was wearing Mrs Kenny's hat but her name is Doris Leveret." Doris Winkle that was, he remembered.

After questioning him further, they told him to go back to the pub and wait. Syd, fully dressed now, was goggling for information. "Well?"

"I'd like a full English breakfast as well as coffee." With hot food in his belly perhaps his ageing body would cease to shake.

"Ah, now that could be a problem." There was a need to husband supplies for the ravenous teams of media personnel due today, all of them on expenses ready to pay any price you cared to name for a bacon sandwich. "I wouldn't if I were you. We can't guarantee the eggs round here are salmonella free, you see."

"Perhaps just bacon, sausage and mushroom?" The landlord

looked to right and left to make sure they weren't being overheard.

"I get my bacon locally. Well, you have to, don't you, in my position. Now I'm not saying he doesn't do a proper job, curing the carcasses—" .

"How about rolls and coffee?"

"No problem."

When he returned, Syd hovered in vain. Mr Pringle refused to answer a single question. Eventually, in a huff, he withdrew to the bar and began restocking the shelves.

Mr Pringle sensed rather than heard the police officer approach. He looked up to find the man blocking out the light.

"May I join you?"

"Please." Syd had reappeared. "Perhaps you'd like . . . ?"

"Tea would be very nice, ta." The landlord went reluctantly to the kitchen. The officer leaned forward, folded arms resting on the table. "Well, sir, we did as you suggested. Went across and knocked up the elderly gent. He wasn't best pleased. Still in bed. He and his wife have separate rooms because she's always been an early riser. All he could tell us was that Mrs Leveret had a dawn appointment together with some other ladies and a flower expert, and they would be out all day gathering specimens for the church. Mrs Leveret had left his breakfast set and his lunch in the fridge. He was rather annoyed at being disturbed."

"Did you manage to find any of the ladies?"

"Only a couple. They're already out and about, spread across the parish. Away from the roads, in among copses, water meadows and so forth. There was a Mrs Joyce Parsons at the church, we spoke to her. She and her gang are in charge of arrangements once the flowers begin arriving. We've left a message to contact us if the lady reappears. Mrs Parsons couldn't remember whether she'd seen Mrs Leveret this morning or not. They'd carved up the territory between them yesterday. Each knew where to go but not necessarily where anyone else would be. The expert is dodging about among all of them but of course *he* wouldn't necessarily know what Mrs Leveret looked like."

"No." Mr Pringle had had sufficient coffee to be able to think clearly. "As I mentioned, Mrs Leveret was wearing another lady's woolly hat. I can't think why." He was about to enlarge on the matter but thought better of it. No point in describing village enmities at this juncture. Syd arrived, the officer thanked him dismissively and poured himself a strong cup of tea.

"Now, sir. A few questions I'd like to ask you, if I may?" Mr Pringle blinked to attention.

"But of course."

"Last night . . . I think you mentioned you'd been dining with friends."

"Mr and Mrs Brown at Woodbine Cottage."

"You described Mr Brown as an old schoolfriend?"

"Yes."

"Was any alcohol consumed during the evening?" Mr Pringle sighed.

"A great deal. I was drunk when I returned, which is why I woke so early with a hangover and decided to go for a longish walk. By the time I reached the marquee there was sufficient daylight to see that piece of canvas which was hanging loose, as well as the body of Mrs Leveret lying inside. And I was completely sober by then." It was disconcerting that the officer made no reply but drank his tea instead.

"You told us a bit about yourself out there, sir. How you've come back to Wuffinge to find your roots—quite an emotional business, that. The sort of thing a man does when he's taking stock. Starts thinking about all sorts of things. Memories can be confusing, too. I'd guess you weren't normally a heavy drinker?"

"No."

"No. There you are, you see. And alcohol can affect people in many different ways . . . more so as they get older, you'd be surprised." Mr Pringle was disheartened as well as frustrated.

"No matter how old or drunk I was last night, officer, or how emotional, it doesn't alter the fact that the body of Mrs Doris Leveret was lying in that marquee at dawn this morning when I looked inside. I cannot explain how her corpse then came to disappear—"

"That is what's been troubling us, sir. In our experience, dead bodies have a habit of staying put. In fact it's the only thing you can rely on them for."

"Obviously someone must have moved her."

"Who d'you suggest might have done that?"

"I don't know!" Mr Pringle ran fingers through hair already dishevelled. "This village is on the verge of a festival aimed at raising a substantial sum of money. Perhaps someone couldn't bear to think of it as being a disaster." The officer sat back, eyebrows raised.

"In that case it's a great pity he or she didn't leave the lady exactly where she was," he said, matter of factly. "You'd have had them pouring over the barricades, willing to pay anything you like for a glimpse of a nice fresh corpse. You wouldn't have needed to send anyone flower-gathering."

"I know," Mr Pringle agreed sadly.

"As it is, all you've got now is a temporarily missing person. We have hundreds of those every week. Still, keep your fingers crossed, eh?"

"Pardon?"

"She might turn up again before the weekend's over. If you find her again, keep her pinned down next time. Tie a proper knot with one of those bits of rope." He was laughing at him. Mr Pringle attempted dignity.

"I cannot think why Mrs Leveret should be wearing another woman's hat, nor why her clothes were so wet." The officer was on his feet.

"Well, when she returns from the water meadows or wherever, perhaps you could ask her. Good morning." Greedy Syd materialized and stood, hand outstretched.

"Pot of tea, £2.50."

"You must be bloody joking!" At the door the officer called contemptuously, "Put it on his bill," and left.

From inside the police car, the other officer beckoned. As the first one reached it, the second put down the radio receiver. "It's all happening in Wuffinge Parva. A woman's reported an attempted rape. Name of Kenny. We're to hold the fort until the WDC arrives."

"Hey?" The first officer frowned. "Check your book. I've heard that name recently . . ." The second flipped over the pages. "The woolly hat grandad was on about. Didn't he say that belonged to a Mrs Miranda Kenny?"

"Yep. 'A woollen hat with an Aztec pattern' to be exact." The first officer got in behind the wheel.

"Better ask her if she's lost that as well. Which house?"

Syd cleared the breakfast things but wouldn't be denied information any longer. Mr Pringle told him what had occurred in a few brief sentences, revealing the identity of the victim this time. What harm was there? There wasn't the slightest possibility of seeing Doris Leveret alive again despite police doubts.

"But she can't have vanished!" Syd gasped, revelling in the drama.

"Sadly, that would appear to be the situation. She is not where I first saw her."

"So where . . . ?"

"That is for the police to discover." Unless they'd already decided it was nothing but a wild goose chase. "However," he turned a warning gaze on the landlord, "there could be serious consequences if either you or I said anything indiscreet at this juncture. Mr Leveret is unaware that anything has happened to his wife."

"That's OK," Syd was unconcerned, "he never comes in here. Fancy toffee-nosed Doris being murdered . . . I wonder where Miranda Kenny was last night, eh?"

With a sinking heart, Mr Pringle realized he'd opened a can of worms. "I must warn you again, until there is an actual corpse—"

"Well, it won't take long to find her. I mean, she can't have gone far. Here!" Wondrous possibilities opened up before Syd's eyes. "Why don't I organize a search party?"

"Oh, I shouldn't bother," Mr Pringle said bitterly, "so far, the police aren't offering any reward."

He went upstairs intending to return to bed but staff were already cleaning his room. One handed him an envelope. "Joyce Parson's daughter came round on her way to school. Her mother said you were to have it straight away."

Inside was a list of addresses of houses for sale, with appointments made for him to view. Joyce was obviously determined his visit to Wuffinge should be a success. The first was for nine thirty a.m. Mr Pringle groaned.

Chapter Four

A two-tone 2CV was parked on the path outside Macavity's Pastures. The man who answered the door to the police had a beard but otherwise his style of dress was local government conventional. If he was surprised to see them there he gave no sign. The first officer said affably, "Mr Kenny?" Oliver pulled himself together.

"That was quick."

"We were in the vicinity as it happens. Is your wife . . . ?"

"Through here." He added awkwardly, "It's been a dreadful night," and called, "the police, darling." The endearment sounded artificial but Oliver Kenny forced himself to continue as if concerned for her welfare, "You'll be in safe hands now."

"Oh, no." At the sight of two male officers Miranda Kenny leapt to her feet. She said with exaggerated distaste, "I distinctly asked for a *woman* detective. I refuse categorically to discuss the attack with you. All men do is slaver over sexual details." The first officer maintained his poise.

"Try not to upset yourself, madam. A WDC is on her way. We'd just like you to tell us what you can about your assailant. We need to send out details as soon as possible, he could still be in the area."

"I doubt it. I was attacked in the early hours of this morning." The policeman looked at both of them in surprise.

"May I ask why it took so long to contact us?"

Oliver Kenny was glancing at his watch. "Miranda will explain. I really ought to leave for work. A meeting with the chief planning officer at ten . . ."

"Let my colleague have a number where you can be contacted, Mr Kenny."

"Yes, of course."

"Oliver, you're not intending to desert me!" Said in a ringing tone, the police tried not to wince.

"You'll be perfectly safe, madam. We shall not leave until the WDC arrives. Thank you, sir." The first officer shepherded Kenny out of earshot into the tiny lobby.

"She came back home in a state but she wouldn't let me call you. Miranda's highly suspicious of the official attitude to rape." Oliver muttered in a lower tone, "I don't think he did anything too . . . violent. Roughed her up a bit, you know."

"I see."

"From what she said, he jumped on her in the dark and made filthy suggestions."

"Right." Oliver had the front door open, patently anxious to disappear.

"We were both awake all night, she was so upset. Well, angry really. She wouldn't let me call you. Then suddenly, about half an hour ago, she changed her mind. Just picked up the phone and—bingo!" He flushed as if angry at himself for making light of the matter. "Sorry, must dash." Nervousness made him slip the clutch and the 2CV bounded like a kangaroo down to the village street.

Once he was out of sight of his own front door, Oliver pulled up and wiped away the sweat. He'd put up a convincing performance; a weak man, too frightened of his boss to stay with his wife. Which was near the truth, he thought, grinding his teeth.

For he'd followed Miranda last night. Oliver's hands trembled at the memory. She hadn't seen him, no one had. For that he must be thankful. And he'd managed to arrive back ahead of her. He'd been frightened when she'd decided to call the police, but did it really matter?

Calmer now, Oliver went through events slowly. There was nothing to connect him with what had happened. No one had seen him, all he had to do was remain silent. It would blow over, he told himself, all he had to do was stay calm.

At Macavity's Pastures, the policeman had returned to the living-room. There was an evil-looking cat on one of the rush-seated chairs. For some reason, Miranda Kenny was on her knees beside it, face buried in its fur as though seeking comfort. The second officer pulled a face at him and shrugged.

"Would you like my colleague to make you a cup of tea, Mrs Kenny?"

"What on earth for?" She certainly didn't appear to be in a state of shock. He pressed on.

"Can you give us any details at all of your attacker. I'm not asking you to describe anything that would cause you distress, you understand." This woman mustn't be given the chance to

60

accuse him of harassment. He waited. There was silence. Perhaps he'd been too gentle. "If you could tell us how you came to be out of doors at that time of night? I take it you were alone."

Miranda Kenny rose to her feet, exuding scorn. Her face was shiny and unadorned apart from glasses, her hair hung lankly from its parting. Today, she had dressed for the benefit of the craft workers as well as for martyrdom, in a colourful Indian muslin shirt, jeans and clogs. To his surprise, he found her attractive.

"I was saving the environment, if you can understand such a concept."

"Ah, yes." The man had met them all in his time. Usually they settled down under the pressure of earning a living or raising children but Mrs Kenny didn't appear to have either necessity. She was obviously devoting her energies to causes. He sighed, inwardly. It was going to be an uphill struggle what with feminism, politics and attempted rape. Briskness was the best form of defence. "Well, madam, let's be as brief as possible: height?"

"What?"

"What height was your assailant, colour of hair, any other physical details? And his clothes. Do you remember anything about those?"

"It was pitch dark."

"Where did the attack take place?"

"I was under the motorway protecting the frogs. Frogs have rights, in case you didn't know." Her voice had the suspicion of a tremble. "We are almost at the start of the mating season, the most critical period . . ." A nut obviously but he felt a twinge of sympathy.

"Looking after these frogs . . . Is that something you've been doing regularly?"

"For about the last four weeks. I don't often go out at night, though." I bet the frogs don't either, he thought. What a silly woman despite her pretentions.

"But your habit of protecting them, was that well-known in the village?"

"Oh, he wasn't a local!" There was a mixture of disdain as well as certainty. She was no longer a supplicant, she was enjoying exercising intellectual superiority. Snob, thought the officer laconically; she couldn't bear the thought of being groped by a yokel.

"You're certain of that?"

"Absolutely." She added simply, "His accent . . . he couldn't have been." But this raised his hackles.

"What about his accent, madam? I gather from your husband, his suggestions were unacceptable, however well modulated." She was an angry red and answered resentfully.

"He was an educated person."

"And that's all you can tell us?" Antipathy hung thickly between them.

"I intend to tell the rest to a *woman*."

"Very good, madam." He rose, the second officer did likewise. "Is there anyone you'd like us to call, any friend. To come and sit with you until the WDC arrives?" Miranda's lip curled.

"You're leaving, too, I assume."

"There's very little point in our staying, madam, as you are unable to give us any information. I'm sure you'll be perfectly safe provided you lock both doors and ask for proper identification before admitting anyone. We shall wait in the car and keep the house under observation until our colleague arrives. I would ask, to save time, if you could jot down anything relevant. Any little detail that comes to mind. To assist with our inquiries." The second officer made a slight gesture with his notebook. "Oh, yes, there was one other matter."

"Yes?"

"Have you recently mislaid one of your hats?"

"I beg your pardon!" He took the notebook and read the description aloud.

"Specifically, 'A woollen hat with an Aztec pattern'?" She looked at him, puzzled.

"I may have been wearing it last night, I often do if it's chilly, but I don't remember losing it."

"Could you check, when you're feeling up to it, and let the WDC know, please." She followed them into the lobby, obviously curious. The second man had a view of the street.

"There's a car arriving now," he called.

The first officer said with some relief, "You won't be on your own, madam. We can vouch for our WDC officer."

"Why did you ask about my hat?"

"Oh, yes." He was half inclined to drop it but remembered

Mr Pringle's quiet insistence. "Had you any reason to lend that particular one to a Mrs Doris Leveret?" Miranda Kenny's face suffused with colour. She was obviously very angry this time.

"What a stupid suggestion!" She walked back into the living-room and slammed the door. The other man grinned at his bafflement.

"Never mind. It's been that sort of day."

"It had better bloody well improve then." He greeted the WDC now getting out of the car. "She's all yours, Shirley. Good luck is all I can say. How the bloke escaped without losing his balls, I shall never know."

Alone in her living-room, Mrs Kenny clenched her fists; she'd done it now, she'd reported it. Serve him right!

Mr Pringle stared glumly at a gnome perpetually fishing in a miniature pond. "We've more in the back garden," the owner simpered. "Ornamental sculptures, the estate agent calls them. Wilf and I simply can't make up our minds whether to leave them or not." Why not dig a big hole and bury the lot, Mr Pringle wondered silently.

The house behind the village street and pub was one of a sporadic, ill thought-out development built during the forties and fifties. He wished Joyce Parsons had thought to consult him before making this appointment. For politeness' sake he had to go through the motions. They were in the living-room. Every chair had a starched antimacassar; he sat bolt-upright for fear of sullying his.

"Make yourself at home, Mr Pringle. I'll just fetch the coffee." He was willing to wager it would be made with boiled milk. Three more houses, therefore three more cups in addition to this. He wondered idly whether one could sample as well as admire the sanitary arrangements.

"Have a home-made biscuit."

He exerted himself. "Did you decorate this room yourself?"

"How clever of you to guess!"

She was a complaisant middle-aged woman who'd lived in Wuffinge Parva since her marriage. By the time they'd reached the third bedroom, Mr Pringle had exhausted his stock of polite phrases. For the sake of something to say, he suggested, "You must have known Major Petrie Coombe-Hamilton?" It produced the now familiar simper.

"Not to say 'know', Mr Pringle. But one did admire him.

Such a gentleman. One of the old school. He once tried to make Wilf buy him a drink—very jovial about it, kept insisting—but we're teetotal, of course."

"Of course." Bad luck, Major, thought Mr Pringle. "His death was a little sudden, from what I've heard?" She sighed.

"He was in the Hope & Anchor that night." Seeing his face she explained quickly, "We're Salvationists, we go there every week. Wilf sells *The War Cry* and I rattle the tambourine, so to speak." He remembered the collecting tin on the hall table.

"I see." He dearly wanted to ask if Syd took a percentage but held his tongue. The woman was shaking her head over the Major.

"We were very surprised. He was his usual argumentative self in the bar, then he took himself off. Next morning he was dead."

"Under the motorway . . . which seems strange as he lived in the opposite direction." She clasped her hands, eyes alight.

"We like to think he'd heard immortal voices and was on his way to the church to seek redemption from his sins."

From memory, Mr Pringle thought it much more likely the Major would have reached for a brandy bottle if he'd had the slightest inkling of what was about to happen.

He thanked her and shook hands. The next house was only half a street away but his hostess wasn't perturbed. "We've both been on the market for six months but everyone who comes here says how much more house-proud Wilf and I are," she told him confidently. "*Au revoir* for the present."

By lunchtime the pain had returned behind his eyes, his varicose vein throbbed and too much liquid was sloshing about in his stomach. You needed stamina for this lark. He missed his car. With luck, Gavin would have it ready by tomorrow.

As he walked back, he saw how activity had increased round the marquee. Craft people had returned in force to stack their shelves. Two sections of canvas were pulled back, Mr Pringle could see the bustle inside. He also noticed security men and one lone police constable, presumably all a missing corpse warranted. Miranda Kenny was back in charge but without her loud hailer.

How extraordinary to think that only this morning, in that very tent . . . He shivered. The sick feeling had returned and he desperately needed to talk to someone. Felicity was out

64

gathering flowers, Ted Brown was due in Manchester on behalf of his electrical firm and Mr Pringle couldn't possibly phone Mrs Bignell before the cheap rate began at six o'clock.

He remembered Joyce would be at the church. He needed to stop her making more appointments. Perhaps he would wander up after lunch, maybe even consult the vicar. He wouldn't sleep tonight until he'd discussed this morning's events. A stranger would do, preferably one with a rational mind.

He saw Mrs Kenny emerge and begin walking towards her cottage. On an impulse, he began to follow. He wanted to discover whether she knew about her hat.

"Mrs Kenny . . . G. D. H. Pringle."

"Oh, it's you." She paused reluctantly, her key already in the lock.

Mr Pringle said diffidently, "We encountered one another in the church, somewhat briefly, on Tuesday afternoon."

"I remember."

"It's impertinent, I know, but might I have a word?"

"What about?" Close to, she'd lost her confident aggression. She also gave the impression of being nervous.

"As you are alone, perhaps I should return when your husband is at home," he suggested, aware of the delicacy of her position. At that, Miranda Kenny pushed open the door.

"I doubt if it was you that was responsible for last night. Go in. Only five minutes. I've scarcely time to breathe today." Mystified, he stepped over the threshold.

It was amazing how three cottages could be so dissimilar. If little Elsie's was squalid and the Browns' comfortable, this was 1990 primitive.

There was a black iron woodburner but it wasn't alight so the room was cold and smelled of old pot-pourri, presumably to counter acrid smoke. Judging by the blackened fire surround, the Kennys had been burning sappy wood. There were soot marks on the ceiling too, above the oil lamps. No electricity of course, nothing out of keeping. The sole decorations were stencilled motifs of decaying leaves.

The floor of randomly laid bricks had sisal mats and what he took at first to be a sprinkling of hay. Mr Pringle pushed it with his toe and decided these were rushes mixed with lavender. Miranda Kenny had striven to recreate medieval discomfort—and had succeeded.

He sat on a rough wooden bench. An open staircase hewn

from planks rose haphazardly towards the upper storey. There was no handrail to mar the perfection, only rough slats across the top. Behind these, he glimpsed a lute. A Homely Touch, perhaps?

His heart sank when he saw Mrs Kenny begin to make tea and his stomach sent anxious reproachful signals when the herbal brew reached it, but now was not the time to be queasy.

He listened to complaints about stall-holders, then explained what he was doing in Wuffinge to satisfy her curiosity. Miranda Kenny gazed disparagingly at her own surroundings.

"We shall be putting this house on the market once we've found a sympathetic location for our next project." Mr Pringle felt confident enough to join in.

"No doubt you are looking for a barn to convert?"

"God—how passé! No, we want an ecological environment in which a house can evolve organically. We'd go underground if it weren't for Oliver's claustrophobia."

And live alongside Mole and Mr Badger, he wondered. Miranda sighed over the weakness of the male.

"I've had to compromise. We shall begin with a tree instead and take it from there." He was impressed.

"You intend to build a log cabin?"

"We shall surround the tree with space and naturalness, with a hole in the roof to let out the smoke from our fire. We shall link arms around the tree and listen to what it has to tell us."

Mr Pringle thought it might prefer to stay in the fresh air and go on being a tree but no doubt such an opinion was heresy. Miranda Kenny continued dreamily as her vision took hold.

"The roof will be a simple rib cage of timber. We shall be the heart, pumping in life." His concerns were more practical.

"What about . . . plumbing?"

"There will be a service core to cater for our basic requirements, naturally," she said irritably. The phrase confused him.

"You mean an Elsan?" But Mrs Kenny was on a different plane altogether, stretching out her arms ecstatically.

"There will be nothing but earth in our living space, around the roots of the tree. It will be the ultimate ecological experience." He was baffled.

"You mean soil? No floorboards?" He was becoming familiar with her sneer.

"Of course we shall use twentieth-century technology, under-floor heating and so forth. We don't *despise* man's inventiveness, but don't you understand? The earth has to be there to remind us of our universe. A house that isn't organic simply has no right to be!"

Certainly not a shabby Edwardian semi with sensible rooms and carpets. Mr Pringle remembered young Michelle, labouring away, threatening her future happiness when all she had to do was build a wigwam round a bush.

On the chair opposite, the tom-cat arched its back with a quiver and subsided again. Macavity must be feeling elated. Not only a raunchy sex-life with Elsie's old mog but now the prospect of a wall to wall litter tray, ecologically insulated and warm to the touch.

"Would you care to share my quiche?" Miranda asked suddenly. Mr Pringle pushed away the memory of how Macavity had been sniffing at it when they'd first arrived.

"Only a very small piece, thanks. You mentioned some event of last night. I trust nothing untoward . . . ?" He flapped a vague hand.

"I was attacked," she said bluntly.

"Good heavens! How very distressing, and frightening. You weren't injured?" Miranda bit into pastry angrily.

"It wouldn't have mattered if I had been as far as the police were concerned. Against my better judgement I called them in and d'you know what?" He didn't. "All they're interested in is—can I describe the guy. It makes me sick!" Miranda Kenny conveniently ignored the fact she knew who the man might be. She was out for revenge, which made it different.

Mr Pringle's brain was turning over rapidly. "Did the police mention . . . Have they any suspicion?" he stumbled in an effort not to reveal too much. "Do they think there was anyone suspicious in the neighbourhood?"

"If they do, they're not saying. Why? More camomile?"

"Er, no thank you. Mrs Kenny, you may think this is a very odd question but bear with me, for it is important."

"As long as it isn't about my wretched hat." She caught sight of his face and slammed down her cup. "Bloody hell! Not you as well?"

"I . . . I . . ." he picked up his courage. "Mrs Kenny, has anyone told you why your hat is important?"

"No they haven't." She stood over him, arms akimbo. "I told

the police that a man jumped out on me in the dark, rolled me in the mud and pinned me down while he whispered Freudian filth and all they says is—have I lost my hat?"

"And have you?" His demeanour quietened her.

"Yes," she said, dropping her pose. "Why, have you found it?"

"No, but someone did who obviously bears you a grudge. Please sit down. What I have to tell you is serious. And if it's any comfort, the police don't believe me, either. They think I was drunk or hallucinating."

He told her the tale, beginning from the moment when he left the Browns' cottage.

"Oliver heard you, I think," she said slowly, "I was getting ready to go out to the frogs and he said the Major must've returned because some drunken old sot was singing away outside."

"I apologize," Mr Pringle was shame-faced. "It was dark and Ted Brown had warned me Eddie Runkle might be out there with his gun, after the vixen. Under the circumstances it seemed a good idea to make a noise."

"Go on." This time she didn't interrupt until he began describing the corpse. When she realized this sober, elderly man was talking about murder, the knife clattered against her plate.

"Are you saying . . . Doris Leveret was lying there, in the marquee, wearing my hat?"

"It's a very distinctive pattern." Miranda Kenny was white-faced; this wasn't ecological, it was real!

"I've looked for it everywhere," she whispered. "After the police left I've tried to find it. I can't remember when I last wore it but even if she'd found it, Doris would never have put it on, not in a million years."

"That's what I thought," Mr Pringle agreed. "It wasn't the sort she would wear." Miranda was bewildered.

"If you found her, why has no one said anything? There wasn't a sign of police activity when I arrived at the marquee— you'd have thought the place would have been buzzing." She remembered scenes on television. "White tape marking the spot, masses of uniformed men everywhere?"

He'd got to the worst bit; would she believe him now? She listened in silence. He waited for her verdict. Eventually she pushed back the lank fair hair with a restless gesture.

"I don't think you're a nerd," she was too worried to care about her intellectual image, "but d'you think you could've blown your mind with the booze? It happens sometimes to older people."

In the end, she wasn't sure whether she believed him or not. Miranda had begun the day with an act of retribution, now it was turning into a nightmare. "We'll find out this evening, I suppose. When Doris doesn't turn up at home." Mr Pringle wasn't so sanguine.

"If the police take the trouble to check, we might. Otherwise we may have to wait till the body is rediscovered. Have you any idea what Mrs Leveret's tasks were today and tomorrow?"

"She would have been at the church most of the time. Joyce Parsons would know, or one of the others. Felicity Brown, for instance."

"Of course." He rose. "Thank you for giving me lunch." She continued to sit cross-legged on her medieval beanbag.

"If Doris really was . . . bumped off . . ."

"No doubt about it, I'm afraid." He remembered the ghastly, distorted features, the swollen tongue half-bitten through.

"Whoever did it might have it in for me?" She'd realized the significance of the hat. She read in his face that Mr Pringle had too. Her eyes widened behind the granny glasses. "Do you think they're likely to try again?"

He tried to reassure her; she would be safe enough among the crowds in the marquee. He reminded her of the constable and security men. "Your husband will shortly return—"

"Oliver!" Her voice was full of contempt. "When I got back last night he wasn't much use, he was hysterical." Mr Pringle had sympathy.

"Dealing with your attacker must have seemed a daunting prospect. Was he a powerful man?" She turned away as if determined not to discuss it.

"All I could tell the police was that he came up from behind and took me by surprise," she said shortly. "I'm well able to take care of myself but when a man does that . . ."

Mr Pringle was surprised. How did this enlightened young woman imagine rapists normally behaved? But Miranda was too full of her own worries.

Had a murder really taken place in Wuffinge last night? It terrified her the more she thought about it. She forced herself to continue, "He must've gone in search of someone else . . .

and found Doris." But surely that particular man wouldn't have done such a thing? She gave a genuine shudder this time. "Doris was older, not so agile," she whispered. "I did put up a fight."

"I'm sure you did."

"Who else knows?" she asked abruptly.

"Anyone who's visited the Hope & Anchor because I had to tell Syd." He wanted to leave but not before he'd managed to calm her. "Your friends will have heard by now. Is there anyone I could telephone? I'm sure they'd want to rally round."

"What friends?" Mrs Kenny sniffed. "In this village, they're mostly idiots." A thought struck her. "I hope for your sake Doris's body turns up soon, otherwise you're going to look a complete berk."

She was over the worst, he decided, and bade her farewell.

Outside, the green was crowded with people. The public loudspeaker system was being tested, a junior brass band was going through its paces. He'd never seen so many people in Wuffinge. He needed peace and quiet in which to think. He felt shy of pushing past strangers so went the long way round the green.

"I say!" It was the young housewife from Reynard's Covert. She gazed at him soulfully as if he was the only man on earth. Mr Pringle's heart turned over—if only he could remember her name! "We met on Tuesday at the church. I'm Michelle Brazier."

"Of course."

"I hear you're planning to buy a house. Ours is for sale." Oh, no!

"Actually, I haven't finally made up my mind—"

"Please," she exerted all her charm, "come and have a look, it might be just what you want." He followed, courteous but weary. "Would you like a cup of coffee?"

"Thank you, no." His digestive tract was under far too great a strain.

"I know you've seen the Balmoral but that's intended for a family. This is just right for one or two."

He wouldn't have thought it possible for rooms to be smaller but these were. The layout appeared to be roughly the same. He tried to pick his way through the minefield of offence and choose appropriate words.

"You've made it a very cosy home . . . Everything matches so well."

"Don't!" Michelle was instantly miserable. "I've worked so hard to rid it of that *ersatz* look!" He didn't know how to respond. "We're moving to a barn. I can't wait to get started!" her eyes gleamed fanatically. "We've found one, at the right end of Wuffinge." My word! Which end was that, he wondered? "We can move out the minute we sell this place," she assured him.

Mr Pringle gazed sadly at the shelves, fitted cupboards and pelmets. Should he warn Michelle that the only way to overtake the Kennys was to burrow deep and commune with the worms? But why be in a hurry to do that when there was all eternity with very little else to occupy one's time? He tried to placate her.

"You seem to have worked very hard."

"Next time I shan't make mistakes. No more matching borders and definitely no plastic."

No more comfort, no more efficient insulation and warmth.

"Have you seen Miranda's cottage, isn't it fantastic?"

"Very—quaint," he ventured.

"What about that minstrel's gallery?"

"Beg pardon?"

"At the top of the stairs."

"Ah." So that's what it was.

"I shall have one, with a harpsichord."

As he followed her up the stairs he searched for a safe topic. "What a pleasant workroom." That was harmless, surely.

"I'm crocheting bedspreads." Polyester duvets were out, she knew that now. He noticed the balls of wool.

"You knit, too, how very talented." Michelle flushed.

"Only mitts and a hat." In the same red and yellow Aztec shades favoured by Miranda Kenny, he noted. "What d'you think?"

"Hmm?"

"Of our house? We'd include all the fixtures, fitting and carpets."

"Ah, yes . . . Well, as I tried to explain—" but she'd suddenly noticed the time.

"Damn, I have to get back! I'm supposed to be helping Doris Leveret and Joyce Parsons till four, that's when Tracey takes over. Look—phone me when you've had time to think about it."

"Surely Mrs Leveret's not at the church!"

Michelle was startled by his cry. "Doris is out picking flowers but she organized the rota."

"So you haven't actually seen her today?"

"I don't think so—should I have?"

"No, no . . ."

She pouted. "I wanted to help Miranda but she didn't ask me."

Oh dear, how childish.

"Why not present yourself in the marquee at four o'clock. I'm sure Mrs Kenny would welcome another pair of hands."

"A person likes to feel needed. If she'd asked, I'd've gone like a shot."

He'd no patience with juvenile petulance.

"I don't suppose the other ladies would let a thing like that worry them." "Grow up" was what he meant but he restrained himself. "Mrs Kenny seems to have a very heavy workload." As well as having had an extremely nasty experience last night.

"I might," Michelle flounced downstairs. "I'll see how I feel." He made his escape.

In the Hope & Anchor, he ignored the sudden silence. Everyone knew. Syd called unnecessarily, "Have they found you-know-who yet?"

"I've no idea." Mr Pringle went upstairs. Drinkers gave one another knowing looks; a nutter, obviously.

From a window, he saw Syd's latest effort at promoting the flower festival. Two flagstaffs now stood on either side of the Bunker entrance; one supported the Union Jack, the other a Nazi swastika, Syd's father's war booty presumably. Between them a banner proclaimed: VIVE L'ENTENTE CORDIALE and from inside, Marlene Dietrich had replaced Dame Vera, murmuring huskily:

Vor der Kaserne, vor dem grossen Tor
stand eine Laterne, und steht sie noch davor.
So woll'n wir da uns wiedersehn
bei der Laterne woll'n wir steh'n

wie einst Lili Marleen
wie einst Lili Marleen.

Chapter Five

When he awoke it was mid afternoon. His joints were stiff and knowledge of all that had happened that morning returned to haunt him. Through the open window he could hear a raucous tetchiness among voices coming from the marquee. All that was necessary had been done; everyone was impatient for the festival to begin.

Mr Pringle watched as canvas entrances were tightly closed and security men began their patrols, talking to one another over their radios. The lone constable had gone. Obviously the corpse hadn't reappeared and he had been withdrawn.

If it remained undiscovered until tomorrow night that would suit him very well indeed, Mr Pringle decided calmly. It would enable him to leave Wuffinge Parva as planned. He hoped he'd enough energy now to walk as far as the church for his need to talk to someone was even greater. He'd had a bad dream; in it, Mrs Leveret's assailant had been Miranda Kenny.

Across the green he saw a familiar figure turn in at Woodbine Cottage: Felicity Brown must have finished her stint of flower gathering. Mr Pringle reached for his hat.

"Oh, hello there . . ." Friendliness was tempered with curiosity. Felicity's smile was slightly cautious. "I've been hearing the most incredible gossip—come in. How are you feeling today? No, don't tell me. Ted was really rough this morning. Fancy a cup of tea?"

"No, thank you."

"I'm parched. I've never walked so far . . . or fallen into so many bogs—I'm weak at the knees." She eased off her wellingtons and indicated he should go and sit in the living-room. "So tell me your version of what's been happening," she called from the kitchen. "You've obviously not been arrested for assaulting Miranda Kenny—which was one tale I heard—but what's all this about Doris Leveret? There's surely no truth in that?" She hovered in the doorway, uncertain whether she wanted to know or not.

73

Mr Pringle replied quietly, "Very early this morning I went for a walk because I couldn't sleep—about four a.m. On the way back I looked inside the marquee and discovered Mrs Leveret's body. I returned to the pub to call the police. Unfortunately that took a little time. When they arrived and went inside, the corpse had disappeared."

Felicity had become very pale.

"It's true then? People were pooh-poohing the idea because it sounded so, well, unreal."

"I fear bad news often is unpalatable."

"But . . . why? You're sure she hadn't had a heart attack?" If death had come, let it be in an acceptable form.

"She had been killed."

Felicity Brown sat and caught her breath. Eventually she swallowed and said, "I know Doris wasn't very well liked, but there's all the difference in the world between that and . . . killing! Who would do such a thing?"

That question had worried Mr Pringle since dawn but he could offer no suggestions. Felicity reached for her handkerchief and disappeared, ostensibly to make the tea. He sat back, eyes closed. When he opened them again she was there with a tray. On it were two small glasses of brandy.

"Here . . . it's medicinal. I shan't offer you any more."

"Thank you."

"And I've brought another cup in case you change your mind."

She didn't ask any more questions until they'd both recovered. Then she said, "The village is agog. We heard various versions of both stories. Most of them favoured you as the would-be rapist. You're the outsider. Wuffinge prefers outsiders when it comes to serious crime."

"Whoever strangled Mrs Leveret was more likely to be local."

"Strangled?"

"That's what it looked like. She was lying face down. When I turned her over, I could see a thin cord round her neck." He kept to himself the fact Mrs Leveret's clothes had been wet. Felicity shuddered.

"Everyone kept saying Doris was bound to turn up—alive, I mean. By four o'clock, they were less certain. We'd picked all the flowers we needed by then. We'd all reported in."

"Did anything unusual happen today, or was anything said?"

"Not that I can remember. We were working hard all morning—Joyce kept us at it. We were one short."

"Of course."

"And that wretched Michelle was no use. As soon as she heard about Mrs Kenny, she became hysterical because she'd shown you over her house. 'Imagine what might have happened to *me*,' she kept saying, 'I might have been raped.'"

"Next time you see her, pray assure her my passions were not aroused." Felicity managed a faint smile.

"We couldn't stand it. In the end, Joyce told her to go and help her precious Miranda instead. That was just before the police arrived. I was ready to leave by then. They asked if anyone had seen Doris today, which made us realize it was serious. They refused to answer questions except to confirm the attack on Miranda. I suppose it must be one and the same person?"

"I've no idea. I fear the Major is somehow involved. I don't know how or why yet—"

"But he's dead!" she cried.

"He is," Mr Pringle agreed, "unfortunately he died in the wrong place."

"Oh, my God, it's so unreal!"

"Look, I'm sorry, I shouldn't have upset you."

"It's not your fault. It just doesn't seem possible, not in Wuffinge Parva. This is a very small, very friendly village—nothing *ever* happens here."

Mr Pringle held his tongue. He thought of all the blood-letting and betrayal down the years; between Protestant and Catholic, land-owner and starving peasant, man and wife. Not a century went by without duplicity, branding, hanging, burning or witch-ducking. Why should 1990 turn out to be different? They were at the end of one of the most venal decades he could remember.

"Would you like me to remain until Ted returns?" Felicity looked at him, troubled.

"He told me not to stay up, he's going to be very late."

"Even if we went to bed, I doubt if either of us would sleep. I should point out, I'm not offering to defend you, Felicity. It's not lack of gallantry—it's a combination of fright and age. If the murderer burst through that door, all I could offer to do is yell."

"We'll hold hands and yell together," she said, comforted.

He returned to the Hope & Anchor to warn Syd he would be late. The attitude there had changed. Before, he'd been regarded as an idiot; a man who'd claimed to have found an invisible corpse. But Doris Leveret was still missing and people were hostile. Syd found it necessary to check whether he would be leaving tomorrow.

"I've had a booking," he announced blandly, "I need the room. Gavin phoned, by the way. He's bringing your car round first thing. He's had a little bit of a problem but he wants to explain about it himself."

Mr Pringle asked for change so that he could phone Mavis, aware that everyone avoided looking at him directly. No one could pretend that Doris Leveret was still collecting flowers. Lewd jokes concerning Miranda Kenny's attacker had ceased as well. The police car parked outside the Leverets' house couldn't be ignored. Villagers needed a scapegoat—and here he was. An inoffensive retired income tax inspector—that was suspicious enough in itself. Who claimed to be one of them? What nonsense. He'd only stayed with his granny a couple of years, until it was safe to go back to London.

Mr Pringle felt hostility like knives in his back. He was the eater of sins; when he left, he would take their collective guilt with him, or so they all hoped. He heard Mrs Bignell's voice, as bright and cheerful as a sunbeam.

"It's me, Mavis."

"Hello, stranger! Had a nice little holiday, have you?" Unfortunately Syd had installed the telephone so that everyone could hear from either bar.

"Very pleasant," said Mr Pringle stiffly. "Just to confirm I will be back tomorrow. Early evening, with any luck. After I've seen some wall-paintings in the church."

"Not staying in Wuffinge whatsit for good then?" she chuckled.

"Er . . . not at present. This is a pay phone, Mavis, in the bar. I'll tell you all the news tomorrow night." Mrs Bignell took the hint, there were no lavish endearments.

"Toodlepip then, dear. I'll have supper ready."

"Thank you very much."

He returned to Woodbine Cottage, noticing how others closed their doors against the danger he represented. More than one bolt was pushed home as he walked past. Little Elsie's curtains were drawn back, though; she waved but Mr Pringle quickened his pace and pretended not to see. He still couldn't remember what the unpleasant experience had been years ago but tonight was not the occasion to worry about it.

Felicity had recovered her resilience. "Everyone's been phoning. Joyce first—had I heard anything further about Doris and did you want to see more houses tomorrow? I told her not at present—hope that was right?"

"Yes, thanks."

"Michelle rang to say Gerry was wondering about taking her over to her mother's until the police had 'arrested someone' and did I think she should tell the police you were the man! Ted rang to tell you not to let *me* out of your sight. He says he's relying on you to shout your bloody head off, never mind yell, if the murderer appears at our front door. Oh, and he hopes to be back by ten o'clock. I've made a casserole, will that do?"

"Marvellous."

"Would you like a drink?" Mr Pringle shook his head. The husband of this fair damozel would demand satisfaction if one hair of her head were damaged.

"A glass of water," he replied virtuously.

Eventually Felicity asked, as she was bound to, "What do you think will happen? Will Doris's body pop up unexpectedly?"

"It depends who's hidden it and what their motives are."

"I suppose they must have been watching when you went into the marquee."

"I assume whoever it was must have been in the marquee itself, hidden beneath the stands. There was plenty of cover."

"That's gruesome!"

"Had they been outside, I would have seen them. It was sufficiently light by then."

"And while you were away phoning the police . . ."

"There was ample time to spirit the body away."

Felicity said energetically, "I can't understand why whoever it was wasn't spotted? So many people would be up and about by then. We're early risers here, you know. People glance out of their bedroom windows all the time."

"Presumably the murderer did nothing out of the ordinary. If you saw a man you knew, who worked as a gardener, wheeling a barrow would you necessarily wonder what it contained?"

"Well, no."

"And if the milkman, postman or any of the vehicles you see every day went past, you wouldn't take the slightest notice. No doubt one or two in the village are accustomed to taking the short, unofficial cut across a corner of the green. The grass is well worn there. If I were driving away from the marquee, that's the route I'd take."

"Cars were going to and fro from dawn onwards," she agreed. "Everyone was hurrying to get the stalls finished. Eddie Runkle was fixing up the entrance signs." Mr Pringle sighed.

"Well if none of you saw a strange vehicle early this morning, the chances are someone in the village is responsible—not only for Mrs Leveret's disappearance but her murder as well."

"Urgh!"

When Ted returned, he and Felicity insisted on accompanying Mr Pringle back to the Hope & Anchor. Unfortunately, Ted sensed the hostility in the bar and took it upon himself to "clear the air". He stood foursquare, nursing a beer. "So, what's the latest theory?" he demanded.

No one spoke. Men stared fixedly into their bitter. "My friend here finds a body, comes back to report it and blow me if someone doesn't go and nick the corpse." Ted stared at each in turn belligerently. "Wasn't you, was it, Spiker?" Wuffinge's oldest inhabitant, habitually speechless, dribbled his fury down his chin.

"You'll finish 'im off, Ted," another remonstrated. "Spiker might look daft but 'e still understands what you're saying."

"Well, it wasn't my old schoolchum here who did it," Ted insisted stoutly, "but I bet there's one or two tonight who said it was, eh?" No takers. Mr Pringle, acutely embarrassed, tried to pretend he wasn't there. "And it wasn't him who attacked Mrs Kenny last night either because you let him in shortly after he'd left us—that right, Syd?"

The landlord, who until their arrival had been accusing Mr Pringle of every crime under the sun was suddenly bereft of words.

"Yes," Ted said ruminatively. "Flick and I waved Pringle here goodnight, watched him set off, listened to his 'orrible singing—sorry, old man—and five minutes later we saw him

78

arrive back here. No doubt you locked the front door after you'd let him in, Syd?" Ted swallowed the remainder of his beer, wiped his mouth and summarized briefly. "Which means, one of you lot first tried to rape Mrs Kenny and then bumped off Doris Leveret—not forgetting disposing of her body after you'd sneaked it out of the marquee early this morning. Whichever way you look at it, it wasn't cricket."

Having cleared the air, Ted patted Mr Pringle on the shoulder, ignoring the angry furore. "Just thought I'd put the record straight, old man. Can't have them blaming you. Got to stand shoulder to shoulder when this sort of thing happens."

As soon as they'd left, Mr Pringle judged it prudent to disappear swiftly up the stairs and lock his door before Ted's well-meaning efforts resulted in Wuffinge Parva's first ever lynching.

As is the way with fête days, Friday dawned heavily overcast. Mr Pringle was up early after a fitful night. As he sat over stale rolls for the final time, two fair-haired Swedish giants ambled into the dining-room. They stared at him incuriously before selecting a table nearer the window. One of them snapped his fingers. Syd burst out from the kitchen. "Who did that?" The finger-snapping giant spoke.

"English breakfast for two peoples. Qvick, please." Syd's jaw dropped.

"Room number?"

"Three." The honeymoon couple had finally emerged.

Mr Pringle deducted several items from Syd's creative accountancy before settling his bill. He waited outside for Gavin. Across the way the marquee looked inviting with the striped awnings now pulled taut over each of the entrances. Ticket-sellers were in position, drinking coffee and chatting to the stall-holders. A platform had been erected to protect the cricket pitch and enable brass bands and morris dancers to be clearly visible. Notices directed visitors to the church, to refreshments in the village hall or to the school playing field which had been transformed into a car-park: all was ready. Mr Pringle remembered his callous hope that the body wouldn't be discovered before he'd had a chance to see the wall-paintings; it wasn't just for his own sake, he decided. Despite the policeman's comment, with so much effort expended on raising money for the new church thatch, a corpse now could ruin everything.

A strange coloured vehicle displaying his Allegro's number plates turned into the pub forecourt. Gavin smiled at him ingratiatingly. "Morning. Lovely day."

By two thirty a line of people stretched back under the motorway as far as the village street and Syd's cousin was doing a roaring trade in the ice-cream at £1 per cornet. Mr Pringle was near the head of the queue, within sight of the church door. Felicity had thoughtfully loaned him a folding stool.

Visitors were to be allowed inside in batches of thirty when viewing began. From time to time Mr Pringle wished he'd accepted Felicity's other invitation to take a quick unofficial peep at the pictures. The wooden shutters had been taken down that morning and provided he put something in the collection plate, the vicar wouldn't object. "They're absolutely wonderful," she assured him. "We were stunned." But Mr Pringle was too shy of his own notoriety to take advantage. This way at least he would be inconspicuous.

There was a stir at the front: people gasped as a Green Man strode into the porch. A child gave a shrill cry of fear, Mr Pringle nearly did the same. It was an awesome sight. The man was tall, completely covered with vines and ivy, hands and face disguised with green dye, his eyes staring out through slits in a mask, with a wreath of laurel on his head. There was an air of menace as well as authority. He raised a hand and people immediately fell silent.

What an incredible sight in front of that ancient building; Mr Pringle was full of admiration. Pagan the Green Man might be, but he blended in with the flints and chalk far better than any religious emblem.

The heavy door opened and the vicar stepped out, his surplice fluttering gently. The sight of so vast a congregation made him hesitant. Mr Pringle heard him clear his throat.

"Welcome to Wuffinge Parva church, ladies and gentlemen, and to the treasures we have discovered on these ancient walls.

"There are five paintings. Three have been so well preserved they're as clear as the day the Saxon artist put down his brush. Two, sadly, have not withstood the centuries. We ask for your understanding and tolerance. Such fragile glories must be protected so that our great-grandchildren may marvel as we do today. Thank you all."

It was well organized despite the absence of Doris Leveret. Mr Pringle glimpsed a harassed-looking Joyce Parsons standing with Felicity and a group of scouts. As soon as the vicar stepped aside, they went into a well-drilled routine. The Green Man held everyone back until the boys were on either side of the queue. Joyce and Felicity signalled when the first thirty tickets had been sold.

The sinister pagan figure beckoned the first group forward. "Keep moving inside the church but do not rush, there is much to absorb." It was a deep, resonant voice. Wherever he'd come from, Mr Pringle was certain it wasn't Wuffinge Parva.

As he moved Mr Pringle did a swift calculation: £2.50 a head (children £1), with a queue three or four wide stretching back over a mile, why there must be close on two thousand pounds already here! That, plus the car-park and proceeds from the marquee, with people pouring in off the motorway, there should be little trouble in raising twenty-five thousand by the end of the weekend.

He was inside the church with assorted treble voices of scouts reminding everyone to take care descending the steps. Curtains concealed the interior. Once through them, the full theatrical effect would be revealed. Mr Pringle advanced.

Greenery almost concealed the walls apart from the five conspicuous oval shapes. As he'd guessed, the massed banks of wild flowers prevented the public approaching too closely.

More green boughs hung from the roof and ferns half-concealed the windows. This was deliberate so that in the dim coolness, spotlights concentrated the attention. The three paintings on the left-hand wall were brilliantly illuminated.

He couldn't grumble that he wasn't near enough, not with such intense primitive colours. In the first picture, amid Celtic twists and scrolls, Noah, his family and animals were boarding an inadequate Ark, watched over by strange deities. Mr Pringle heard the comments on every side.

"Oh, look, isn't it amazing. Smashing!"

"Reckon he wasn't a sea-faring man, though . . . that Ark'd sink first time it went in the water."

"Must've been a monk, Dad. They were the first Christians who came over here."

"Is it true that these are the oldest pictures in England?"

Which was why so many had come, of course. Most of the crowd weren't interested in the paintings as such, but in the unique link with the past. Mr Pringle listened as each onlooker found something to identify.

"Look at his face, Jimmy. Doesn't he remind you of someone?"

"Your uncle Phil, you mean? I dunno. I've never seen him with no clothes on—"

"Ssh! We're in a church."

The second painting was a mystical puzzle. Mr Pringle wasn't familiar enough with biblical allusion to understand. It was beautifully executed and satisfying. He gave himself up to enjoyment until a hand tapped at him to move him on. Next was the Garden of Eden painting he'd seen previously. He was able to listen to those behind him as he examined the details.

"Wicked eyes that little devil has."

"Aren't they great?"

"Incredible."

By contrast, the final two paintings were a disappointment. Dark Perspex concealed barely visible figures. Mr Pringle peered, as did everyone else, but the lighting on this side was low. A second Green Man, less authoritative but muscular, patiently answered questions.

"The history of Man's downfall, we believe. The plaster underneath is in a loose powdery state . . . Most unfortunate, yes, madam . . . The latin inscription? We think the first word is *descenditi*, to do with going down; Man's fall from grace. Never mind, three pictures out of five . . . It's a wonderful find, isn't it?"

And in answer to the same query on everyone's lips: "Yes, we believe these could be some of the earliest pictures, although we'll have to wait for the experts to give their verdict, of course."

Mr Pringle made his way out into the sunshine, back to the present. It was time to go home to Mavis.

"I don't know," she said querulously. "You come back with a bruised face and a split lip. Even your car looks different. Why is the boot such a funny colour?"

"The shape's more or less the same but Gavin's brother

Keith, he's in charge of the paint shop, is colour blind. He has to do the mixing by numbers." Mrs Bignell didn't understand.

"Who's Gavin?"

"He repairs wrecked cars."

"Wrecked!"

"I had this little accident . . . A hearse ran into the back of me." Cod Mornay, straight from the oven, threatened to fall from her nerveless, gloved hands. Mr Pringle caught it then hopped about the kitchen in agony.

"Put it down and stick your fingers under the cold tap or they'll blister," she said automatically then, in disbelief, "you've only been away four days."

"That wasn't the only thing that happened," Mr Pringle confessed, a trifle reluctantly.

"Go on."

"I found a body in a tent but it disappeared."

"What, the tent?"

"No. The body. It was wearing another lady's hat." Mavis Bignell sat, heavily.

"Bugger the hat," she said. "Start at the beginning and tell me exactly what you've been up to."

Later, wrapped around her wonderful thighs, he murmured, "When they find Mrs Leveret, I fear the police may want me to go back to Wuffinge. Will you come with me? I don't think we'll be in any danger. The murder had nothing to do with my visit."

"I'm not going looking at houses," she said adamantly. "What's wrong with this one? Apart from the fact it needs decorating from top to bottom."

"Nothing. It's solid and the hall's the right size." Absence makes the heart very fond indeed.

"I'm definitely not staying at that pub." Mavis was indignant, "Syd sounds a nasty piece of work."

"We could try and find a bed and breakfast place."

"Who would want to kill that poor woman?"

That he could not answer so said instead, "The Browns said they'd like to meet you."

"I'll think about it." He knew from experience that this was Mrs Bignell's final word; for the time being.

* * *

They didn't have long to wait. "Wake up," Mavis marched into the bedroom grim-faced carrying morning tea and the newspaper. "Get dressed because they'll be here to arrest you any minute."

"What?" He jerked awake, heart pounding.

"You're famous all of a sudden. They've found that body of yours and they think you're responsible."

"What!" Print danced in front of his eyes. DEATH OF FESTIVAL ORGANIZER, Mr Pringle read.

The body of Mrs Doris Leveret, 61, was discovered last night in the River Wuffen on the outskirts of Wuffinge Parva. Her hands and feet had been tied and string was wound round her neck. Police suspect foul play.

Mrs Leveret was organizer of the Wuffinge Art Festival which opened yesterday.

Commented local resident Michelle Brazier, "An old man has been seen in the village. Yesterday he raped my friend. We've all been afraid to go out." Mrs Brazier, 27, drew attention to the high level of vermin. "Foxes have eaten the dog food and left a smelly mess beside my dustbin," she said. She confided that she and husband Gerry, 28, would shortly be leaving the area to live in Barnes.

Mavis was unsympathetic. "So much for going back to your roots," she said, "and never mind the murder—who's this woman you're supposed to have raped?"

"I never even saw her before last Tuesday!"

"I expect a lot of rapists say things like that. You didn't tell me Mrs Leveret's hands and feet had been tied."

"They weren't, not when I saw her."

"Vermin!" She said in disgust. "I keep telling you the countryside's not healthy." As he shaved, Mr Pringle wondered venomously if Michelle Brazier had improved the prospect of selling her house? Probably not, he concluded.

There were two phone calls. The first, a straightforward request from the police to attend the Incident Room newly set up on Wuffinge Parva green, and make a statement. The second was Ted Brown.

"Seen the papers, old man? Rape and murder—you shouldn't be allowed out! Seriously though, any idea what's going to happen next? Coppers have been knocking on doors since first light. We're all being asked the same question—when did you last see Doris Leveret."

"They want to interview me later today."

"Flick guessed they would. Listen, come and stay with us. You can't possibly waste more money at greedy Syd's."

"Mrs Bignell and I were planning to find a local B and B."

"Not a chance," Ted said cheerfully. "Thanks to Doris, the general public as well as the media are pouring into the village. Little Elsie has put up a sign—teas & coffees by the river Wuffen."

"Good heavens!"

"On the other hand, Michelle Brazier has taken her For Sale notice down. The council sent the Pest Control officer round first thing this morning."

"Serve her right."

Ted laughed. "Flick's sentiments entirely. Journalists are demanding exclusive rights to the story of Miranda's rape."

"Oh dear, oh dear!"

"She's one hell of an angry female at present—I caught a glimpse of her. I'd say the very next pressman who knocks at her door takes his life in his hands. It's all happening at Wuffinge Parva—come and enjoy the fun!"

Chapter Six

According to radio reports, all motorway exits to Wuffinge Parva were blocked. Mr Pringle was baffled. "There are no motorway exits to Wuffinge Parva. There's a sign to the church but no indication how to get to it."

"It's what they always say," Mavis replied. "Every time I switch on the radio: The M25 is blocked at the entrance to the Dartford tunnel . . . There is a sixteen-mile tailback on the M1 in Northamptonshire . . . A lorry has overturned on the M62— it never varies." Their road had become a single lane with passing places. She nudged him. "Slow down. You can't possibly see round the next bend."

"I've been here before, remember. I know this area." She viewed the scenery dispassionately.

"I do dislike the country. It's full of spiders and things— Look out!" They'd arrived at the end of the five-mile tailback to Wuffinge Parva. After a few minutes, she reached for the Thermos flask. "We've got to go forward now because of all those cars behind us. It's disgusting! Just because they've found one poor woman's body—the police should have had more sense than to tell everyone."

"We don't know if it was they who found her and I doubt if they could keep it a secret for long." They inched forwards. "I shan't be able to park in the village. There's nowhere apart from the school playground and that must be overflowing."

"You can't abandon it—there aren't any verges."

"There's a possible place," he wanted to re-establish dented credentials. "I don't think the lady of the house will object."

Attached to the For Sale notice outside the Petrie Coombe-Hamilton residence was a newly scrawled sign: TRESPASSERS WILL BE SHOT.

He'd already turned off the road and the gap immediately closed up behind him. Mavis looked at him frostily.

"I'm not committing suicide, I'm staying right where I am." As he went to open the gate, she wound down the window, "Where d'you keep the first-aid?"

"In the glove compartment."

There were scissors, a packet of aspirin, two elastoplast and a bandage. Mrs Bignell handled the scissors speculatively.

"Would these be any good for extracting bullets?" He pretended not to hear.

Miss Petrie Coombe-Hamilton bellowed through the letter-box, "Yes. What d'you want?" Mr Pringle bent to explain. She opened the door a crack. "Oh, it's you. I thought you'd been arrested."

"I have an appointment to see the police," Mr Pringle said, stiffly. "However, I also have a request: may I leave my car here? As you can see, the festival is proving quite an attraction."

Guinevere reacted vigorously. "Ghouls! I'm ready for them, though." He saw, stacked against the umbrella stand, two shotguns.

"Oh, I say!"

"One of those drivers had the impertinence to ask if he could use the lavatory! Daddy would've loosed off straight away. I sent him off with a flea in his ear but I held my fire." She was full of the lust for battle, he could see it in her eye.

He asked apprehensively, "Might my companion wait here also, until I've established whether Mrs Brown is at home?"

It wasn't an arrangement he would have chosen, given different circumstances. There was no opportunity to describe Miss Petrie Coombe-Hamilton's peccadilloes. "Hurry up," she cried as he hurried back to the car, "don't want any of those other stinkers getting the wrong idea."

"Why've you brought me here?" Mavis demanded.

"This is one of the houses I looked at. Rather inconvenient, but I haven't told the owner yet of my decision." She was incredulous.

"But it's huge!"

"Ssh! It's a temporary parking place, that's all. I'll try not to leave you too long . . . Miss Petrie Coombe-Hamilton, may I introduce Mrs Bignell." The two women sized one another up.

"I must say you don't look the sort to have a spare twenty thou, either." Miss Petrie Coombe-Hamilton sought to soften the remark with one of her explosive braying laughs.

"Oh, we're very deep. At the Bricklayers." Mavis turned on Mr Pringle a most acidic eye. "I might as well look the place over, while I'm here." He quailed. "Don't be long, will you

87

dear." She gave her hostess her full attention. "Lead on. There's a nasty smell of damp rot coming from somewhere, isn't there?"

Mr Pringle hurried past the line of cars, past harassed officials urging drivers to keep moving. Wuffinge was bursting at the seams. Men had brought their wives, children munched candy-floss, youths skidded round the green on motorbikes, everyone was having a wonderful time. Except Doris Leveret.

The church roof would surely benefit. There was a stream of visitors pouring out of the marquee, most carrying purchases. As for entertainment, it only needed a gallows and the hanging of the murderer to complete the festive atmosphere. Mr Pringle swallowed as he recalled the most likely contender for that role.

The large black and white Incident Room caravan was conspicuous. He tried to approach it discreetly but one of the villagers, on unofficial guide duty, spotted him.

"There's the man!" he roared. Mr Pringle abandoned discretion and moved rapidly. "'E was the one who found 'er first," the villager told fascinated bystanders. "None of us knows where 'e 'id 'er yesterday." Mr Pringle took the steps in a bound. Inside, the atmosphere was sweaty. Air-conditioning kept the computer cool but didn't reach far enough.

"I have an appointment—"

"Take a pew." The officer resumed his phone conversation. Mr Pringle looked about. It was impressive; there were notices and memos pinned haphazardly, laden desks with a battery of phones, and pretty policewomen staring intently at their computer screens. He hoped he'd be interviewed by the slim blonde one.

"Now, sir . . . Detective Inspector Andrews." The officer was also slim and blond but his expression meant business. Mr Pringle sat straighter in his chair. "You were the first person to find the body, I believe."

"I was, but at present I'm in rather a quandary." He had a sudden ghastly vision of what might be happening even now at the Petrie Coombe-Hamilton residence. "We were delayed because of the traffic. If I could return a little later to make a statement? I've had to abandon my companion—"

"We've got all the time in the world, Mr Pringle," DI Andrews's smile didn't include his eyes. "So, let's begin at the beginning. What was your original reason for coming to Wuffinge Parva?"

It was no use. The inspector had his list of questions. All of them required answers. He'd also had a computer and intended to commit those answers to disc. Every few minutes or so the machine bleeped and made him curse. By the end of an hour, Mr Pringle was exhausted.

"Her-clothes-were-wet . . ." DI Andrews hit the keys in no particular order. "Blast!" He looked up. "How wet?"

"As if she'd been out in a deluge but I don't believe it had rained that night. Mrs Leveret may have been in the river more than once." DI Andrews appeared to frown.

"Why should someone drown her, fish her out and drown her again?"

"I've no idea, considering she was strangled," Mr Pringle said wearily. "I saw the cord plainly, as I told your colleague yesterday. When I moved the body the ligature was clearly visible."

"You shouldn't have touched her, Mr Pringle."

"I wanted to make sure Mrs Leveret wasn't alive—she was face down. When I turned her over, her tongue was protruding—it was a terrible sight. But her hands and feet were not bound. They moved freely."

"Hmm. Why did someone then hide the body?"

"I have absolutely no idea."

"Why did you rush off yesterday?"

"I did nothing of the sort." He was sharp. "I returned home as I'd always intended to do, once I'd seen the paintings."

"And have you any idea why Mrs Leveret was killed?"

"None," Mr Pringle said firmly. "I met the woman briefly, by chance, on Tuesday afternoon. That is all I can tell you." He rose. "I must retrieve my companion. May I return to sign my statement later?"

"No need. This'll be ready in seconds." DI Andrews thumped but this time the computer not only bleeped, its screen went sulkily blank. Mr Pringle hurried away. Goodness knows how long it took to placate a microchip.

Outside there was garish quality about the proceedings. Brass bands were marching, pushing their way through crowds they'd never anticipated. Morris dancers bounced, jaded fashion, on the wooden platform over the cricket pitch, and the loudspeaker was hoarse with appeals concerning lost children.

Mr Pringle knocked at Woodbine Cottage. Felicity opened the door with relief. "I thought you'd got lost. Isn't this dreadful."

"Awful. What's it like at the church?"

"Extremely hot. The vicar decided to close down and turn off all the lights for half an hour. There was nearly a riot but I don't see what else he could've done. He'd been advised the rise in temperature could damage the paintings."

"Have the experts arrived?"

"They're due tomorrow, after the evening service. It's the two restorers who are responsible for them during the festival—they're the ones dressed up as Green Men."

"Of course! What an excellent idea that was."

"Where's your friend?"

"I had to leave Mrs Bignell in the care of Miss Petrie Coombe-Hamilton. I trust all is well. That woman has two loaded rifles in her hall, ready to loose off at trespassers."

"Oh, heavens! Her father had similar habits but at least he usually missed. His eyesight was poor."

"I hope to be back shortly."

Let there not be another body waiting for him, Mr Pringle prayed as he hurried away. Wuffinge Parva had had a sufficiency.

Guinevere had difficulty turning the handle. Once open, she ricocheted backwards, which she found hugely amusing. She brayed delightedly when she recognized Mr Pringle, staggering like an elderly colt.

Mrs Bignell, only slightly flushed, carried a glass. "We found Daddy's secret cupboard." Her enunciation was slow but emphatic.

"Have you indeed."

"Come in, come in," Dragging him by the sleeve, Miss Petrie Coombe-Hamilton galloped towards the kitchen. "Mavis has been teaching me how to make cocktails! We've had a White Lady and a Motor-Car—"

"A side-car, dear.'

"We're having a Manhattan next. It tastes so much nicer than tea!"

There was a row of bottles along the draining board. On a saucer were two tired-looking glacé cherries. Miss Petrie Coombe-Hamilton surveyed them affectionately. "These are the only ones we could find. We keep transferring them from drink to drink but I don't think they'll last much longer."

She and Mavis consumed them in a ceremonial farewell.

Mr Pringle sank into the driving seat. "You know, you may have started that woman on a downward path."

"If she runs hard, she might catch up with the rest of us," Mavis agreed.

"I wonder if I should've done something about those rifles?"

"Don't bother," she patted his thigh affectionately. "We got rid of all the ammunition."

"How?"

"We had a target practice in the attic."

"What!"

"Guinevere taught me how to shoot in return for me showing her how to make cocktails. It's not difficult once you get the hang of it. I kept falling over to begin with. When the gun goes bang it doesn't half knock you on the shoulder. I should have some bruises to show you tonight."

"Did you kill any birds?"

"Oh, no. Frankly, I didn't try very hard. Guinevere enjoyed herself, though. She yelled her head off each time she hit one. I blew another whopping great hole in the roof but she said it didn't matter. What's one more when half the tiles are missing anyway? The pigeons were a bit upset."

"I'm not surprised."

"One of them had diarrhoea."

"Mavis, spare me the details." They drove in silence for a minute but Mrs Bignell was troubled.

"Guinevere does go on about her father. Keeps saying how thankful she is that he's dead. He wasn't shot, by any chance?"

"It was natural causes," Mr Pringle replied sternly.

"Even though he was found in the wrong place?"

"A doctor examined the body—he would hardly miss a bullet hole."

"No. And the sort we were using would've blown his head off. Thank goodness for that," Mavis sighed. "Otherwise . . ."

"Quite."

"Guinevere carried on about the Leveret woman as well. 'Very common', she described her. She was in Guinevere's bad books because she'd once upset Daddy."

"Oh, when was that?"

91

"Before he died, I expect," said Mavis placidly. "It's living in the country that does it, you know. It turns people queer."

Felicity took her upstairs to unpack. Mr Pringle gazed at the crowds outside number eight. The tea and coffee sign had been withdrawn. "Elsie's a shocker," Felicity said, returning. "She's been charging 75p a cup and telling everyone Doris was dragged out of the river at the bottom of her garden. If she and Eddie had had any red paint, they'd have added a pool of 'blood'."

"As a matter of interest where was the body discovered?"

"Jammed beneath the bridge. I'm not sure who saw it first—there's three claiming that honour. The police arrived at dawn, taped the area off and began combing the ground. They weren't there long." Mr Pringle shrugged.

"Presumably because Mrs Leveret had been killed elsewhere. They may have simply been trying to establish if that was where the body entered the water."

"Ted didn't think so. According to him there was another corpse years ago, a drunk who fell in. He ended up at the same spot. It's the effect of the current on the bend."

"I'd better go and sign my statement."

It was placed before him with an air of quiet triumph. Mr Pringle read it carefully; he needed to watch his step. If the village believed him responsible it was only a matter of time before the police thought so too.

"I understand you called on Mrs Miranda Kenny yesterday," DI Andrews said, apparently carelessly.

"I was not responsible for the attack on her." Eyebrows were raised.

"Did I say you were? We do take age into consideration, you know." Mr Pringle was mortified. "What was her reaction?"

"She was annoyed the police had shown so little sympathy."

"I'm not interested in either the incident or her pique, Mr Pringle. What I meant was, what was Mrs Kenny's reaction to the news of Mrs Leveret? I presume you'd gone there to tell her?"

"I'd gone to ask about her hat. The one Mrs Leveret was wearing."

"And?"

"We agreed it wouldn't have been to Mrs Leveret's taste, therefore it was unlikely she had put it on herself." DI

Andrews's eyebrows went even higher. "Mrs Kenny realized someone with a grudge might have been responsible. It's no secret that one or two in the village disapprove of Mrs Kenny. It occurred to her that the murderer might try again."

"One or two think it was *her* the killer was after and not Doris Leveret—and that's no secret in this village either. So, that's all you can tell us?"

"It is. There is another matter, however."

"Yes?"

"It concerns a former Wuffinge Parva resident, Major Petrie Coombe-Hamilton . . ."

"Ye-es?"

"He died in the wrong place."

"Died? You mean he's already buried?"

"Yes, in the churchyard."

"Mr Pringle, you're not suggesting we should apply for an exhumation order?"

"Oh, no! Not at all." The Major's ghost would come after him with a shotgun.

"Then why bring him up? The doctor must've been satisfied before he signed the certificate?"

"I'm not suggesting foul play but the Major went in the wrong direction when he came out of the pub the night he died."

"So he was pissed," DI Andrews said flatly. "Let's hope the gentleman died happy. Good afternoon, sir."

As he stepped outside, flashbulbs went off. Mr Pringle blinked, thus ensuring immortality as a slit-eyed rape and murder suspect.

He hurried back to the sanctuary of Woodbine Cottage. "I'd hoped for another look at the paintings but there are too many pressmen outside."

"If you feel like risking it, we could go via the river bank. The Wuffen loops round this half of the village and there's a tow path."

"Of course! I'd forgotten. Does it go as far as the church?"

"Not quite. There's a track past the vicarage and we can cut through the garden. Reg won't mind."

"Reg?"

"The vicar."

"I'd forgotten. What about the crowds?"

"We should be safe. I don't think strangers will know about

the path." Mrs Bignell declared she too was ready for a breath of air and wanted to see the exhibition.

The church windows shone out brilliantly in the dusk. Outside, the queue had dwindled but the line continued through the churchyard. "They've got a hope," Felicity murmured. "It won't stay open past six o'clock."

"Who's on duty?"

"Ruby should be but I think Reg intended calling in the security firm to help clear the place. We'd no idea so many would come, you see."

"They wouldn't if you hadn't had a body, dear," Mavis said cheerfully, "the poor woman's probably paid for the thatch by getting herself strangled."

"Well I hope everyone felt uplifted after they'd been inside," Felicity said with asperity. "These paintings were inspired by the love of God, not hatred and wanting to kill someone."

She led them round the back of the church to a small narrow door. "The vicar's own private entrance."

"I don't remember it."

"It was probably done after you'd left Wuffinge. A previous incumbent was arthritic, it saved him having to use the steps inside the main door. It goes into the Norman apse by the choir stalls. Mind your heads."

The day was nearly over. Ruby and the scouts had gone but the two Green Men were still there, backed by security men. "Five more minutes . . ." one called. "Hurry along. The church is about to close."

"Reg!" There was a whispered consultation and Felicity beckoned. "Follow the last ones as they go through, that way you'll be less conspicuous."

"Here, dear," Mavis shoved a five-pound note in her hand. "Put this in the plate." She gazed heavenwards. "He's done his bit for me. He took Herbert Bignell, you can't say fairer than that." The last customers were ushered in, Mr Pringle and Mavis joined them.

"These three are the best," he murmured to her. He lingered in front of the last picture, finding new delights to savour. Mavis watched him enjoying himself and gave Felicity a contented wink. As far as she was concerned, the paintings were lively and colourful but had no other significance. She approved the fact that their message was plain.

"You and the vicar ought to get postcards done, Felicity. They'd sell like hot cakes, especially one of him." She pointed to the figure of Adam. "He's got a dirty mind, you can tell just by looking at him . . . and as for that little devil!"

Mr Pringle took her arm. "Over here. Sadly, the plaster was too fragile to be restored—oh, dear!" He'd accidentally bumped into one of the lamps, tilting the beam so that it shone over the two dark pictures.

"Goodness!" The crazed surface was clearly visible under the glare. "I am sorry—how careless of me."

"Here, let me." The taller of the two Green Men reached up and adjusted the shutters. Gloom was swiftly restored.

"You can tell how hard you must've worked on the others," Mavis was impressed. "No chance of bringing these to life then?"

"None," the man answered shortly.

"There's a bit of a word on this one?"

"We think it's *descenditi* . . . to do with Man's descent into Hell." Mavis peered more closely.

"If that's what this is about . . . When the light was on you could see this chap's expression . . . He doesn't look terribly upset about it."

"Please—not too close."

"Sorry, dear." Mavis straightened up. "I wouldn't be surprised if Herbert looked like that, till he found out where he'd been sent."

"Seen enough?" The vicar was obviously worn out.

Mr Pringle said quickly, "We must go. Thank you, again." He snatched a final glance at the mystical, magical panel. "Wonderful," he said simply and led the way back.

Behind, he could hear Felicity asking, "Have the police been, Reg?"

"Yes. We're off to make our statements as soon as we've locked up."

"Try and have an early night," she said sympathetically. "You look bushed."

"I will."

Mr Pringle waited, holding the curtain aside for her to pass. The Green Men were replacing the screens now, while the security team disconnected the lights.

"Everyone was on edge this morning but now we're all too tired." Felicity said sadly, "Poor Doris. She worked hard enough to make this festival a success. The more I think about it, the more unreal it seems."

She and Mavis walked down the path. Mr Pringle stared back at the one lit area below the pulpit where the boxes of ticket money were stacked. How many thousands had been earned in Wuffinge today? There would be a repeat of it tomorrow and whenever the pictures were shown in the future. Mavis was right; they would safeguard church fabric from now on.

Outside, the churchyard was deserted. In the gloaming they heard distant brass bands while overhead the motorway kept up its roar. Despite this, it was peaceful. Bats skimmed past them, squeaking excitedly.

"Do those things bite?"

"No, no," Mr Pringle assured her. Mavis stared at the wreaths, pale under the rising moon.

"Is that the chap who died in the wrong place?"

"It is."

"Well, I'm not stopping. He might pop up to tell us what happened—I'm not sure I want to hear." They walked beneath the lych arch. "When we get home, Felicity, I'll make you one of my specials. Ever so effective they are; cure coughs, keep out ghosts, everything."

Behind them, the church crouched as if wanting to hide the marvels it contained. Had the Major been on his way here that night, to see the pictures for himself?

Reassured, Mr Pringle began to follow the womenfolk. He'd no idea why Mrs Leveret had been strangled but here at least was surely a valid reason for the man to have turned left instead of right.

In the police caravan, DI Andrews summarized the day's results so far. "She wasn't liked and everyone thinks that somehow the Kenny woman was involved."

"It's not a woman's way, strangling," his sergeant, John Mather, objected.

"There's always a first time. Didn't her husband tell us she believes in equality?"

"He's a far more likely candidate."

"Possibly, if we knew why . . ." Andrews drawled. "Definitely hot and bothered according to the lads who saw him on

Thursday morning. Wonder what Mr Kenny was up to the previous night?"

"The thing is," said Ted, "why should anyone *want* to kill Doris?" They were back in the living-room with the french windows open to enjoy the warm evening "She was harmless enough. She'd put one or two backs up since she returned but not enough to bring that kind of retribution."

"Guinevere didn't like her but she'd never have strangled her," Mavis said with conviction. "She'd have used her gun."

"I don't quite see Miss Petrie Coombe-Hamilton as the killer," Mr Pringle agreed. "As for strangling, that would require strength. Mrs Leveret must have fought back, her hands weren't bound initially remember. But when it came to carrying her body out of the marquee . . ." he shrugged. "It had to be someone strong."

"Guinevere's very strong," Mavis assured him. "And she's a little bit loopy."

"How would you go about murdering someone, Mavis?" Ted asked with a grin.

"Use a soda syphon. Blind whoever it was with the contents then bash 'em on the head."

"If ever you're found unconscious and soaking wet, old man, the police will know where to turn." But that reminded them too acutely of Doris.

"What about Miranda Kenny?" asked Felicity reluctantly. "We've been told she was attacked but there's been no corroboration as far as I know. The police began questioning some people. When Doris was found, they gave up. We've only Miranda's word that it ever took place at all."

Ted said slowly, "She goes out in the dark, comes back later looking all het up and tells her husband—who's a bit of a twit, by the way—"

"He's not that stupid."

"She's the one who wears the trousers," Ted insisted.

"Are you both implying there wasn't an attack?" asked Mr Pringle.

"I'm saying it's a possibility. Miranda's a strong person, physically as well as mentally. If she had been in some kind of—fight—and came home in a state, it would be one way of explaining it to Oliver."

"You're right, old girl."

"By 'fight', you mean strangling Mrs Leveret?"

Felicity sighed, "She's the only one I can think of who really did detest Doris."

"Does anyone know why?" demanded Mavis.

"Nothing big, just lots and lots of little things. They rubbed each other up the wrong way, always have."

"But what about the hat?" asked Mr Pringle. "Who ever heard of a killer leaving something as obvious as that?"

"Someone else did that," Mavis said promptly, "someone who didn't like Mrs Kenny found it and put it on the other woman's head."

"You mean—found a dead body and put a hat on it?" Mr Pringle said doubtfully. "That's awfully far-fetched."

"It's possible," Mavis said darkly, "in a village. It wouldn't happen in London."

"It's a theory I cannot accept. What you're suggesting is that Miranda Kenny met Doris Leveret—why should she anyway?"

"She might've asked for a meeting," said Felicity.

"That late?"

She shrugged. "It's possible, especially this week."

"All right, for the sake of the argument, the two of them meet. Mrs Kenny strangles Mrs Leveret—where?"

"You mean, where in Wuffinge Parva?" asked Ted. "There are hundreds of places."

"It must've been near the river otherwise why were her clothes wet when I found her?"

"That's easy," Ted replied. "If Miranda made out she was off to guard her frogs, she might suggest a meeting over there. It's not far from the river."

"So . . . Mrs Kenny strangled Mrs Leveret and lugs her body to the nearby Wuffen, then what?"

The three of them looked at him blankly.

"What d'you mean?" asked Ted.

"I mean that while Miranda Kenny rushed back to Macavity's Pastures, to convince her husband she'd been attacked, and while we three were carousing here, what happened to the corpse of Mrs Leveret, last seen being deposited in the Wuffen?"

"Mrs Kenny had lost her hat in the struggle," said Mavis. "She didn't realize it until the following lunchtime when you told her where it had turned up. That's when she realized she'd have to say it came off while she was being attacked—no one would expect her to miss it under those circumstances."

"Right," Ted agreed. "That's another reason for Miranda to claim she was jumped on."

"But you still haven't explained how Mrs Leveret's corpse arrived in the marquee."

"Or how it disappeared afterwards," Felicity reminded them.

"Give us a chance, dear," Mavis protested. "We're none of us experienced at this kind of thing."

"I fear I cannot accept that Mrs Kenny was a killer," Mr Pringle shook his head obstinately. "Her reaction when I told her about Mrs Leveret as well as the hat, was one of complete disbelief."

"Yes but Pringle, old man, it probably wasn't the hat she was reacting to. I mean, if I'd left Doris bobbing down the Wuffen and a stranger turns up and says he saw the hat on Doris's body—in a tent—"

"Doris's head."

"Don't be pedantic, Flick. You do see what I'm getting at? Miranda Kenny had just been told the most incredible thing—and she *knew* the body was no longer in that tent because she'd been working there all morning. She must've wondered whether she was listening to a bloody lunatic when you started telling her that tale, old man. She'd be startled, all right."

"It's the most unlikely hypothesis I've ever heard. During my time in the Revenue, I was told many tales but none as wild as that."

"Did you ever come across a dodge I could use?" Ted asked wistfully.

"Ted!"

"But who was responsible," Mr Pringle demanded, "for transporting a dead weight all the way from the Wuffen to its temporary resting place inside the marquee?"

"Eddie could've done it!" cried Felicity. They stared. "Because Doris wouldn't have been near the church by then. She'd have been washed down near the bridge just as she was this morning. In fact, her body may not have got that far. It would have floated past the gardens here. Eddie may have seen it as it went past."

"Old girl, you're brilliant!"

"Who's Eddie?" asked Mavis.

"Little Elsie's brother . . . and as for who little Elsie is—"

Ted was about to continue when his wife said quickly, "They're brother and sister, Mavis. They live in the dilapidated cottage and they *loathe* Miranda Kenny."

"But why put the body in the tent wearing another woman's hat?" said Mr Pringle pedantically. "And how had Eddie come by that hat? I thought he spent Monday to Friday in Milton Keynes."

"He sometimes comes home on Thursday instead of Friday," Felicity told him. "He's been prowling round for weeks, trying to shoot that vixen. He might've stumbled over it." Mavis was horrified.

"You don't mean—there really are foxes in Wuffinge?"

"And wolves," Ted said heartlessly, "but we're lucky when it comes to snakes, only a very few adders come slithering out of the river—"

"Urgh!"

"Ted—stop frightening our guest."

"Sorry, Mavis . . . especially after those wonderful cocktails. When I'm a widower, will you marry me?"

"Returning to our hypothesis," Mr Pringle began.

"You mean, the hat? Eddie could have found that when he was prowling after the fox as Flick suggests," Ted replied. "Then, when he discovered Doris's body he thought he'd make trouble for Miranda Kenny. The marquee was her domain, remember. Just the sort of thing Eddie would do."

"So why did the body disappear?"

"He'd be watching, of course," Felicity said thoughtfully. "When he saw you dash off to the pub, maybe he had second thoughts. Eddie's not that stupid. He'd know he might have left some trace which could've implicated him. It could've been self-preservation that made him do it. No one would remark on his old van. As you were saying before, someone who's part of everyday life in Wuffinge. That just about sums up Eddie and little Elsie."

"And where would they—store—the article?" asked Mr Pringle.

"The privy," Ted said promptly, "down the garden. As soon as it was dark, drag her out, dump her in the river. She was bound to end up under the bridge."

Mr Pringle thought about it.

"It's plausible . . . if one can accept the initial premise: that

Miranda Kenny *would* be stupid enough to strangle Mrs Leveret. I must say I still find that impossible."

"Maybe she never intended to, old man. Maybe things simply got out of hand. They have had some frightful spats in the past."

"But Mrs Kenny is intelligent," Mr Pringle insisted. "Naïve, I grant you, but to let emotion get out of control . . . and commit such an act here, where everyone knew the situation?"

"The female is deadlier than the male," Ted announced heartily, "and far more hot-tempered. Look at Flick here. She flew off the handle the other day when I'd used a shirt to mop up a spot of diesel. I bet Mavis acts unreasonably sometimes."

"Only if he's done something silly." Mavis considered her partner, "When he does, I could thump him."

"But neither of you ever have," Mr Pringle pointed out, "because you bring us down to size in other ways. So, I believe, would Mrs Kenny. She knew how to make Mrs Leveret feel inferior. I'm sure she saw through her pretensions to have had a grammar school education."

"I was surprised when Doris repeated that tale to you," said Felicity.

"I'd suggested she was in little Elsie's class at school."

Ted laughed. "Doris Winkle wouldn't like that!"

"Ted, the poor woman is dead!"

"I know, I know."

"Why is it," Mavis demanded to know, "that whenever little Elsie's name comes up . . .?"

"Shall we tell her, Pringle?"

"Bed," Felicity announced firmly. "Come on, all of you. I'll explain tomorrow, Mavis, in private. It's a subject which gets Ted excited."

"Not these days, old girl." Ted began collecting glasses and coffee cups.

"None of this answers the question that continues to puzzle me," the image of the Major as an art-lover was beginning to trouble Mr Pringle, "as to why Major Petrie Coombe-Hamilton—" he was interrupted by groans.

"I thought we'd managed to get through the whole evening without a single reference to that, old man."

Mr Pringle replied sheepishly, "Nevertheless, I fear there has to be some connection. I wonder what conclusions the police have come to?"

"They've probably solved it by now. I hope they tell us soon, then we can all get a good night's sleep."

In the Incident Caravan, DI Andrews was alert. "Oh, yes? Tell me more."

Without his make-up and mask, in jeans and a T-shirt, Robert, the taller of the two Green Men, still had an authoritative air.

"You were bound to discover, from your records."

"I agree. But I want you to tell me now."

"Just over six months, with full remission—"

"And the charge?"

"A painting which was sold for two point eight million pounds . . . turned out not to be entirely—genuine."

DI Andrews said without thinking, "No picture's worth that."

Robert smiled sardonically. "There I agree with you, but my work was as good if not better than the original. A second-rate Dutch interior became a masterpiece—"

"And is that what you've been doing up at the church? Creating masterpieces?"

"Oh, no." The voice was vehement, "Certainly not. Reg gave me the chance to put my talent to use, and I asked Peter along. *Restoring* work of such antiquity is a serious matter. Peter and I happen to be experts."

"Hmm."

"I was foolish over the other business, granted, but you'd be amazed how expertise such as ours can be under-valued in the art world." The voice became bitter. "Neither of us has paper qualifications, only talent."

"So what did you get paid?"

"For the interior? Two thousand."

"Bloody hell!"

"Exactly. Which is why I turned Queen's evidence."

Oh yes, thought Andrews. He assesed the man shrewdly.

"I'd been promised ten," Robert continued. "My 'employer' reneged, which was stupid. He ended up in Winson Green. I went to Chelmsford where Reg was prison chaplain."

And if he hadn't reneged, would you have turned him in? wondered Andrews.

"I shall require a full statement."

"Gladly. I want to make it perfectly clear that we had nothing

102

to do with the Leveret woman's death. Peter and I were in the church throughout Wednesday evening and didn't finish until the early hours. We had to wait until the women had finished decorating before we could complete restoration of the final picture. It's been a race against time the entire week."

"And the vicar?"

"Reg and Peter were installing wiring for the lights. A power cable had to be run from the vicarage because the church hadn't a sufficient supply."

Which tallied with the vicar's statement. The computer had been abandoned; Andrews picked up his pen. "Right, let's make a start. Name?"

In the adjoining cubicle, DS Mather had reached the same stage with the second Green Man. "Name?"

"Winstead. First name, Peter."

In the outer office, WDC Tyler said kindly, "I shouldn't bother to wait. It could take ages." The vicar was anxious. He'd made no mention of Robert's prison sentence in his statement, but now he decided to tell Tracy Tyler.

"There won't be any trouble?"

"I don't see why. They were both working at the church with your blessing?"

He nodded. "A second chance is how I look on it." He hesitated. "The three of us were together throughout Wednesday evening, as we have been every evening for weeks. We neither heard nor saw anything of Doris Leveret."

"Well, that probably clears the matter up."

DI Andrews was sarcastic. "He needs his head examined." WDC Tyler disagreed.

"He probably couldn't afford to employ anyone else. Anyway, he claims to have been in the church whenever the two of them were working on the restoration. He's no fool."

"It's fortunate those paintings are part of the walls," said Mather, "otherwise they might've been tempted to nick 'em."

"Which doesn't make either of them a murderer," Tracy insisted.

"I agree, worse luck," Andrews yawned. "Come on. Time for beddy-byes. We've done enough for one day." He picked up his jacket.

* * *

103

Mr Pringle was allowed to join Mavis in bed after inspecting the dormer thatch for spiders. During the night, he awoke from a troubled dream. "Of course!" he muttered, "how stupid of me not to think of it before." It wasn't the complete answer but it enabled him to slumber more peacefully.

Chapter Seven

In the police caravan the following morning, DI Andrews was peevish. He'd no reason to be, most of the reports he'd asked for were on his desk. Some of their conclusions were vague however and this irritated him. He was curt with DS Mather.

"All they're committing themselves to is that she'd been strangled and been dead for longer than twenty-four hours. We knew that much. They also agree she could've been dead as long as seventy-two but they refuse to be more specific at this stage, which is a big help. Oh, and she was dead before she was dumped in the river."

"None of which contradicts granddad's story."

"What about the woolly hat?"

"We showed it to Mrs Kenny last night. She agreed straight away it was hers. Although the weather's warm, she still uses it when she goes on frog patrol because of the dust blown down from the motorway. Claims as it's such an automatic habit, putting it on, she càn't be certain when she last wore it."

"Oh, great!"

"Unfortunately, she keeps both hat and her scarf stuffed inside her wellies which always stand in the porch. I had a quiet word with her neighbour. She confirmed it."

"Blast! In other words, where anyone could've pinched it." DI Andrews took the hat from the plastic bag and turned it over in his hands. The earflaps had been untied so that it now resembled a bonnet. He found the label. "Aztec Products. Made in Korea."

"It's a mail order company. D'you want us to check?"

"No point."

"Forensic found hairs from the deceased as well as others, presumably Mrs Kenny's."

"What about the ligature?"

"We're waiting for news on that. Should hear later this morning."

"Right. I want another chat with Mrs Kenny when we've finished the interviews. I want to recall all those who were out

105

in Wuffinge after midnight on Wednesday when Mrs Kenny
went on patrol. I don't care if they do have alibis, I want all of
them double checked."

"Right."

DI Andrews raised his voice to everyone in the caravan. "A
meeting in half an hour, folks. I want the map marked up with
Miranda Kenny's route including the spot where she says she
was attacked plus all known sightings of Doris Leveret from
Wednesday afternoon onwards. Someone try and get the coffee
machine fixed by then."

"We've had to send for the man. As it's Sunday he said he
couldn't promise when he'd get here."

"Oh, great."

Sunday had also begun badly in Woodbine Cottage. Mr Pringle
and Mavis heard Ted's indignant roar as they were dressing.
"Those bloody moles! Look at my lawn!" From the safety of
their room, they gazed down on the destruction in the back
garden.

"Did animals do that? Dig up those heaps of soil?"

"Yes."

Mavis shuddered. "Wild creatures running about underneath
the grass—will they dig through the floorboards?" It was his
turn to comfort, for she had soothed away his terrors last night.
He'd awoken more than once with the image of that dreadful
swollen face still so vivid in his mind.

"Moles stay below, they don't molest us humans."

"How d'you get rid of them?"

"Owners of lawns have been pondering that question for the
last two thousand years."

"Here . . ." Mavis had another worry. "If we walk outside,
how can you be sure they won't nip up for a quick nibble?"

The phone rang as Felicity was preparing breakfast. They
were in the dining-room, reading accounts of yesterday's events
in the Sunday papers when they heard her say, "Oh, lord,
Joyce—I never gave Cyril a thought . . . Yes, of course I will.
Yes . . . yes . . . Ten o'clock? Who's in charge? No, neither do
I. Would you? Oh, yes . . . well, I'll ask him. Ted?"

"Yes?"

"Can you take over the harmonium? Joyce has the list of
hymns."

"Oh, bother! Why can't she do it?" Felicity stuck her head round the door.

"Because crowds are already arriving even though the marquee doesn't open officially until eleven a.m. and Reg has asked if we can come to the rescue *now*. The public has to have somewhere to go. We can't let them into the church until morning service is over. If Joyce is in the marquee she can't play the harmonium at the same time."

"OK, OK." He rose. "Hope there's nothing in E minor."

"The police want to interview Miranda Kenny again. Michelle's offered to take over but she's so unreliable Joyce feels she ought to keep an eye on her."

"Understood."

"And we've all forgotten about Cyril Leveret. I'll simply have to go round . . ." Ted ambled through to pick up the phone and Felicity reappeared.

"You heard all that? Mavis, would you mind taking over here? The eggs are done and I've turned the sausages over under the grill. It's Doris's husband. She used to do everything for him. I'm going round now to get his breakfast."

Mavis protested it was no trouble. Ted returned and propped *Hymns Ancient and Modern* against the marmalade jar.

"I normally deputize during Joyce's summer hols," he said plaintively. "If there's half a dozen in the congregation then, it's a full house. She says the whole village could be there this morning, plus outsiders . . . Blasted stupid idea, this festival!"

Full of sympathy, Mr Pringle ate in silence while Ted thudded stiff fingers on the table top.

"We can certainly arrange for a WDC to be present, Mrs Kenny—"

"I want a woman police officer to conduct the interview. You can listen in if you think it necessary."

"Mrs Kenny, I am in charge of this inquiry."

"I refuse to answer questions about rape from a man."

"Difficult", the notes had described her after the first interview: it was the understatement of the year.

"One moment, Mrs Kenny." DI Andrews left her and breathed his fury over the slim, blonde WDC next door. "Tracy, if you don't squeeze every last ounce of information out of her—including whether or not the attack ever really happened—"

"It's like that?"

"It's a possiblity."

"Anything else?"

"Why ask a mere male?"

"He's worse than I remember, Ted. He's not just ga-ga, he's utterly confused. Keeps saying why did Doris go off and leave him high and dry?" Felicity's face had lost its wholesome fresh colour again. "I tried to make him understand she was dead but Cyril shouted it was a lot of nonsense and the police had no business saying things like that. He mumbled something about Doris having gone to speak to Leonard and when she came back they must sort things out because there wasn't any more money."

Ted said gently, "Steady, old thing. Sit down, it's obviously been a bit of a shock."

"I'll get you some coffee." Mavis disappeared into the kitchen followed by Mr Pringle. As they shut the door, they heard Ted say, "Now then, kitten, tell huggy bear all about it," and Felicity began to sob. "Cyril's in such a state, Ted . . . completely out of touch . . ."

"Dear oh dear," Mr Pringle perched on a stool. "I suppose the shock to an elderly mind . . . I wonder who Leonard is?"

"Never mind him, it's Felicity I'm worried about." Mavis put the coffee in the microwave to reheat it. "She's got a heavy day ahead. Look, we don't have to rush back to town, do we?"

"No?"

"I could get the lunch, maybe even help with the festival in some way. I'm sure Ted would be glad of support."

"So long as he doesn't expect me to play the harmonium."

"Keep him company. I can manage here."

WDC Tyler was making heavy weather of Miranda Kenny. They had reached impasse, with Mrs Kenny claiming she wasn't surprised that no one believed her story but could show the police where the attack took place. Doubtless there would still be signs of the struggle.

DI Andrews believed they had already found the spot, near the river. He showed her the place they'd marked on the map. Miranda frowned.

"I'm sure it was much nearer the motorway bridge, where I normally go on patrol in fact."

"The marks of the struggle are consistent with a body having been dragged into the river, Mrs Kenny."

Miranda was angry. "Which means you stopped looking for the place where I was attacked because you'd found the spot where Doris was killed. That's not very thorough."

"You believe it was the same person, Mrs Kenny?"

She was sarcastic. "Two thugs abroad the same night in a village this size? Or has there been a prison breakout we don't know about?"

"Why d'you think no one heard you shouting?"

"Did anyone hear Doris?"

"No one has admitted to doing so, so far."

"That's because of the motorway. The noise drowns out everything. I couldn't shout at first—he came from behind and clamped a hand over my mouth—no doubt he did the same to her. I screamed like hell when I broke free but there are no houses in that lane, no one to hear until much nearer the village and I'd stopped shouting by then because I was out of breath."

"How d'you explain the marks on the river bank?"

"I've told you, it must have been where Doris went in. Obviously she had to have been pushed in somewhere and the river is overgrown there, with plenty of cover. It was dark, no street lights." The young policewoman didn't respond. Miranda's sarcasm increased, partly out of fear. Surely even the idiotic police would arrest him soon!

"If you're suggesting I had anything to do with the *strangling* then you really are being stupid." DI Andrews was unperturbed.

"For the sake of argument, let's suppose you were the attacker, not one of his victims," he drawled. "After you'd run off, he finds Mrs Leveret. Things go badly wrong. What d'you, as a killer, suggest might have happened next?" Miranda Kenny stared, half-inclined to laugh.

"You're completely mad. I complain to you about an attempted rape and now you accuse me of being the murderer? It's ludicrous."

"No doubt it is, Mrs Kenny. But you know the habits of people in this village, so I repeat the question: what do you think the killer would have done, assuming him to be a local, after his attack on you had failed?"

"I've told you before—*my* attacker wasn't a local man." How many clues did they need, for Christ's sake!

"For the sake of the hypothetical argument, let's say he was."

She shrugged.

"It's a waste of time but all right. This hypothetical local must have attacked Doris and she couldn't defend herself. She was older—I've no idea what she was doing out at that time of night—I certainly didn't see her. Perhaps she recognized the man."

"His voice might have been unfamiliar to you but not to her. She was from Wuffinge originally." Miranda didn't bother to reply. She's obviously not going to shift on that one, thought DI Andrews.

"And you say you didn't see Mrs Leveret either when you went on patrol or when you ran back?" Tracy Tyler repeated.

"I did not."

"You claim not to have seen anyone, in fact."

"Look." Fear made her loud. What had begun as revenge had now become a threat. "No doubt there were one or two people. I mean, I heard the odd sound—probably someone walking their dog—but I wasn't paying attention. I was thinking of all the things that remained to be done before the marquee could open the following afternoon. It's been a huge undertaking for a village this size."

"Of course."

"It has caused—friction. But I repeat, if you're accusing me of harming Doris Leveret in any way, you must've been listening to gossip."

"We did that yesterday, Mrs Kenny. We sorted out who's got a grudge, who was trying to implicate their neighbour, who sounded reliable and who didn't—all part of standard procedure. An orderly process of elimination. Now we're down to common factors. Names that keep cropping up. Cross-references. Stories which don't quite tally. You know the sort of thing. Your name crops up quite often, Mrs Kenny."

"I'm sure it does." Miranda made herself stay calm. Of course she could handle this, she was intelligent, twice as bright as the man goading her. "There are plenty who would prefer to see the village crumble and stagnate. I want to preserve what's best here but that also means encouraging change. In some people's eyes, that's unacceptable. It's partly because Oliver and I are newcomers—we always will be in Wuffinge Parva."

110

"What were Mrs Leveret's views? Was she for change or against?'

"I've no idea."

"We can't ask her husband, he's too upset. But your arrival had repercussions for her, didn't it? You were the stone which sent ripples through Mrs Leveret's comfortable little back-water. Was the festival entirely your idea by the way?"

"Nothing that happened in the village was entirely my idea. At parish meetings, we take a collective decision—"

"But who *proposed* the flower festival? It'll be on record in the Minutes but it'll save time if you tell us now." Miranda Kenny sat back, arms folded.

"I'm perfectly certain you must have asked other people as well as checking the Minutes. I'm not answering any more questions without consulting my solicitor."

DI Andrews craved strong coffee. The thought of grappling with another feminist—for he was willing to bet that's what it would turn out to be—was too much. Some things were better left. He gave Miranda a polite smile which still didn't include his eyes.

"If we require your further assistance we'll be in touch, Mrs Kenny. Just one question before you leave, do you know anyone in the village by the name of Leonard?"

"Do you mean Len Runkle?" she frowned. "Or there's Leonard De'ath—quite a few, in fact."

"A Leonard known to both you and Mrs Leveret?"

"We knew all of them, at least by sight. This is a village."

"And you can't think of any Leonard, from Wuffinge, who might have been your attacker?"

"No, I can't."

When she'd gone, WDC Tyler said uncertainly, "You don't really think she did it, do you?"

"Ever study *Macbeth* when you were at school?"

"Yes."

"Women don't always do their own dirty work, you know."

Tracy Tyler ran through her knowledge of Oliver Kenny.

"I wouldn't have thought *he* was the type to kill anyone."

"I don't suppose Macbeth thought he was, until his wife got started on him."

The inspector was staring out of the window when another message came through. "The ligature was several strands of

111

ordinary garden twine," DS Mather reported, "the green sort you buy in garden centres."

The inspector focused his gaze on distant flower beds, a much prized feature of Wuffinge Parva, full of blooms neatly tied and staked. "There's a nice little task for a Sunday," he murmured, "finding a ball of twine that matches. How many dwellings are there?"

"I dunno. There's three hundred and seventy voters on the electoral role. We should've finished interviewing the last of them by lunchtime."

"After that, you can start on gardener's question time. Should keep you out of mischief. Don't forget the allotments, there's sheds a-plenty over there. I suggest you organize a team, John."

Mr Pringle was required to stand adjacent to the harmonium so that, "if the back falls off you can stick it up again before the bellows fall out". It was no idle threat. Ted's answer to a lack of expertise was to pound heavily, causing the instrument to rattle.

The pews weren't back in position and the few chairs were insufficient for the mass of visitors. Latecomers could scarcely move. There was an excited buzz. Doris Leveret, Winkle that was, who'd bossed them about, had been strangled by the stranger seen hanging about Wuffinge. It must be true because Michelle Brazier had said so in the newspapers.

To see that same stranger beside the harmonium caused amazement. Maybe the police would arrest him during the service? It added to the anticipation.

Oblivious to their whispering at first, Mr Pringle wondered if the two Green Men would attend. He was curious to see what they looked like in real life but none in the congregation matched them in height or build.

There was a suggestion of decay in the air. Greenery which had added so much to the magic on Friday and yesterday, was wilting fast. Felicity and her colleagues had sprayed with reviving compounds but it was no use; wild flowers shrivelled on the stem.

"Oy!" Ted's whisper recalled him to duty. Mr Pringle had to cue him when the choir were ready to process down the aisle. He peered over the massed heads. At the back was a gaggle dressed in starched ruffs and blue gowns.

"Yes, they're there." Unfortunately the Voluntary Joyce had provided was beyond Ted's skill. From a limited repertoire, he had found a march by Souza and launched into it. Those fortunate enough to be seated, leapt to their feet. Fighting their way through them came the choir, arriving in chaos at the steps to the apse. Grey-haired lady choristers glared in their direction. "They've got there," Mr Pringle whispered unnecessarily, "they're finding their places." It was an inadequate description for the melée that was even then sorting itself out.

To distract from the noise, Ted attempted an arpeggio which dwindled to a diminished seventh and was quickly abandoned in favour of a C major chord. Silence. The bewildered congregation settled themselves; the vicar appeared and mounted the steps to the pulpit.

Like many this morning, he looked as though he hadn't slept. He nodded to Ted and failed to exhibit surprise at seeing Mr Pringle standing beside him. Slowly but surely it began to dawn on his flock that if the stranger wasn't the killer, and his presence unfettered and free appeared to confirm it, someone else—a member of their own small community in fact—must be responsible.

There was a drawing together. Despite the crush, families huddled, trying not to brush up against a neighbour's elbow. Long forgotten petty hatreds began to resurface as women looked at one another with suspicion and men positively scowled. Despite the heat, the temperature dropped by several degrees and all trace of brotherly love evaporated.

Established Wuffinge families were out in force. Children not seen in church since their christening sat and fidgeted. Mr Pringle recognized some faces; Ruby from the council house surrounded by her menfolk, all of them Runkles, all peas in a pod. Nearby was her cousin, little Elsie. Eddie must be the man on her left—goodness, he'd aged! Mr Pringle recalled that last night Eddie had been cast as a possible murderer. Before he could wonder at it, the vicar rose.

"When the wicked man turneth away from his wickedness that he hath committed, and doeth that which is lawful and right, he shall save his soul alive . . ."

These words commanded everyone's full attention for once but when the familiar responses began, Mr Pringle found his thoughts drifting. *CRASH!* Dust filled the air.

"Be quick, old lad!" Ted watched in anguish as Mr Pringle

scrabbled among the debris, struggling to replace the bellows. "Don't nod off again," he begged. "Psalm 77 next—it's a real swine!"

Miranda Kenny was in no hurry to leave Macavity's Pastures for the marquee. Oliver affected not to notice.

"I think the police suspect me."

"Suspect you of what?"

"Of strangling Doris Leveret."

"That's ridiculous!"

"It's the real reason they wanted to question me again, not about the attack."

"But how . . . I mean, why? What reason did they give?" stammered Oliver.

"Nothing but village gossip. But they obviously believe I made up the story as cover for having killed Doris." When Oliver remained silent, she said sharply, "Just what did you tell them yesterday?"

"I? I simply answered their questions. They wanted confirmation of the time you returned here, the state you were in— nothing I said contradicted your statement. I told them how upset I was—"

"You!" Contempt was barely concealed. "Well?" she demanded. "What are you going to tell them next time?"

"Why should there be a next time?"

"Because you, Oliver, are my husband. Theoretically, the person closest to the one whom they now suspect of being a strangler." He looked relieved.

"That's all right."

"What?"

"As your husband I can't give evidence against you."

"Is that all you can say? You—turd!" She slammed the door with such force, the lute fell to earth with a clatter. Macavity leapt to safety in his chair.

"If they suspect you, my dear wife," Oliver muttered into the emptiness, "then I'm truly glad!" If she could have seen his face at that moment, Mrs Kenny would have been very frightened indeed.

"It smells wonderful," Felicity said gratefully.

"Lunch will be ready in half an hour, provided our menfolk are back."

"They'll have gone to the Hope & Anchor. Ted always needs a drink afterwards. I hope Joyce can take over this evening."

"Could you show me where you keep your cornflour? Ta. What's happening about Mr Leveret?"

"Ruby's cooking his lunch. She worked for Doris even though she loathed her but she's sorry for Cyril."

"Poor old thing . . . ga-ga, you said?"

"Yes."

"Who's this Leonard his wife went to see?"

"We don't know." Felicity frowned. "There are several in the village, but we don't know which one."

"Odd the way Mrs Kenny's name keeps cropping up."

Felicity shrugged. "I just can't believe her capable."

"Do the police know about the two of them quarrelling?"

"I had to tell them about one incident," Felicity admitted, "I was there when it happened. It was when we were discussing who should be in charge of ticket sales. Quite a responsibility considering the sums involved. Doris and Miranda were at one another's throats. Excessively polite, of course, but *so* hostile. In the end, Reg suggested he should look after the money."

"Who was the most put out?"

Felicity considered. "Doris, definitely. She took things to heart more than Miranda did."

Mavis added stock to the gravy. If Mr Leveret was broke, was that why his wife wanted to get her hands on the ticket money? In Mrs Bignell's experience, raffles at the Bricklayers often produced less than anticipated. As for the mystery Leonard, someone must know who he was.

"We've been given a possible lead by Syd at the pub."

"How much did it cost?" asked Andrews sourly.

"He forgot to tell us about two other guests who stayed there earlier this week. They left Wuffinge on Friday morning for Sweden. One gave a home address in Uppsala. Syd claimed there was something fishy about their behaviour."

"With hindsight, I daresay there was something fishy about a lot of people's behaviour this week. However, it's worth a try."

"It could tie in with Mrs Kenny's conviction that the man wasn't a local."

DI Andrews sniffed. "She never mentioned a foreign accent. I'd have thought she'd be the first to identify that."

* * *

115

Mr Pringle said apologetically, "Would you mind if we stayed late this evening? I'd like to test a theory about why the Major died where he did but it means waiting until the vicar is free."

Mavis shrugged. "If you think it's important, dear. If we do, we ought to offer to help Ted and Felicity clear up. They can't start until the experts have finished."

They were washing-up following lunch. Ted and Felicity had returned to the church.

"I'll wander up and ask Ted now," Mr Pringle agreed.

"And I'll go and have a chat with Guinevere. There's something I want to ask her."

"Mavis, do take care. The killer hasn't been apprehended yet."

"Listen, dear, I've coped when they've been smashing glasses in one another's faces at the Bricklayers. It's not murderers that worry me, it's spiders and moles and things. D'you think Felicity would mind if I borrowed her wellies?"

Guinevere was in a temper. "Those dreadful policemen have taken all of Daddy's guns."

"Why?"

"He didn't have a licence for them."

"Isn't that illegal? I thought he was a magistrate?"

"Yes, he was. That's why he said no one would dare challenge him."

"Ah."

"All I've got left is great-grandfather's blunderbuss."

"What's a blunderbuss?"

"Through here, I'll show you." Miss Petrie Coombe-Hamilton led the way to the glassed-in verandah. "The police poked about of course but they didn't find it because Daddy always kept it in a hockey bag." She unbuckled the stiff canvas. "See."

It was a ferocious-looking weapon, with a wide barrel and a short flared muzzle. Mavis eyed it with respect.

"It's fearfully heavy," said her hostess, "try it." Mavis agreed that it was.

"What sort of ammunition does it use?"

"That's the marvellous thing; you can stuff just about anything inside. Shot, stones, anything. It has a flintlock action. Aiming is difficult and the kick's an absolute pig but it works every time."

"Do you need a licence for it?"

116

"I didn't ask," Guinevere said simply. "Shall we try it out on the pigeons?"

"D'you think we could have a cup of tea instead? I've brought you a little present." Miss Petrie Coombe-Hamilton was enchanted with the bottle of Angostura.

"This is the first time anyone's given me a present since Mummy died. Daddy always said gifts were a waste of money." The mean old bastard, thought Mavis Bignell.

"You'll find a few drops makes all the difference to a cocktail." Guinevere gazed at her new friend, moist-eyed.

"Shall we try it out?"

"Tea first," Mavis said firmly, "and then I want to ask you a question." But at the end of half an hour she had acquired more information than she'd bargained for.

"There are five Leonards in the village," she told Mr Pringle proudly. "It was a common name fifty years ago. Mrs Leveret had a brother called Leonard Winkle, he went to Canada. Guinevere's father was Leonard Eric. There's Leonard Runkle and his cousin Leonard De'ath, a cabinet maker, and the landlord of the Hope & Anchor is Sydney Leonard Grice because I saw it on the licence above the door."

Mr Pringle, who was at Ted's table surrounded by books, was astonished.

"Where did you learn all this?"

"From Guinevere. I asked if she knew which particular Leonard Mrs Leveret might have been seeing. She said it could've been any of them—except Daddy for obvious reasons—as Mrs L was such a busy-body and probably sticking her nose in where it wasn't wanted."

"That could be true," he murmured and returned to his book.

"I thought you'd be interested. Normally you're as keen as mustard when someone's been bumped off."

"Mavis, I shall lie awake yet again if I start worrying about Mrs Leveret. Her death was so dreadful it fills my mind and prevents me thinking clearly."

"I'm sorry, dear."

"The police have the investigation in hand. There were at least half a dozen officers inside that caravan and more, I gather, have been interviewing every male in Wuffinge between the ages of sixteen and seventy. Such knowledge I find sooth-ing. It enables me to concentrate on the other mystery."

"But it wasn't a mystery if the Major died from natural causes."

"That has never been the point at issue."

"D'you still think there's a connection?"

"It seems illogical if there weren't. So much violence within such a short time. I have discovered a possible link although a little tenuous. Ted and Felicity have accepted our offer of help, by the way. The plan is to begin clearing at eight."

"It'll be a late finish. I'll make some sandwiches to leave in the fridge."

"There is a further errand I must make, to a house I visited earlier." Mavis looked at him in alarm.

"You're not still thinking of moving to Wuffinge?"

"No," he said with a certain amount of regret, "and in fairness, I must make that clear to the lady concerned. Would you care to accompany me?"

As they walked, she said conversationally, "I met a wild animal on the way back from Guinevere's but a cyclist was passing and he killed it for me."

"Good heavens!"

"He said it was a weasel. What happens when they go pop?"

"D'you know, I'm not sure. I shall have to look it up."

Mavis remembered the blunderbuss.

"I think I've found a way of getting rid of those moles."

"Mankind will be forever in your debt. But each creature has its rightful place in nature's cycle, you know."

"Not in London they don't, thank goodness. Are we staying overnight?"

"Felicity suggested it. I said we'd be glad to accept, there's so much traffic heading back on a Sunday night."

"Now I know why," Mrs Bignell said ominously. "It's people who've been to the country realizing their mistake before it's too late."

"The lady we're about to visit is extremely house-proud," Mr Pringle explained tactfully as they entered the gate. Mavis took umbrage.

"I trust I know how to comport myself," she said grandly, then, "my God—look at all those gnomes!"

"Ssh! They have several more round the back."

She remembered to smile fulsomely as the door opened and Mr Pringle made the introductions.

"What lovely lobelias." The gnome owner looked puzzled. "Where?"

"In your neighbour's garden," Mavis improvised quickly. "That's what I like about the country. Always chock-a-block with lobelia flowers." It seemed prudent to change the subject and she walked further inside. "What a lovely sunny living-room!" Mr Pringle breathed again.

He introduced his questions casually, as they were leaving.

"No doubt the Hope & Anchor was too crowded yesterday for one of your regular visits."

"Oh no, we went," the woman assured him. "Wilf said we should take advantage and spread the gospel."

"No doubt your husband occasionally misses the Major's repartee?"

She said cautiously, "I wouldn't put it quite like that. More of a bully, Major Petrie Coombe-Hamilton could be."

"On his last visit, I believe he was arguing with Mrs Kenny?"

"Among others, yes, he was."

"What was the topic, do you remember?"

She wrinkled her forehead. "It was something to do with frogs," she declared. "Do I mean frogs? To do with an animal's habits, anyway." It was better than he'd hoped. Mr Pringle hid his excitement.

"The last of the Petrie Coombe-Hamilton line," he announced sententiously.

"After his daughter dies, you mean."

"Give Guinevere a chance," Mavis said cheerfully. "She's not ready to die yet. She's over the moon at the prospect of leaving Wuffinge."

"After so many years, Miss Petrie Coombe-Hamilton will feel it keenly, none the less," Mr Pringle added quickly.

"I don't know about that but the family has been here since the Conquest. You will let the estate agent know?"

"Oh, yes . . ." Guilt came over him as he realized he should have been honest, but the woman didn't appear to notice.

"I was right, wasn't I?" she simpered.

"Beg pardon?" She indicated the other For Sale notice further along the street.

"Not house-proud one little bit, is she? Never cleans her windows."

"No. No indeed." He couldn't remember a single detail but felt sure it might be true.

"I don't think she has any gnomes, either," said Mavis innocently. Mercifully, the woman was already out of earshot.

The police had come up with better results than Mrs Bignell or Guinevere.

"Seven males between the relevent ages have Leonard as one of their first names."

"Show me those who use it, either in full or as Len." WDC Tyler tapped the keys and information rolled on to the screen.

"Which of those hasn't got an alibi?" At the command, two names remained. Tracy Tyler ran her curser down to the second.

"Len Runkle was on his way home at midnight on Wednesday, or claims he was. He and his brother had been playing darts over at Yoxford. His brother dropped him off outside the Hope & Anchor—says it must have been about midnight—but Len's wife can't confirm what time he came in because she was asleep."

"Right. We'll have those two in again. Have either of them any form?"

"Sorry. Nothing doing because it's Sunday. We should have that information first thing tomorrow."

"Fair enough."

"What about greedy Syd, he's Sydney Leonard? The vicar is Reginald L. W. Terson, and our Chelmsford chum claimed to be Robert L. McCormack. I can't check without interrupting them at the church."

"Forget the pub-owner. The other three can account for Wednesday."

"Shouldn't I add them to the list, though? To keep it tidy?" DI Andrews shrugged.

"Why not?"

"I forgot—there is one other: Edward L. Brown, Woodbine Cottage."

"We'll check him later, the rest you can do tomorrow."

"Thanks."

Chapter Eight

"None of the wallpapers matched in that house, did you notice?" Mr Pringle grunted. Patently, he hadn't. "I might as well talk to myself," Mavis grumbled, "I thought you wanted a second opinion."

"I'm sorry." They were back at Woodbine Cottage. Mr Pringle looked up from the pile of reference books. "The gnome woman has answered one of my questions but there is another enquiry I'd like to pursue. It involves a visit to the village of Wenhaston. Would you care to come?" Mrs Bignell gazed out at the lowering sky.

"We could be in for a bit of a storm. You go, dear. I'd rather chat to Felicity when she gets back. What is there at Wenhaston anyway?"

"A Doom," he said, and left it at that.

Outside, he manoeuvered his car into the line of those already leaving Wuffinge. The weekend was nearly at an end.

Away from the crowds he drove on wider roads in open countryside. Nearer the sea, trees were stunted and the land covered with gorse. Majestic Blythburgh church was on the skyline. Mr Pringle turned left off the main road. The much humbler Wenhaston church was ahead. He parked in the lane and walked past a vast yew and old cracked gravestones.

It was a high-ceilinged building, a proper church unlike the one at Wuffinge. A curtain concealed the bellringers' ropes but facing him hung the semi-circular wooden panel depicting the Day of Judgement.

Mr Pringle gazed at it. Painted, probably by a monk, it illustrated the church's spiritual power. Here were figures rising up in response to the last Trump, the Judgement itself presided over by St Michael and the Devil, and those who were doomed, terrified creatures behind red-hot chains, about to be consumed in the fires of Hell.

Beneath was a text with the phrase he sought: *descenditi maledicti*. Depart, ye cursed; and the estimated date of the panel, 1480. A medieval decoration, that was all. Mr Pringle felt sadness welling up inside. Now he knew, just as the Major had done through reading about mammals, that the Wuffinge wall-paintings were not unique.

The Major had set off that night to break the news but death had overtaken him, a coincidence which still puzzled Mr Pringle but the possible answer to that lay elsewhere. Should he take it on himself to complete the Major's task? He discarded the idea. Far better that the real experts should do that later tonight.

The storm clouds had rolled away when he emerged, his sadness tinged with melancholy. So much in England was a mere five centuries old. Here there were no queues waiting to see the Doom, he was alone. It would have been marvellous had the Wuffinge paintings been Lord Wuffa's work but it wasn't possible. Mr Pringle began the drive back.

Felicity eased off tight shoes. "Hot buttered tea-cake," Mavis put the tray in front of her, "a strong pot of tea, scones, jam, whipped cream and cake because you and I cherish our figures, not starve ourselves like some daft women."

"What a wonderful spread."

"Well, my dear, I've yet to find the man who didn't admire a bit of flesh provided it was well-shaped." Mavis smoothed a skirt which flared from a dainty waist over her comely behind. "It's what first attracted Mr P, did I tell you? I was posing for an art class, deputizing for the regular model. It was love at first sight. I've still got his picture but I don't show it to everyone, it's far too private. Have a scone. Do we wait for Ted?"

"He's helping Reg check the takings. There's so much money . . ." Felicity gestured helplessly. "I'm glad Reg offered to take responsibility for it."

"What was the arrangement with the craft people?"

"They paid a nominal fee plus a percentage of their sales. Miranda set up a foolproof system whereby no one could cheat. It seems to have worked."

"What happens now?"

"We repair the roof using top quality Norfolk reed. We might even refurbish the inside. Joyce suggested we finance a village bus, it's certainly an idea. There's the school, which needs a computer. It's so exhilarating to have cash, Mavis. Normally we're counting the pennies."

"If you run short, you can always exhibit the paintings again."

Felicity shuddered. "I don't think I could face another festival, not for a long time. You two have been a Godsend."

"We've enjoyed ourselves."

"I'm afraid you've seen very little of the countryside. Ted and I hoped you'd go out for walks and enjoy the fresh air."

"I don't think so, thank you," Mavis replied politely, "there aren't enough pavements for walking."

In the police caravan DS Mather was dispirited and didn't bother to conceal it. "Two hundred and twenty-seven samples of twine."

"How many?"

"Exactly. Keen gardeners they are in Wuffinge. Keep spare bits of string. One bloke's been hoarding scraps since the war, he argued about handing them over to the police." Mather had revised his opinion. "I reckon any one of them could've done it. What surprises me is that whoever it was left the piece of twine in place. I'd have expected him to have taken it home."

"Perhaps he couldn't get it off," DI Andrews suggested. "It was well embedded."

"Any chance of a coffee?"

"The repair man refused to come out because his firm no longer pay overtime at the weekends." DS Mather swore darkly.

The phone rang. DI Andrews answered it.

"Incident Room." His expression changed. "Yes, sir. Yes, I do understand. We were following up a lead—No sir. Of course . . . Yes . . . Yes . . . No, no longer an offence over here. A full report, yes, and our profound apologies, sir. Good afternoon." He hung up before he exploded, "Bloody Syd! That was the Swedish embassy complaining we'd been harrassing two of their citizens with our inquiries—I'll give him fishy behaviour!"

"Felicity . . ."

"Yes?"

"What do moles eat?"

"Worms, I think." She lowered the colour supplement. "Why?"

"We were discussing it this morning. I might have an idea for getting rid of them."

She chuckled. "I wish you luck. So far Ted's tried just about everything. He's even put traps in their tunnels but they've found the answer to those."

"Tunnels?"

"Yes, they travel up and down, eating all the worms. When they've cleaned out one stretch, they dig another somewhere else."

Mavis became excited. "And that's where they live? In those tunnels?"

"I suppose so." Felicity was vague. "I don't think they nest or anything."

"You'd think it would be easy to catch them."

Felicity laughed again. "They're cunning. I know Ted tried to thump his spade through a mole hill once."

"What happened?"

"He put his back out."

Mavis gave a smug smile. "I've got a much better idea."

Mr Pringle arrived back to find Mrs Bignell waiting impatiently. "Can I borrow your car?"

"Yes, of course."

"I shan't be long."

Wuffinge was almost back to normal; the temporary school car-park was deserted, only the police caravan remained to mar the scene. He walked along Beggar's Row to number eight.

"That's odd," Felicity was watching from their window, "he's usually more than ready for a cup of tea."

"Pringle's an odd cove altogether," said Ted. "He was the same at school. Quiet, shy, a bit of a loner. It was his sister who was a menace."

"Enid? He doesn't speak of her if he can help it. What was she like?"

"Lumpy," Ted said decisively, "and overbearing. Rather like Doris Leveret in that way."

"D'you think he and Mavis will move up here?"

"Don't know, old girl. I hope so, naturally, but I'm not sure if the country would suit a luscious peach like Mavis. She needs sophistication."

Felicity said slyly, "She's arranging a surprise for you."

"Can't wait!"

"No, you old ram; she's going to rid our garden of moles. Don't ask me how, but she's convinced she's found a way."

"Bless her auburn heart," said Ted, amazed.

"You only need a few drops, Guinevere. A flick of the wrist is sufficient."

"What are we having tonight?"

"Champagne cocktails."

"Whoopee!" Miss Petrie Coombe-Hamilton gallumped around the kitchen.

"It's not proper champagne but it's got bubbles in it and with the brandy, you'll hardly notice the difference. Now, watch how much Angostura I add to the lump of sugar. Like so."

Guinevere said admiringly, "I wish I'd been trained. It must be fun, being behind a bar. I suppose you just chuck people out if they're the wrong sort?" Mavis Bignell reviewed the Bricklayers' clientele of a Saturday night.

"Sometimes, if they're provocative, we have to call in the ashtrays," she admitted. "What d'you think of it?" Guinevere licked the frosting off her glass.

"It tastes jolly good!"

"The best thing about champagne cocktails is that it would be a sin to waste the rest of the champagne."

"Or the brandy."

"Brandy will keep, but not necessarily, so shall we have another?"

"Rather!"

A little later Mavis said confidentially, "I hope you won't mind, dear, but I'd like to ask a little favour." When she learned what it was, Guinevere's enthusiasm was boundless.

"We don't have to reply on that old blunderbuss. Daddy had lots of souvenirs at the end of the war, plus some fuses."

"I shall have to rely on you for the technical side but it seems quite straightforward to me," Mavis said airily. "All we have to do is send a blast down that tunnel. At the very least, it'll give those moles a headache."

"Oh, we can manage better than that. To do the job properly you need to block both ends to prevent them escaping. What a pity we haven't any ferrets."

125

"Guinevere, I'm not asking for a massacre!" Her hostess gave one of her disconcerting braying laughs.

"Trust me, Mavis. First thing tomorrow?"

"After breakfast, yes."

Mr Pringle sat on the sofa while the kittens kneaded him with playful claws and Eddie cleaned his gun. Little Elsie pottered to and fro.

Had Eddie seen the Major on that fateful night? It was the Browns' suggestion that Eddie might have been involved with the disposal of a corpse which had put the idea into his head. There were night prowlers in any village. If Eddie hadn't seen the Major he might know who had, but could he be coaxed to tell?

"I'm not interested in what happened on Wednesday. It was my misfortune to find Mrs Leveret as everyone knows. What took place between that time and the moment when her body was finally discovered is not my concern."

Eddie Runkle's teeth were as twisted and broken as those of his sister. He exhibited them as a token of his understanding.

"I would like to ask a few questions however—nothing to do with Mrs Leveret—but were you in Wuffinge late that night?"

"I might have been," Eddie looked along the line of the barrel, "on the other hand, I might have been someplace else."

"But if you were back last Wednesday," Mr Pringle persisted, "that means you're not always in Milton Keynes from Monday to Friday?"

"No, I'm not," Eddie conceded, "on account of I've been driving for only two days a week for the last few months. Cutbacks, they call it."

"We live in difficult times."

"Not if you know how to claim benefit." Mr Pringle chose not to pursue this topic.

"Mrs Leveret wasn't well liked."

"She was not," Eddie agreed. "Was she, Elsie?"

"She wasn't."

"She was an interfering old sow, 'specially considering she was only Doris Winkle before she married."

"On the other hand," said Mr Pringle, "the Major was a respected figure."

Eddie said coolly, "You could say that. Not everyone would agree with it."

"Not likeable," Mr Pringle amended his description. "A man who could be relied on to do what was right, as he saw it."

"He was a dratted nuisance, always trying to cadge drinks. Never bought a round, he was that mean. In the old days he even fired at kids who went scrumping. Not lately, though. His eyesight weren't so special." Mr Pringle seized on this.

"Especially in the dark?"

"Couldn't say," Eddie pulled a cleaning rag through the barrel.

"The night he died, it would have been pitch black beneath the motorway bridge." Eddie wouldn't be drawn. "I believe the Major had a dicky heart?"

"No one knew that." They were treating one another warily now.

"Miss Petrie Coombe-Hamilton happened to mention it to my friend. A man with both a weak heart and bad sight could be taken unawares. Accidentally, of course."

"What are you suggesting?" Mr Pringle wasn't suggesting anything, he was fishing for information. Eddie sucked at a favourite tooth before saying deliberately, "The Major's dead and he's buried. Natural causes."

"And may he rest in peace," Mr Pringle replied. "Was it you who found him?"

"T'wasn't me who phoned the police."

"No." Mr Pringle appreciated the distinction.

"Len did that, I believe." Another Runkle. Mr Pringle looked pointedly at the weapon in Eddie's hands.

"The night the Major died, were you out after the vixen?" There was a pause.

"Might've been. Been going after her for weeks."

Greatly daring, Mr Pringle suggested, "I wondered if it was possible that the Major had suffered some kind of shock. The sort of—accident—that could bring on a heart attack. That was the cause of death, I believe." Eddie was silent.

"The accidental discharge of a gun for instance. That could come as a shock, especially in the dark, even if a man was simply attempting to rid the village of vermin, for the sake of his neighbours and friends."

"That vixen's a menace."

"I can believe it."

"I seem to remember now . . . she did go past me that night . . ."

Mr Pringle advanced very carefully indeed.

"Close, was she?"

"Damn close. I lets her have it, only I missed."

"Bad luck."

"There was nothing to prove what I'd been aiming at."

"No." Mr Pringle understood the dilemma.

"It was extra loud 'cause I was under the motorway bridge."

"At that hour you could hardly have expected anyone else to be there." Eddie's tongue loosened a fraction.

"Why the silly old fool should be visiting the war memorial at that time of night, I shall never know."

There was an implication there. Mr Pringle couldn't bring himself to work out what it was, not here and now. Instead, he forced himself to ask, "How can you be sure?"

"He was coming from that direction otherwise I'd have seen him ahead of me. I kep' my eyes skinned all the way up the lane. After I'd fired, and he hollered, I nearly died of fright as well." Mr Pringle stared. Eddie said defensively, "He only screamed the once. He'd fallen by the time I reached him. I got my flashlight on him—he was choking an' spewing. It was over damn quick. He gave a cough—an' that was it. All over. Nothing I could do."

"No." Mr Pringle's mouth was dry.

"I looked him over but there wasn't even a scorch mark. You could see marks in the concrete though, so I moved him a little bit. Didn't want any awkward questions even if it was an accident."

"Of course." The Major had had a skinful as well as a quarrel. The explosion was too much for a weak heart—but had he reached the church? Was he on the way back? Mr Pringle's mind was in chaos, he needed time to think. To divert Eddie, he said as casually as he could, "I'm surprised you risked firing with Mrs Kenny also in the vicinity."

"She wasn't there that night. I made sure, I always do."

"Wasn't she guarding her frogs?"

"No." Eddie gave an evil grin. "That's all pretend, that is, 'specially at night."

"Oh?"

Little Elsie wandered out from the kitchen.

"We know what she was doing though, don't we Eddie?" She had an expression Mr Pringle remembered.

"Good heavens, she wasn't doing that, was she?" he exclaimed.

"Sometimes she did," Eddie assured him, "down by the river. Didn't give a toss what happened to the frogs then, she didn't."

"She's daft," said Elsie. "It's damp down there. Why don't she do it indoors like everyone else?"

"She's got a nerve," Eddie said with feeling. "Comes round here criticizing. Anyway, me and Elsie's got a surprise planned for that dratted Miranda Kenny." Brother and sister were full of conspiratorial glee but Mr Pringle's thoughts were elsewhere.

"Eddie," he asked abruptly, "was it you who found her hat?" Eddie stopped grinning. Elsie dodged back into her kitchen. "Look, I've no wish to interfere but the police probably believe the person who put the hat on Mrs Leveret's head was responsible for what happened to her both before and subsequently."

"Mrs Kenny's hat was on Doris's head when she was found."

"Yes, I know . . ." Mr Pringle hesitated then said uncertainly, "You don't mean, when she was in the river the first time?"

The face opposite clammed tight shut.

"Look," it was awkward but he had to push a little harder. "When I touched her, the clothes were saturated. She must have been pushed into the river after she'd been strangled, then presumably taken out and dumped in the tent."

"If you know so much, why don't you tell the police?"

"They've already worked out that for themselves."

"So's everyone in this village."

"Of course they have." He wouldn't achieve anything further; Eddie was working himself into a rage.

"I've answered every one of their dratted questions, been in that caravan three times—and they let me go."

"What happens if they discover you only work part time? I shan't tell them, naturally."

"What if they do? Coming back here on Wednesdays doesn't mean I killed Doris Winkle. There was plenty of others out and about that night, including Mrs Kenny." Eddie rose, indignantly. "I'll thank you to take yourself off. You told us you weren't here to ask about that. The Major was all you were interested in, you said. Now you're pretending to be a policeman—I'm not answering any more questions."

"I beg your pardon, Eddie. And you, Elsie. It was impertinent and I apologize. But I fear the police may wish for more information."

"Let 'em ask. I got a clear conscience. You can't believe I'd have done that to Doris Winkle?" Face to face with him, Mr Pringle couldn't. Threaten to hit a newcomer with a heavy hammer was one thing, strangling a Wuffinge Parvian was a different matter entirely; it went against the village code. A gun might be fired accidentally, too close to a man with a weak heart, but to squeeze the life out of someone in cold blood . . . ?

All the same, somebody had.

"Discover what you were looking for, old man?"

"Yes, thank you. You have a most comprehensive selection of books on Suffolk."

"They were for my benefit, originally," Felicity told him, "I knew nothing about the area. I keep dipping in. There's so much *ancient* history around this area, isn't there?"

But not the wall-paintings, alas. And how many knew that beforehand?

There was a knock at the door. Felicity went to answer it and when she returned, her voice sounded odd.

"It's the police, Ted. They want to talk to you again."

However innocent, it is difficult to remain insouciant under such circumstances.

Ted, at his heartiest, demanded, "This won't take long, will it? We're due to begin clearing out the church at eight—it'll take most of the night to finish."

"Not long at all, sir, no. We simply need to check what your middle initial stands for; you are Edward L. Brown, I believe."

"Edward Leonard, yes." DR Mather's expression didn't change.

"In that case, sir, would you mind returning with us to the Incident Room."

Chapter Nine

"It was rum," Ted said as they began making their way towards the church. "They wanted to know where I was between five and seven p.m. on Wednesday evening. They weren't interested in what happened later, around the time when Doris was presumably being strangled. I was driving back to Wuffinge for dinner with Flick and you between five and seven, old chap, but I can't prove it." Ted had lost something of his carefree manner; his wife tried to restore it.

"Of course you can't," she said warmly. "But you definitely arrived home shortly after seven. Will it help if I tell them that in the morning?"

"It might. Yes, of course it will. Make an appointment to see Andrews, he's the one in charge." Ted began shedding his worries. "It is dashed odd though. I mean—between five and seven? What on earth was supposed to be happening then?"

"Goodness knows," said Felicity. "We were putting up the last of the greenery, Doris was supervising, then we all went home. I never saw her again."

They skirted the activity on the green as craft workers cleared away debris from their stalls. A crew had arrived and were dismantling the marquee. Sections of canvas flapped loosely against a darkening sky. Everyone seemed determined to distance themselves from Wuffinge as soon as possible. Outside the Hope & Anchor, Syd and his barman were disconnecting the coloured lights.

"You don't have one of those phones in your car, Ted?" asked Mavis. "You might have talked to someone between five and seven."

"I used to, until it was nicked. Nowadays I phone Flick when I stop for petrol, but I didn't fill up on Wednesday."

"And you didn't bother to call later because we'd already spoken at lunchtime," Felicity reminded him.

"That's right. As I said, the fuzz didn't seem particularly fussed. Told me to try and come up with something. Andrews is a sensible bloke. If you tell him I was taking corks out of bottles by seven fifteen, I'm sure that'll be the end of it."

"Why that particular period?" Mr Pringle wondered aloud.

"They're filling in the gaps. They had this diagram on the wall, times and locations, you know the sort of thing. Doris Leveret's movements throughout the day until the moment she disappeared."

Felicity shivered. "Gruesome!"

"I'm surprised such evidence was on public view," Mr Pringle remarked.

"Oh, they'd used a code. Fortunately it wasn't difficult to decipher," Ted smirked. "They'd reversed her intitals: L.D. instead of D.L." But might those letters also stand for Leonard? He had the impression Ted was being less than frank about his movements.

They'd reached Lovers' Lane and were walking two abreast, men in front, women behind. "In case there are wild animals," Mavis explained.

"Can you show me where the Major was found?" he asked.

"Approximately, yes. It was one of the Runkles who called the police."

"Which one, d'you know?"

Ted frowned, "Len, I think. He and his brother are responsible for keeping the war memorial and churchyard tidy. Whichever it was was on his way to work ten days go and found the Major lying where he'd fallen. About—here." Ted paused to allow Felicity to catch up. "This is where they found him?" She nodded.

It was about three yards from the bridge. Mr Pringle glanced at the verges.

"Which side of the road?" She pointed to the left, which again corroborated Eddie's story. As a countryman the Major would automatically face oncoming traffic.

Mr Pringle moved on and Ted fell into step. Under the bridge, he snatched a quick glance: the concrete support had many pock marks, any one of which could have been made by a bullet. Ted said, "That still bothers you far more than this business of Doris?"

"I try to put that out of my mind altogether."

Ted was sympathetic. "Glad it wasn't me who found either of them. Bad enough being interrogated. Hello . . . ?" Out of the gloaming a figure approached from the direction of the church. "I'm surprised old Oliver lets his missus out at night after what happened," he muttered.

"Shh!" Felicity whispered. 'She'd be very hurt if she heard you say that. She still values her independence, you know." Mrs Kenny drew nearer. "Evening, Miranda."

"Oh, hello." She halted reluctantly.

"What was the grand total we made out of the marquee?" Felicity enquired, friendly fashion. "Beyond our wildest dreams, I trust."

"I don't know whether I'm permitted to say."

"Quite right," Ted said stoutly, "don't tell a soul until Reg has everything safely stashed in a night deposit box."

"He's planning to do that after he's taken the experts back to the station," Felicity told him. "Incidentally, have you heard what their verdict was, Miranda? That surely can't be a secret any longer? I trust those really are Lord Wuffa's paintings?"

Miranda struggled to keep control. Her voice was unsteady.

"The experts are at the vicarage having supper. I wasn't permitted to see them and Reg refused to tell me what they thought." Then, to everyone's embarrassment, Mrs Kenny began to weep.

"What a pity," Felicity said lamely.

"As I'm not wanted any more, I'm off home." And she walked away, head high. Felicity was astonished.

"For heavens' sake, what was all that about? Surely Reg hasn't upset her."

"He must be tired. You all are," Mavis answered. "Perhaps he spoke out of turn."

"I shan't offer to accompany Mrs Kenny home. She might feel insulted and kick me in the goolies," Ted said comfortably.

Miranda returned by a circuitous route, to give herself time to recover. She'd begun the day in fear, now she was angry, her self-esteem badly dented. Never mind if she had sought revenge, the tables had been turned: Mrs Kenny had been rejected.

Entering her front gate, she argued fiercely that none of it mattered. She had her causes; she was sole leader now of village women who depended on her.

"I'm back," she called. Silence. "What's for supper?" There was an edge to her voice. "Where are you?"

"Upstairs."

She went into the kitchen. There was nothing in the oven, nor any tasty smell. Miranda bounded up the stairs.

"I hope you don't expect me to cook tonight, not after the day I've had. Hey, what are you doing?" A suitcase lay open on the bed.

"What does it look like?" Rational behaviour deserted her. How dare Oliver even think of . . . A different sort of fear gripped her as she realized just what his intentions might be. It made her shrill.

"Where are you going?"

"I'm leaving. For good."

"You can't!"

"Oh, can't I?" He'd been waiting for this moment and relished it. "You never thought I'd have the courage, did you? Well, you were wrong."

"I . . . I . . ." For once, Mrs Kenny was lost for words.

"You needn't worry, you'll be all right. I'm letting you have the car—I've always hated it. As for this house . . ." Oliver bounced on the suitcase lid to shut it, "you can have that as well. It never was a home—it's a sham. I've cracked my head on the beams too many times to want to stay—I'm sick of the place."

"But why?" she wailed, "why are you doing this?" He misunderstood deliberately.

"I'm giving you the house and car so you won't have any claims on me. If you're interested, I'm off to a nice little flat with gas central heating, wall to wall carpet, and steak and chips in the freezer whenever I want it."

"You're pathetic!"

"Possibly." Oliver looked at her. "But then, so are you." He'd stopped baiting her now. "I saw what happened on Wednesday night." Miranda went white beneath the tearstains.

"D'you intend telling the police?"

"Is it likely?" He pulled on his jacket and picked up the case. "The taxi should be here soon, I'll wait outside." He paused for the last time, to enjoy the sight of her misery. After years of posturing there were signs that reality was beginning to take hold. "I've put up with you for nine years. Nine years of pretence, that's enough for any man."

His detached appraisal was chilling. He stared as though she were a specimen rather than a woman.

"It wasn't worth it," Oliver Kenny said loudly, "I was

infatuated but you didn't even love me, did you?" She wanted to contradict but the words wouldn't come. "Well, serve you right, my dear Miranda, because I'm off." She stumbled down the stairs behind him.

"You can't leave me, not after what's happened. Where will I find you?"

"You won't. Not you, not the police, no one."

Miranda suddenly found her courage and shouted derisively, "You'll be crawling into those council offices tomorrow morning, tugging your forelock as usual. I've only got to pick up the phone to find out where you are!"

"Wrong. I finished there on Friday. I'd worked out my notice by then." He'd stunned her this time.

"You had the whole thing planned?"

"Right from the moment you began fancying that chap. You thought you were being so clever . . . thought I hadn't noticed." Oliver placed his doorkey deliberately in the centre of the hall table. "Please note the symbolic gesture. With this key, I discharge all my marital obligations. Count yourself lucky. Not many two-timing women end up with a house and a car. You don't deserve either. It's up to you how you pay the mortgage, of course. I've written to the building society and the bank, explaining that from now on you're responsible. As an independent-minded person I know you won't object. Oh, and I've closed the joint account. You can begin earning your living tomorrow. It'll be a new experience, the sort you're always preaching about. I hope you enjoy it. Don't bother trying to trace me, it'll be a waste of time."

A different terror gripped Miranda now, to the exclusion of everything else.

"If you saw me that night . . . Was it you who . . . ?" Oliver almost laughed.

"You'll never know, will you?"

Joyce, harassed, met the four of them in the church porch. "Am I glad you've arrived! Good evening, Mrs Bignell, Mr Pringle—we've had such an unpleasant scene."

"We've just met Miranda."

Joyce lowered her voice. "Michelle Brazier's in there, bawling her head off. I was about to fetch Gerry."

"What happened?"

"We'd begun clearing the flowers and the Green Men, Peter

135

and Robert, were dismantling the lights. It's the first time we've seen them close to. The tall one, Robert, is quite good looking and that wretched Michelle started flirting—you know what she can be like."

"I do," sighed Felicity.

"Miranda Kenny arrived to hand over the cash, wads and wads of it zipped inside her jacket, which is marvellous. She and Reg began checking it, when Miranda suddenly spots what's going on and rebukes Michelle, to put it mildly.

"Next minute, floods of tears and the girl comes out with loud accusations against her dearest friend. 'You're jealous,' she tells Miranda, 'you think you're clever enough to attract everything in trousers.'"

"And how did Miranda respond?"

Joyce went extremely pink.

"Very, very rudely despite being in church."

"I'm not surprised. What a stupid, spoiled child. We must send her home or we'll never finish."

"Shall I take her?"

"No, Ted," Felicity gave a brief laugh, "she might claim you'd tried to rape her."

"Let's you and I do it," Mavis suggested. "The men can stay and help Joyce."

Mr Pringle waited until they had the sodden, snuffling Michelle outside.

"Mavis, it's nearly dark and this village contains violence. Promise me you will not let Felicity out of your sight."

"Don't you worry, dear. She says owls fly about at night as well as bats. I shall keep tight hold of her hand."

Inside it was hot and foetid. The vicar, having shed his cassock, was in his shirt sleeves helping the other two lower spotlights and fold tripods. Mr Pringle felt awkward in his presence and couldn't manage more than a brief nod. Ted went to fling the door wide and let in air but the vicar called quickly, "Not yet, if you don't mind." Spotlit below the apse was the table stacked with boxes of money.

"Sorry, Reg. Forgot. Be glad when that lot's in the bank."

"So will we."

Joyce indicated a stepladder. "If we could clear the ceiling greenery at this end, we shan't be in their way."

Mr Pringle dearly wanted to ask the question uppermost in

his mind: had the Major spoken to anyone in the church on the night of his death? He would have to wait until the vicar was alone.

His hands shook slightly as he held the ladder steady for Ted to climb. The five wooden screens were back in position on the walls, he noticed.

"Put the rubbish in these plastic bags and stack them in the porch," Joyce instructed. "Everything will be collected tomorrow."

"Right. Anyone got a knife?" asked Ted.

"Will my penknife do?"

"Thanks, old man." He began to slash at the string. "No point in undoing knots."

The three nearer the apse worked swiftly and in silence. The taller Green Man, Robert, passed to and fro but made no effort to speak. The incident with Michelle had obviously put a blight on conversation.

"Wish I'd thought about it before, we could've nipped into the pub on the way here," Ted muttered. "It's going to be a damned thirsty evening."

"If we finished early, we could call on our way back?"

"It's not very likely. Got any beer, Reg? We'll drink it outside, so as not to offend the . . . er . . . ." Ted acknowledged the presence of the altar. The shorter of the Green Men murmured something and disappeared.

"Peter thinks there's some lager."

"Great." Ted resumed his hacking and more dead ferns showered down. "What was the experts' verdict?" he asked ingenuously. "Have they come to any conclusion?"

"Perhaps it would be best if I announced it from the pulpit next Sunday."

"Rather. That should guarantee to pack even more of 'em in than this morning. And whatever happens, you, dear Joyce," Ted said pointedly, "are to play the harmonium."

One by one the spotlights were extinguished and the church became a shadowy place. Peter re-appeared with their beer and resumed work without waiting to be thanked.

"Pringle and I won't be long," Ted announced.

They settled on trim, dry grass between the tombstones and swigged gratefully.

"Not exactly a talkative pair."

"No."

"I mean, there's no need for secrecy now. The festival's over, everyone's seen the ruddy paintings including the experts—I say!" The obvious thought had finally reached Ted. "You don't suppose *they've* given them the thumbs down?"

"I fear they may have done."

"Why?" He looked at him, surprised. "Come on, spit it out. Pictures are your thing—Mavis told us about your collection. What's your considered opinion?"

Mr Pringle wondered how much he dare reveal. Ted, whom he hadn't met since schooldays, whose middle name was Leonard, who was still assisting the police with their inquiries.

"I'm not an expert, especially on such ancient paintings," he procrastinated.

"But you were rootling among those books and you disappeared to Wenhaston this afternoon," Ted protested. "You must have had a reason?"

"I wanted confirmation."

"Of what?" Mr Pringle decided to make a clean breast of it. Whatever else he might have done, Ted Brown was a most unlikely strangler.

"The paintings are delightful but of a much later period than we had hoped. Certainly not from the time of Wuffa. He was king in these parts about thirteen hundred years ago."

"What date d'you put on them?" demanded Ted. Mr Pringle hesitated again. "Look, old sport, if you're worried I'll spill the beans, forget it. As far as I'm concerned, it's Reg who'll have to do that, poor beggar. It'll be a tremendous blow to Wuffinge pride but at least the damn things exist. We've earned enough to repair the roof, so look on the bright side, eh?"

If their lack of uniqueness didn't concern Ted, Mr Pringle thought others might feel it deeply.

"I believe the two which haven't been restored can only be medieval and the remaining three must have been painted after the Norman Conquest." Assuming they weren't fakes, he thought, but kept this to himself.

"As late as that!" Ted was dismayed. "What makes you so sure?"

"The rabbits in the Garden of Eden." It was the simpler of the two explanations.

"Why? I like that picture best of all. Masses of jolly little animals. Probably what the artist saw from his wattle hut every morning." He gestured at the village with his beer can. "It hasn't changed much in the last thousand years, which is why Flick and I settled here."

"Unfortunately rabbits weren't introduced into England until the Normans arrived in 1066. It's unlikely a painter in AD 600 would have known what they looked like."

"Oh, shit!"

"The Major guessed. I think that's why he didn't want them exhibited."

"Oh, bloody hell!" Ted swore again at the loss of a cherished illusion. "All those stories you and I believed as gospel—King Wuffa's paintings my dad used to say. Now you tell me they're nearly five hundred years too late—what a let-down!"

"I'm awfully sorry." They heard Felicity calling them.

"You lazy pair! Are you out on strike?"

"We won't tell anyone," Mr Pringle urged, "not yet."

"Trust me. Pringle and I are enjoying a well-earned break," Ted replied.

In the church, Joyce was alone. "They've finished." She indicated a neat pile of boxes. "Those are the lights. Reg asked if we'd put them in the porch as well as the tables and trestles. A firm's collecting them tomorrow."

"Where's he gone?"

"To take the experts to catch a much later train than they'd intended. They weren't best pleased apparently—poor Reg. The other two, Robert and Peter, wanted their supper. I told them we could manage. Reg warned me he'd be back late so we're to lock up."

Mr Pringle knew he ought to do something. So many aspects were wrong, and yet . . . The Major had died of natural causes. There was no suggestion Doris Leveret's death was in any way connected with the paintings. Paralysis overcame him. Ted spoke and the moment was past.

"What about the key?"

"We'll put it through the vicarage letterbox. There's a meeting of the festival committee on Tuesday afternoon. We'll have to wait till then to find out how much profit we've made— something to look forward to at the end of the worst week I can remember."

"I'd be tempted to ask him tomorrow."

Joyce smiled indulgently. "You're no church-goer, Mr

139

Pringle. Mondays are a vicar's day off. Nobody disturbs Reg on a Monday if they can help it."

They worked on in silence for a while.

"The festival expenses must be heavy," Mr Pringle said interrogatively. "Apart from the marquee, two expert art restorers can't have been cheap?" Felicity heaved another bag of rubbish up the steps to the porch.

"Peter and Robert were friends. Reg assured us they were working for far less than their normal fee."

"A rather—taciturn pair."

"Hardly surprising with Michelle Brazier lusting after 'em," Ted snorted.

When every scrap of greenery had been taken down, Ted handed Mr Pringle the broom. "You sweep up. I'll give the girls a hand with the trestles." The church was empty apart from the stacked pews. Ancient flagstones sloped down towards the apse. Mr Pringle worked towards them in long sweeps, piling rubbish against the step. Joyce saw it and laughed. "You've discovered the easy way?"

"Hmm?"

"Here, I'll show you." She took the broom and pushed the pile across a crack between two flagstones. Smaller items disappeared. "No doubt we shouldn't but everyone does."

"Is there a vault beneath?"

"I don't think so. It's never been used if there is. Just a gap below the stones."

"A considerable amount of dust must have accumulated after thirteen hundred years."

"No doubt one day it'll be full but until then we'll keep on shoving it down the crack. It saves a lot of extra work." The moon had risen and silvery light spilled through the leper window. Mr Pringle was reminded of his first afternoon in Wuffinge.

"Did one of the Green Men wear a gold ring?"

Joyce thought for a moment.

"Yes, Robert did, I think—the taller one. Can you help me line up the first pew?" Mr Pringle tugged obediently while she slid her end over a mark on the floor. "That's it. The rest will be in parallel now."

They dragged the heavy benches over the stones.

"Hope we haven't made too many scratches." Felicity yawned. "Ruby will polish them out, bless her."

"She's the caretaker?" asked Mavis.

"Yes. That's why the brass is so well cared for. Golly, I'm bushed."

"Pringle and I will finish off," Ted ordered. "You put your feet up." They slid the last pews into position. "That do?"

Joyce glanced round briefly.

"Perfick."

"Let's go home."

Ted turned the massive key in the lock. "Wonder how old this is? It weighs a ton."

"Victorian," Joyce replied. "Sorry to disappoint you. It's a copy."

"Hang on while I nip next door with it."

Mavis looked contentedly at the empty sky.

"No owls or bats."

"They've gone to bed, sensible creatures." Joyce yawned this time. "Reg deserves a lie-in tomorrow, I hope he gets it." The four of them walked back silently. On the green, the police caravan made a sinister shape with one window shining yellow in the darkness. "I do hope they find whoever it was soon," she remarked uneasily. "A few more days and people will be quarrelling openly."

"Who's the favourite suspect?" asked Mavis.

"Anyone named Leonard—except you, of course, Ted. There's also a whisper that Miranda Kenny might not have been attacked after all."

"Dear me," said Mr Pringle. In Wuffinge, nothing was what it purported to be.

Chapter Ten

The following morning, Ted enquired at the Incident Room whether he could go about his lawful business and was assured that he could.

"It's like being reprieved," he announced breezily over breakfast. "God, what must it be like for innocent chaps who are banged up, eh? What time are you two pushing off?"

"About eleven," Mr Pringle replied, "I'd like to tidy Granny Pringle's grave before I go."

"Don't leave it another fifty years before your next visit."

"We'll be seeing them again soon," Felicity smiled happily. "We're invited to stay with Mavis on the fifteenth so you can take me to the theatre for my birthday."

"Fine. Let's make it a foursome and you three choose what it's to be. Well, must dash." He kissed Mavis goodbye and Mr Pringle followed him out to the car.

"Sorry to disappoint you about the paintings."

"It's the same for both of us. You had faith in the legends. In a way, I'm glad it was you who broke the news, rather than Reg's experts. Everyone will feel foolish. It's like being caught believing in Father Christmas."

"It doesn't alter the quality of life here. Your own piece of Eden, you called it?" Ted's ebullience returned.

"Right first time, old chap. Take a few deep breaths of that country air, look at the view. It may not be spectacular but it's England at its best. A place where a chap can feel at home. See if you can twist Mavis's arm about moving back, eh? I approve of her, you know. Quite an improvement on Wuffinge's home-grown sexpot!" He grinned in the direction of number eight.

Mavis had a particular reason not to hurry their departure. She sent Mr Pringle back to linger over the newspaper while she went upstairs and kept watch for Guinevere. Outside, a dilapidated Morris Minor estate pulled up. Mavis waved eagerly, "Good morning." Miss Petrie Coombe-Hamilton brandished the canvas hockey bag.

"Morning. Ready for business?"

"Just a moment while I speak to Felicity."

For reasons best known to herself Mrs Bignell did not disturb Mr Pringle and kept her voice low when she went through to the kitchen.

"Guinevere and I are about to deal with the moles. May I borrow your wellies?" Felicity chuckled.

"Help yourself. Try not to ruin Ted's lawn, he only finished feeding it last week."

"Did he really?" Mavis was surprised. What did grass eat? Compost perhaps?

If Felicity had gone outside, she might have deduced the nature of the remedy. Guinevere was dressed in her shooting clothes; a tweed jacket with a leather shoulder patch, plus a game bag which she'd slung over her shoulder. When Mavis re-appeared, she produced from it various wartime souvenirs.

"I don't know what these are capable of. You don't read German by any chance?"

"No, dear." Mrs Bignell carried the shell gingerly. "Does this go inside the blunderbuss."

"Unfortunately it won't fit. I thought we could stuff it down the tunnel with the rest of the junk."

"Felicity is anxious we don't spoil the grass." They were in the back garden and Guinevere squinted at newly turned piles of earth.

"Actually, these are fresh diggings. Look, they lead round to the front . . ." she began to pace along the route, "across the flower bed, beyond the path and over there, on to the green—d'you see?'

"So they do. Those moles must've been busy last night."

"It must be their latest tunnel so why don't we stop it up at this end and aim the charge toward the green?" Guinevere suggested. "That way the row of cottages won't be in any danger."

"Danger!"

"Oh, you know. Vibration, that kind of thing."

"Guinevere, this is safe, isn't it?"

"Absolutely. Damn, I forgot to bring a spade. D'you know where Ted keeps his?"

Once equipped, Miss Petrie Coombe-Hamilton set to with a will and exposed a very small hole just inside the front fence.

Into this she packed an assortment of items from the hockey case, culminating with the blunderbuss.

"I thought if we jammed the muzzle in and let rip, it would trigger the whole thing off."

"Give the moles a headache, you mean."

"Rather."

"Not murder them or anything nasty, just send them away?"

"We've been clumping about in our boots. They won't be asleep down there, they're probably halfway to Bury St Edmunds. We'll make sure they don't come back, that's all." Reassured, Mrs Bignell asked if she should warn anyone.

"They used to during the war. Knocked at people's houses when they were about to explode a bomb."

"Sadly this isn't a bomb," Guinevere said with regret. "Now, are you ready?" Mavis retreated to the porch and put her fingers in her ears.

"Ready!" she cried. Mr Pringle heard her from the dining-room and he wandered over to the window. The sight of Miss Petrie Coombe-Hamilton's trouser-clad posterior as she took up a curious stance, fascinated him.

"What's going on?" asked Felicity from the kitchen.

"I've no idea."

"It's a scheme Mavis has devised to rid us of moles." Realization came swiftly.

"Oh, good Lord—" but he was too late. The flintlock proved as reliable as Guinevere had promised.

The noise of the explosion wasn't overpowering but the crash as crockery fell from shelves made Felicity scream. Further along at number eight, loose chunks of thatch tumbled into the garden. Outside, sections of tarmac lifted as shock waves thundered in the tunnel. Turf and vegetation hurtled into the air in a direct line across Wuffinge Parva green.

The Incident Room rocked, the lights went out but busy officers were slow to react. "What on earth was that?"

"No idea. Petrol tank exploded?"

"Sounded more like a gas main."

"Take a look outside, for God's sake!" DS Mather departed hastily.

In the outer office, a small voice asked, "Why has my screen gone blank?"

"So's mine."

"Oh, Christ! The power's off." Panic built up and multiplied.

144

"I was in the middle of saving—"

"I'd only just switched on—"

"Shut up!"

"Did you do a backup last night?"

"No, did you?"

"Have a heart, it was Sunday and we were so late—"

"Shut up!"

"But that means we haven't a single copy!"

"SHUT UP!" From the doorway DI Andrews re-established his authority. "Now, will someone tell me what the problem is in here?" The nearest computer operator summoned up her courage.

"We may have lost all the information on the discs."

"What d'you mean—all?" In the meaningful pause that followed, DS Mather burst back in with his report.

"You'll never believe it, some crazy woman was trying to kill a mole." DI Andrews fought to control his rage.

"Tell the woman from me, that suicide is no longer considered a crime in England and Wales—and I'd advise her to try it."

"At least we've solved the problem of what to send Ted and Felicity as a thank-you present. Six cups, saucers, plates and one milk jug should do it."

"There's no need to exaggerate."

Mr Pringle was wrestling with an established bramble root in Granny Pringle's grave.

"Mavis, I wasn't exaggerating."

"It was just a bit more—explosive—than we'd anticipated." Mavis was sulky. "I hope the police let Guinevere go soon. I told them we were only trying to help."

"You succeeded beyond everyone's expectation, not only with the moles. Macavity was last seen heading for the motorway."

"Guinevere was ever so surprised. She wasn't sure what sort of gunpowder was inside the shells."

"No doubt scientists will provide a detailed description at the trial."

"We weren't trying to *disturb* anyone. All we wanted to do was make sure the moles didn't come back." Mr Pringle plunged a fork beneath the root.

"You're being too modest, Mavis. Wild elephants wouldn't

return after the earth moved like that. Locals believe they're atop the San Andreas fault. From now on you can safely claim to be a part of Wuffinge Parva's history. It's a pity Guinevere couldn't produce a licence, however. DI Andrews struck me as a man who'd lost his sense of humour this morning. Now . . . one big heave!" The grave gave up its weeds and Mr Pringle nearly toppled over. "Whoops!"

"If you jab your foot with that fork, you could get lock-jaw."

"My tetanus jab is up to date."

Mavis, bored, got up to stretch her legs and examine the old church. An oddity struck her.

"That's a very silly place to put a window. Why is it so low down?" Mr Pringle began to explain about lepers having to listen to the word of God from outside, about the level of the ground being much lower during previous earlier centuries, when he stopped in mid-sentence.

"Good Lord!"

"What's the matter?"

Sunlight glinted on the misshapen panes. He felt suddenly breathless. "You are right, it is far too low. What's more, I saw a hand wearing a ring trying to open it."

"I heard you ask Joyce last night. She said the tall Green Man wore one."

"But when I saw the hand, it was *pushing* upwards."

"Well of course it would, if he wanted to open it."

"Mavis, how tall was Robert? Roughly?"

"At a guess, over six foot."

"And that window is less than two foot from the ground?"

"About eighteen inches."

"If a six footer was pushing upwards, think how awkwardly he'd have to lie beneath it?" When she continued to look puzzled, he said, "To push like that, he must have been *below* the level of the flagstones. Come on."

"Where are we off to?"

"Next door. I want to borrow the key to the church." But there was no response to his knocking.

"Joyce said Monday was the vicar's day off. He's probably gone out."

"Damn."

"Don't swear. I bet she knows where there's another key. I'll take the car and go and ask—you finish that bit of weeding."

It was difficult to concentrate at first but as he worked pieces

146

from the kaleidoscope fell into a new pattern. When the Allegro pulled up again, the grave was tidy and Mr Pringle was ready to put the rest of his theory to the test.

"Ruby had the spare," Mavis waved it. "She asked us to drop it off when we'd finished." He unlocked the door. "What are you going to do?" There was a trace of apprehension in her voice.

"First, I need to look at the two pictures which couldn't be restored, preferably the one with the lettering. That means taking down the screen. Then I want to lift a couple of flagstones to see what's beneath. What I shall need, is a crowbar." Mrs Bignell looked at him in horror.

"You're talking like a vandal!"

"I need proof, Mavis. I think the Major was inadvertently caught up in a conspiracy—and it could prove the legends were right after all."

"I thought that had been done." Mavis indicated the screens. "Aren't those Lord Wuffa's pictures? Now where are you off to?" Not surprisingly perhaps, Mr Pringle couldn't find a crowbar in the church.

"There's a toolbag in the boot," he called. When he returned and began levering the cover from the wall, she couldn't believe her eyes.

"What will the vicar say!"

Mr Pringle only grunted as he lifted it down and set it against a pew. Next he began unscrewing the Perspex.

"I hope Reg Terson will be pleased. If not, I shall want to know why."

"Pleased! But what are you doing that for? I know you're interested in pictures, dear, but they have had two restorers working on those for months . . . and what about the experts who were here last night?"

"I don't believe there were any."

"What? Don't be silly. Joyce told us they'd missed their train. She said the vicar was taking them to catch a later one."

"Joyce repeated what she'd been told," he replied. Mavis felt increasingly nervous now the screws had been loosened.

"I don't know what you mean but I hope you've not forgotten that police caravan? You must have committed half the crimes in the book by now."

"Catch hold while I undo the last one."

"Me? I'm not going to be your accomplice!"

"Mavis, if it falls, the Perspex could shatter."

"Oh, all right." She took the weight in both hands. "It'll have my finger prints all over it—I shall have to confess." Mr Pringle got down from his stool.

"I'll take over now, thanks." He set the darkened sheet aside. "Now, let's see what's beneath all this thirteenth-century camouflage . . ."

"You're not going to touch that painting? You must be mad—that's a sacred work of art!"

"I'm willing to bet that it's only concealing what's beneath." He slid his penknife under the loose paint. "Yes, here we are. I've lifted off two tiny flakes but already you can see there's another colour. Now, let's keep these scraps somewhere safe . . ." Mr Pringle seized a hymn book and placed them inside. "We'll keep them for the real experts to examine."

"I told you—they've all gone now."

"I meant genuine art experts not figments of someone's imagination."

"What do you mean?" She was unwilling to accept the obvious conclusion. 'You don't mean the vicar was telling fibs?"

"I fear so, yes."

Bewilderment gave way to worry. "You're not doing more damage? Please don't get carried away, dear." For Mr Pringle was chipping away with abandon. He stopped when he'd uncovered an area approximately two inches square. "What will it cost to repair that!" she cried in despair. He was deaf to protests as he examined the tantalizing piece of information.

"The first of the real paintings, I think," he murmured happily. "But what are they? How infuriating—if only one could just keep on and on. And why didn't they reveal these in the first instance?"

"If you think I'm going to let you scrape off any more, you're mistaken." Mavis was red with indignation, "I'm off to fetch the police myself. I shall tell them you've had too much sun." This time her words reached him and he smiled gently.

"It's all right, Mavis. I've stopped. I've proved all I needed to know. They exist all right."

"What do?"

"Lord Wuffa's pictures."

"Oh, to blazes with Lord Wuffa! I want you to put that Perspex back and then we can nip off home before anyone discovers what you've done."

"Not yet. I want to lift that flagstone near the leper window and see what's underneath."

"Oh, my God!" Mavis looked round fearfully. "I'm sorry, I shouldn't have said that, not in here." She watched resignedly as he began to lever it up. "Oh, well . . . I don't suppose you can do much damage to a thick chunk of stone. But you'll never lift it with that little crowbar. You need Ted's garden fork. Stay there, I'll get it."

Outside the sun was warm. Mavis jerked the fork from Granny Pringle's grave, muttering, "I blame you for some of this, you know. You should have brought him up to respect other people's property." Feeling slightly ashamed, she hurried back inside.

The tines slid easily into the crack. "I shouldn't be surprised . . . if they didn't use something like a fork . . . themselves!" Mr Pringle strained hard.

"Who?"

"Whoever it was . . . that did this before—Ah!" The stone lifted, pivoted and fell backwards with a crash. Mavis jumped.

"Oh, my nerves! They'll give way altogether at this rate!"

But Mr Pringle was already peering into the hole. "Is my torch handy?" She found it in his toolbag.

"The batteries are flat. Can we go home now?"

"In a minute." He sat back and looked round the church. "They always had spare candles, to go on the altar and for when the lights failed. Now where did they keep them?" He scrambled to his feet and began to wander round, "When it was Granny's turn to do the altar flowers, I used to help. We'd give the candlesticks a rub . . . then we'd come over here." He'd reached the pulpit and was examining the panels beneath. "Yes, just as I remembered. A storage cupboard at the bottom, see. Candles, matches. Plates for communion bread—"

"You're not to touch those, they're consecrated!"

"Don't worry. I mean no disrespect. All I intend to do is borrow a couple—and this old copy of the parish magazine to shield the flame." Mr Pringle struck a match and lit the first wick. He caught sight of her face. "Mavis, I shall leave sufficient money in the collection box to pay for any damage."

"You'll need a bank loan at this rate, that's if you haven't been certified by then. This is a church, you know."

"Can you hold the second one above the hole, otherwise I

149

can't see what I'm doing." Reluctantly, Mrs Bignell edged nearer the opening.

"Yes . . ." his voice was muffled as he leaned further in. "There's at least one block of stone which I can reach if I'm careful, and another beyond that. I'll just lower myself . . . very gently."

"You're not going down there!"

"Of course I am." She watched with dismay as he eased himself forward, legs dangling, then dropped out of sight. Head and shoulders bobbed up above the level of the floor and Mavis let out a pent-up breath.

"You're still in the land of the living."

Mr Pringle stretched up, leaned forward and ran his hands round the window frame. "This is what I saw from the outside the first day I came. A hand reaching up to open this—or rather trying to. Whoever it was, presumably Robert, was interrupted by the arrival of Doris Leveret and her ladies. And thanks to you, we now know why this opening is so low down. Look . . ." Mr Pringle indicated the distance from the window to the hole in which he was standing. "That wasn't intended as a window when this place was built—it was the entrance door itself!" He was ecstatic with discovery, Mavis couldn't bring herself to scold. "Don't you see?"

"It makes more sense, seeing you standing there. I mean, it's too low for anyone outside to see in whether they'd got leprosy or not."

She allowed herself to walk a few paces back to consider the aperture's proportions. "And it's the wrong shape. Too narrow. But if it went down a couple more feet it would be just right for a narrow little door."

"Which is what it was. They weren't as tall in those days, remember. That would bring it to the level of this block of stone." Mavis measured the gap with her eye.

"Maybe if there was a sort of threshold, then another step, that would take it to where you are now."

"Well done! Now, where's my candle?"

"You're not going any further down?"

"Of course I am!"

"There could be skeletons! Wild animals! Rats!"

"It smells perfectly dry down here. If there's anything living, it could only be a church mouse. And don't worry about dead bodies, they used coffins in ancient times before putting them in a vault." He disappeared from sight calling, "It's a sort of chamber, Mavis . . . it goes forward, underneath the apse. The Normans must've built that over the top. Two more steps down . . ."

"Do be careful," she quavered. His voice was faint but she could hear the excitement. "Remember what the doctor warned about your cholesterol."

"I'm perfectly all right. I'm on the floor now. That's made of stone, too. Lighter coloured. Beautifully laid out, with a sort of inset mosiac, like a carpet. Goodness, I do believe it could be Roman!" He was increasingly cheerful with each new find. "Trust the locals to use what was already here. It could've been a Roman Temple—they often converted those to Christianity. There's a sort of stone table at this end. It must've been an altar. I wonder which God they used to worship? Probably Ceres in this part of the country. Can't see a single skeleton, thank heavens!" The echo of relieved laughter bounced off solid walls and Mavis felt herself go limp.

"What about mice?" she croaked.

"There aren't any. There's plenty of dust below the step. Centuries of Rubys have been sweeping it through the cracks but it's dry, powdery stuff. I don't believe this was ever used as a vault. No sign of a coffin. Hang on a minute . . ." The flickering light travelled away from her and from above Mavis could only stare into the darkness.

"Where are you? Have you found some bones?"

"No. There are stone benches along the walls . . . must be seating, I suppose. Maybe this was a council chamber . . . with the stone table in the centre?" He'd lifted the candle high for she could see the luminance as she peered over the edge.

"Mavis, there are paintings down here! All along the walls. Every square inch is covered in pictures! It's a kind of mural. Bright colours, gloriously clear. Absolutely wonderful!" She could hear incredulity as well as excitement now. "Mavis, *these* must be Lord Wuffa's pictures. There's no question about it this time—they're primitive little figures . . . so full of life! Almost as clear as the day they were painted!"

"They aren't camouflaged like the ones up here?"

There was silence for a few, unbearably long seconds and when he spoke this time the eagerness had evaporated. Mr Pringle had a stange inflection in his voice.

"Oh, yes . . . genuine . . . without a shadow of a doubt.

Even I can see that . . ." Then, almost in a murmur, "There's no chance these could be fakes. Lord Wuffa's pictures . . . Oh dear, oh dear . . . What would Granny Pringle have said." The suspense was too great.

"Look out," Mavis cried, "I'm coming down."

In the Incident Room, power, information and a certain degree of calm had been restored. "We found we could recall everything from the master disc," the computer operator announced importantly.

"I don't care where you got it from, just see you don't lose any of it ever again."

"No, sir."

"There's plenty coming through now," DS Mather was reading from the paper rolling out of the printer. "Hello? Some of our hayseeds have form."

"Any of our Leonards featured yet?"

"Not so far. Most of it's what you'd expect; speeding, non-payment of debt, poaching." Mather rifled through another yard. "Hello? Our Chelmsford chum has been less than frank. R. L. McCormack is an alias for Robert Simmons. Also known as Bob Reeves or R. D. Davenport . . ."

"Punch him up," Andrews ordered. Information appeared on the screen.

"Born 1955 . . ." DS Mather summarized rapidly. "His speciality is fine art. Imitative rather than original—"

"We knew that much."

"Yes, but look. Another conviction in '82 for receiving stolen property. We ought to let the trusting Reg know about that."

"Later," Andrews decided. "Check if there's anything known about the other one, Peter Winstead. And I want to speak to the lab—"

"Sir," called WDC Tyler putting down the phone, "that was Felicity Brown. She'd just come back from giving Mr Leveret his breakfast and asked if she could see you."

"What about?"

"Something Mr Leveret mentioned. He gave Mrs Brown the impression he wasn't actually married to his wife."

Mr Pringle and Mavis sat side by side, flanked by candles. The flames flickering in mockery over the exuberant, cavorting, naked figures that surrounded them.

"Sort of seventh-century graffiti," Mavis was visibly shaken.

"Or sixth. I can't remember Lord Wuffa's exact dates. He was once thought to be a candidate for the burial chamber at Sutton Hoo."

"What's that?"

Mr Pringle leaned back against an illustration that could have come from the pages of the Kamasutra.

"About twenty miles from here under a mound, archaeologists excavated a huge ancient burial chamber containing a wooden ship nearly ninety feet long. It had been dragged up out of the water. Goodness knows how the men of the time managed. Using tree-trunks as rollers, I suppose. Inside the ship were glorious treasures; gold, silver, jewellery, you know the kind of thing. It's all on display in the British Museum. But there was no skeleton, nothing to say who the chieftain was, or why he'd merited such an honour. An epic poem exists, called *Beowulf*, and describes the burial but even that doesn't name the warrior king."

"And this Lord Wuffa," Mavis nodded at the mural, "he was dead before that time?"

"Yes."

"They wouldn't waste a great big ship on a randy old goat like him, would they?"

"Possibly not."

She sniffed. "Or a poem. He's the sort you cremate and try to forget."

"There's a village not far from Sutton Hoo, Rendlesham; that's where the Wuffinga tribe are thought to have had their Great Hall. No one's really sure. All this was over thirteen hundred years ago."

"If that was their Hall, this was definitely where they came for a night out. Wuffa's Brothel."

"It gives a new perspective to archaeology, certainly."

"They came here to be naughty," she said, disapproval building up, "very naughty indeed. You can't tell me these stone benches were designed this width for sitting on? It's a wonder to me they didn't put a mirror in the roof. And that thing in the middle of the floor, dear, was never intended as a table or an altar. There's a word for dirty old men like your Lord Wuffa: voyeur." Mrs Bignell had recovered from the initial shock and picked up her candle for a more detailed tour of inspection.

"I am broad-minded, you cannot deny that. I have to be, behind the bar at the Bricklayers, but these pictures are disgusting. I don't care if they are antique. I mean—look at this one. See where he's putting his whatsit? And such a smile on his face, he should be ashamed!"

"Nevertheless as a relic, the chamber must be unique."

She rounded on him. "Much good will that do." Mr Pringle remained silent. "You couldn't show it to anyone. Suppose they put it on television—what would the Prime Minister say?"

"She'd want to privatize it."

"She'd want it demolished. Otherwise her lot would never stay in Parliament—they'd be queuing up down here with their floozies." Mavis leaned forward to examine a detail.

"Oh, my word! This must be when your Lord Wuffa was getting on a bit. He's using a funny little gadget. I saw one just like it in Tottenham Court Road once. Fancy it being invented in AD 600."

"By the fifth century, the Romans had departed leaving our ancestors with the appurtenances of civilization."

"Now you can't blame this on the Italians, dear, it just isn't fair. Pompeii was one thing, this is entirely different." She was massively indignant now. "It's not titillating, it's far too *explicit*." And gathering herself for her verdict, Mrs Bignell pronounced: "I don't care what you say, mucky pictures like these put me off nooky altogether."

"Then by all means let us go back up."

Felicity Brown, still in a state of shock following the explosion, fidgeted in the crowded Incident Room.

"Won't you come through, Mrs Brown."

She followed uneasily. "It feels like betrayal, coming here behind Cyril's back."

"How is he this morning?" DI Andrews guided her into the inner sanctum, keeping up a genial flow. "According to my officers, he's beginning to pick up. Takes more of an interest in what's going on."

"He's finally accepted Doris is dead, if that's what you mean."

"Take a seat. Can I offer you a coffee? Our machine's been repaired. At least, I hope it still works. The chap had only just finished when World War Three began out there." Felicity smiled wanly.

154

"I thought an aircraft had crashed."

"So did my sergeant. What a stupid woman! Guns like that should be in museums. At least she'll never get her hands on one again. So . . . Cyril Leveret came out with interesting information?"

"I don't know if he meant to," Felicity began hesitantly, and paused.

"I realize how you must feel, but we must have all the facts. We won't embarrass anyone but we do need to know anything that could be relevant."

"Cyril's worried about the funeral. He asked me what he should say to the undertaker because Doris's surname isn't really Leveret."

"Did he say what it was?"

"No."

"No inkling at all?" Felicity shook her head emphatically.

"Ted might know. He and Mr Pringle talked of Doris the other night. Ted knew the house where the family lived before they moved away. Doris was the only one to return, after she'd—supposedly—married Cyril."

"We've learned much of that. Does your husband know what she did after she'd left Wuffinge? We're still checking what we've been told."

"I was in the kitchen part of the time. I'll ask him tonight."

"If you would. What about Mr Leveret?"

"I doubt if he'd tell you even if he knew. He won't respond to threats, either. I don't think he cares any longer."

"My information is that Doris Winkle left here to train as a nurse." Felicity nodded. "And that she married?"

She nodded again. "She claimed her first husband had died. There may have been a divorce. Women of our generation are often shy about admitting it."

"Do you think Mr Leveret could have been confused about that?"

"I don't think so," Felicity said slowly. "This morning he was agitated but that's nothing new. He remembered the mobile library calls today and had put books ready on the hall table."

"He knew what he was doing, in fact?"

"Yes. I cooked his bacon and egg. He had the paper but he kept staring out of the window. When I put the food in front of him, he said: 'Will it matter that Doris's name wasn't Leveret. I don't want unpleasantness at her funeral.'"

"What did you say?"

"I asked what he meant. He wouldn't explain. I think Cyril's had to answer too many questions lately. Anyway, I suggested the vicar should come and discuss it but Cyril wouldn't have that. He muttered something about the undertaker then he took the newspaper into the study and shut the door. It's no use trying to talk to him when he's in that mood. And that's all I can tell you."

"Thank you, Mrs Brown."

"What will happen at the inquest?"

"I'll have a word with the coroner."

"Thanks," she said gratefully. "Cyril's very frail."

"And if you could ask your husband if he remembers anything more?"

"I will. By the way . . ."

"Yes?"

"Ted must have been on his way back between five and seven on Wednesday. He was in the kitchen by ten past seven, opening bottles." DI Andrews's expression didn't change.

"I see."

"He knew Mr Pringle was expected by seven thirty, you see."

"Yes." Happy that she'd cleared the matter up, Felicity departed. Andrews watched her walk back across the green. What was to stop a man parking a little way from home and then turning up precisely when he was expected? It was exactly what a killer would have done.

Mavis helped Mr Pringle replace the flagstone and watched as he screwed the sheet of Perspex back in position. "What about the screen?"

"It's splintered. I doubt if it will go back up."

"You can't just leave it," she scolded. "People will know what we've been doing."

"I don't care . . ." He tightened the final screw. "It's high time this charade was exposed. It contributed to the Major's death."

"For the last time, he died of natural causes, you told me so yourself."

"He died of a heart attack."

"He was an old man," she insisted. Mr Pringle dropped the screwdriver into his bag.

"Mavis, I'm sure the Major knew about the chamber. He may even have known what lies beneath this painting."

They gazed up at the indecipherable figures and ancient lettering.

"Tell me again what those words mean?"

"*Descenditi malediciti*—depart, or I believe it can also mean descend, ye cursed. It's a quotation, maybe even a pun in this instance, intended to warn those about to use the chamber of an all-seeing God. It's on the eyeline as you climb back up."

"They never carried on down there after this bit had been made a church?" Mavis was horrified.

"Who can say?"

"And you think there could be another dirty painting underneath?"

"There's something there, we've already proved it."

"What I can't understand is how anyone could go on being a vicar—standing in that pulpit week after week—knowing what was in that cellar?" Neither could Mr Pringle, but he tried to reason it out.

"There were obviously those in Wuffinge who always knew. Whether they told the vicar, who can say? It's possible some passed their entire ministry in ignorance of what lay beneath their feet. It's been kept secret for centuries, remember." Mavis picked up the church magazine they'd used to shield the candles.

"The Major was a church warden. On the back page it lists the officers of the parish church of St Boniface, Wuffinge Parva."

"Who was the other?"

"Mrs Doris Leveret."

"Ah . . ." Mr Pringle took off his spectacles and rubbed his eyes. "That could explain it." Mrs Bignell preferred not to hear. She rose.

"If you're ready we should make a move, dear. We need to give Ruby the key and take Ted's fork back. It's all tidy in here—Oh!" She gave a guilty start. "The vicar's arrived," she whispered, "he's standing at the back." Mr Pringle rose also.

"Good morning," he said politely. The figure in his shabby working clothes remained where he was.

Mavis called, "We borrowed Ruby's key, vicar. We thought we'd take a last look around . . ." but her voice trailed away.

"Mavis, would you mind waiting for me in the car." She moved with alacrity, skirting the man who continued to stare at the broken wooden screen propped against the wall below the painting.

Chapter Eleven

"What we have is the pattern of deceased's movements from two fifteen onwards on Wednesday afternoon." DI Andrews had called another meeting. On the wall behind him was a plan of Wuffinge brought up to date with various coloured markings.

"So, to repeat, from two fifteen approximately," he pointed at a blue cross, "deceased returned home for a quick late lunch with Cyril Leveret. He can't remember anything significant being said, she was in and out within half an hour. Other members of the WI were already at the church when deceased got back. She stayed there, in full view of everyone, for the rest of the afternoon.

"According to Joyce Parsons, certain derogatory remarks were made from time to time, about Miranda Kenny, by Mrs Leveret as well as everyone else. Mrs Ruby Runkle was particularly snide. Others had been upset by Mrs Kenny's manner but Ruby hinted at something else: claimed Mrs Kenny was quote 'no better than she ought to be' unquote. Very original. Unfortunately she refused to say anything more to us. Claimed it was nothing to do with Doris Leveret's death— which indeed may be true.

"However," Andrews paused, "it ties in with what Ruby's husband Len claimed to overhear while on his way to poach in the manor house grounds—which we shall overlook—and Eddie Runkle's description of what he saw when on the trail of a fox.

"According to those two, plus a sighting by a Mr Charlie Braithwaite out late exercising his dog, Mrs Kenny was very friendly with our Chelmsford pal, Robert Simmons, alias R. L. McCormack, Bob Reeves, alias etc. etc. Yes?" WDC Tyler had raised a hand.

"Has Mrs Kenny admitted her relationship?"

"We haven't talked to her since you and I saw her on Thursday. According to these three statements, Miranda Kenny was making the running with Simmons and this was known in the village. She was also at odds with the deceased.

"So . . . to return to Wednesday afternoon: by five o'clock the ladies were finished at the church. Mrs Leveret returned home—at least we *think* she did because her husband is uncertain. Anyway at some point between five and seven p.m. after a quick cup of tea, she told him she was off to talk to Leonard. Something to do with money—have we discovered anything about Cyril Leveret's finances?"

"Sorry," DS Mather was apologetic, "the bank are being difficult." Andrews swore.

"Keep pressing. We need to know."

"Sir."

"Deceased returned saying she hadn't been able to talk to Leonard—in private." DI Andrews looked round the group. "By which we assume she at least managed to see the man although in the company of someone else. She left the house again after ten thirty p.m. to try and see this Leonard once more. We assume she did because Cyril Leveret took a sleeping pill and went to bed at ten thirty but claims that's what she told him. He also remembers her saying she would be 'very late' getting back. Why, we can't establish until we hear it from the man himself. Anyone disagree with that so far? Any questions? Anyone want to add anything?"

"When granddad went back to the pub on Wednesday night, did he see Mrs Leveret by any chance?" DI Andrews shook his head.

"A fox, that's all. Pringle admitted he was pissed that night. Said he was taking care not to trip over guy ropes by the marquee so didn't notice anything."

"Nobody claims to have seen deceased and no one knows which direction she might have taken to meet up with Leonard." It was stalemate; in the Incident Room, officers shifted irritably. One put up a hand.

"Sir, did Oliver Kenny know about his missus and Simmons?"

"We think he must have done. We shall ask him."

Mr Pringle was no longer the eager seeker after truth, he was dishevelled, even his moustache drooped. He'd been waiting to speak to Reg Terson alone, to ask him questions. Now the time had come he was a little afraid and uncertain how to begin. Terson ignored him and crouched instead in front of the broken screen. It was an automatic reaction to that which made him say, "I'm sorry about the damage."

"It won't go back up again."

"That hardly matters." The hands gripping the edges of the screen tightened perceptibly. "That medieval painting is nothing but camouflage for what's beneath."

The Reverend Terson was suddenly very still.

"Mrs Bignell and I have discovered the truth about Lord Wuffa's pictures," Mr Pringle said quietly. "We found the way into the chamber. We've replaced everything. The front pew is on its original mark, concealing the crack between the stones."

"If you know what's down there, you'll realize the nature of what lies beneath this." Terson straightened up and gazed at the picture.

"Nothing the church would want revealed, I imagine?" The haggard, boyish face almost managed to smile.

"Have either of you spoken to anyone?"

"No," Mr Pringle shook his head. "Nor shall we. I owe a loyalty to Wuffinge."

"I didn't know about the chamber when I first came. No one does. They wait a while before they tell you. A testing period. Will he keep silent or is he the sort to tell the Bishop?"

"Was it the Major who told you? I presume the secret has been kept by officers of the church."

"Not necessarily. It's been handed down by a responsible person. There are always two who know. For the last five hundred years or so, one has always been a Petrie Coombe-Hamilton. Each has to swear to keep it secret and when he becomes the sole survivor, entrust it to one other person. It's up to the two of them to decide whether or not to tell each new vicar, which is how they've been successful in keeping the secret. Many of my predecessors have come and gone in ignorance." Mr Pringle found it astonishing that any would stay, once they knew. Guessing his thoughts, the Reverend Terson added curtly, "I was considered safe. Too easy-going to make a fuss."

Or too weak, wondered Mr Pringle. The end of the questioning was in sight, at last.

"It was the reason the Major was so unhappy about the festival?"

"That wasn't because of the chamber," Reg Terson replied. "We needed money to repair the thatch. As well as the mural below there were legends of other wall-paintings in here. I decided it was worth investigating and knew Robert was talented enough to undertake the task—"

"Those three paintings are fakes!" Mr Pringle's voice rang out in condemnation, "You're not trying to pretend . . . ?" Reg Terson flushed.

"That's not entirely correct."

"What do you mean?"

"Traces of paint were there beneath the layers of plaster but that was the problem, they were mere daubs."

"Too indistinct to be of interest, you mean? Did you inform the Major? He must have been extremely worried they would turn out to be of a similar nature to those below."

"I told him traces of paint had been found, that was all. When Robert suggested he could . . . improve them, I took the risk and told him to go ahead. It was damnably stupid." Mr Pringle agreed.

"Those fakes . . ." he began again.

"They weren't fakes," Terson was unwilling even now to accept blame, "not to begin with."

"But once those daubs had been embellished, you knew they'd be spotted. It could only be a matter of time. The Major guessed because of the rabbits, didn't he?"

"Rabbits?" To his amazement the vicar patently didn't understand. "I know nothing about rabbits. The Major managed to push his way in one night and realized what was going on."

"The night he died?" Such a simple explanation after all!

"I wasn't here, I'd gone up to London on business. Peter had been careless for once about locking the door. He and Robert were busy 'ageing' the paintings when they heard a noise and found the Major standing there. There was the most enormous row. He was drunk. He'd already had a dust-up with Mrs Kenny. Two arguments in one night was too much for a weak heart. The doctor was satisfied," Terson said defensively. "He signed the death certificate."

Mr Pringle spoke as though he hadn't heard. "So, the three of you decided to turn the traces into full blown pictures to deceive a gullible public—which amounts to forgery and deception."

"That wasn't my idea, that was Peter and Robert."

Mr Pringle was pitiless. "You condoned it, which amounts to the same thing."

"No!" The vicar continued more quietly. "The whole business got out of hand. I invited Robert here, I admit that, and his colleague Winstead. Robert and I met at the prison where I was chaplain. I wanted to give him an opportunity to put his talents to honest use."

Mr Pringle wasn't impressed.

"Didn't the Heritage people have reservations? An ex-convict permitted to uncover the earliest known paintings in Britain?"

"They weren't told," Terson wasn't apologetic, he obviously thought it a stupid question. "The committee left everything to me. I reported back that the authorities were satisfied."

Mr Pringle hardened his heart. "From the beginning it was an enterprise intended to deceive. The weakness was that it was bound to be exposed—I spotted one error. You were fortunate no one else did during the weekend. No wonder your two friends were anxious to disappear." The vicar began to gabble.

"I couldn't prevent what happened. Robert refused to stop once he'd uncovered traces of paint. He was an expert at copying. He kept on, using medieval missals as a guide, transforming what was there into beautiful works of art. He hid from me what he'd done until it was too late. Once he and Peter showed me the first painting, what was the point in preventing them doing two more? We had to hide the remaining traces, otherwise everyone would have guessed." Mr Pringle could understand but he couldn't forgive.

"You had the authority of the church. You could have refused to allow it to continue. The Major would have been your ally."

"You've no idea what you're talking about," the vicar argued fiercely. "Robert and Peter saw the chance of making big money. Robert encouraged Miranda Kenny with ideas of a festival—he'd been meeting her late at night. She was silly enough to believe herself in love. Robert is an educated man, he gets a kick out of enticing women, particularly those with intellectual pretensions. He hinted he was uncovering masterpieces. He convinced her he knew experts who would confirm the paintings were genuine, that Wuffinge would benefit. He

163

and Peter concocted the whole scheme, there was nothing I could do."

"Except tell the truth."

"About what lies beneath this church!" he exploded bitterly.

"Yes . . ." It would take courage to expose that, Mr Pringle acknowledged. "A pity you didn't listen to the Major."

"I couldn't halt the festival without giving the committee a reason, don't you understand?" he insisted. "It was out of control by then but it wasn't my fault." Wisely, Mr Pringle refused to grant expiation. He began to brush the dust off his clothes.

"What about those?" he asked, indicating the dark paintings.

"Robert uncovered them later, after he'd finished the first three. We were amazed—he genuinely hoped to restore them but when he began the work, some flakes came off and he saw colour beneath. At that point, we decided to leave them as they were, for fear of any contrast with the others."

"Which would have revealed the deception immediately."

"Peter took infra-red photographs. That's when the nature of the subject matter was revealed."

"You hadn't told them of the chamber?"

"No. The irony is, the Major did that. He was so drunk, he must've let it slip during the shouting match. When I returned from London, the two of them were full of questions. I refused to answer, pretended I didn't know. It was a shock, seeing that photograph. Peter kept on searching. Eventually, he found the right flagstone."

"Last Tuesday?"

"After the Major's funeral that morning. We had moved the pews so the WI could bring in their trestles. That's when Peter spotted the crack. Once I'd gone back to the vicarage, he and Robert began to explore."

"The deception was bound to be discovered. Oh, of course!" The truth was suddenly obvious. "You planned to escape as well."

"No!" The protest was a lie.

"It must've been what you intended, there was no reason for you to stay. You couldn't have remained as vicar. From the start the three of you must've planned to share the proceeds and disappear. Doris Leveret's death put a stop to it. You couldn't go once that happened, it would have given the game away. You had to stay until an arrest was made—and pray that

164

no one would spot the deception. Did she discover what was happening? Did the Major tell her?"

"He must've done," muttered Terson thickly.

"Come, you must have thought of nothing else since her murder. Which of those two was responsible, Peter or Robert? Or was it a joint effort? Did one of them pinion the poor woman down while the other squeezed the life out of her? Surely you questioned them?" Mr Pringle was too angry to notice the effect his words had. "Yet you continued to do—nothing? The Major had to tell someone, he'd taken an oath, and Mrs Leveret was his fellow church warden. Someone had to know about the chamber. Was it Mrs Leveret?"

"I'm not sure," Terson stammered.

"You *must* know." Mr Pringle was remorseless. "Did she appeal to you to stop the festival? Whichever of them was responsible for her death, it is your duty now to tell the police."

"No! You can't assume . . . They were in the church on Wednesday evening."

"How can you be sure?" Despite Terson's desire to spare his friends, Mr Pringle couldn't feel compassion. If only Terson had shown a little courage at the beginning, none of the dreadful charade need have happened. But it was a waste of time trying to persuade him. The police would deal with the matter, he must do what was best for Wuffinge.

"I trust you will at least guarantee that the church roof will be repaired," he said severely. The vicar stared as if he'd taken leave of his wits.

"The roof?"

"This building may have been intended for other purposes originally," Mr Pringle said sternly, "but my granny worshipped here all her life. She was a good woman. It is for her sake as well as the rest of the village that the thatch must be renewed."

If he'd hoped to impress, he was disappointed. Reg Terson broke into wild laughter.

"You think that's all that matters?"

"In the end, yes I do." The vicar made a great effort to control himself.

"You're right, of course. Doris Leveret is dead. No one knows about the chamber now except you and I. In future, no one shall know. I shall seal the crack. No one will discover what lies beneath these stones. The building can be reconsecrated privately and continue as a place of worship. As for the paintings, I shall announce they are of a much later date and valueless. Interest will gradually fade."

"You're deluding yourself over that," Mr Pringle said involuntarily.

"Not if they are plastered over again. A valid excuse would be that exposure during the festival has already damaged them. I must know, however, what you intend to do."

"Return to London. I shall not come and live here—" They were interrupted. The heavy oak door swung open and DS Mather walked in.

"Might I have a word? Oh, sorry to interrupt, vicar." He stood there, waiting.

"I was just leaving," Mr Pringle told him. Reg Terson gripped his hand.

"I can rely on you?"

"What? Oh, yes." Why should he expose his granny's church to trampling paparazzi? "A pity that a place of worship cannot benefit from man's carnal appetites." The smile opposite was miserable.

"You and I agree that's not possible."

"We do."

"We'll take the key back to Ruby, the fork to Felicity and then be on our way."

"Certainly." Satisfied, Mavis fastened her seatbelt.

"I've enjoyed my little visit but I shan't be sorry to get home. That mural left a nasty taste."

"The vicar wants us to forget it exists."

"I'm not surprised. You needn't worry about me. I shan't say a dicky-bird. I'm only sorry you had to see them." Puzzled, Mr Pringle pulled up outside Ruby's house. "It's bad for your cholesterol," she said solemnly. He picked up the key.

"I shan't be long." When Ruby answered, he asked, "May I come in?"

"If you like." She waved vigorously at Mavis in the car and stepped aside. "She's very nice, your lady friend. I'm in the middle of me washing so come through to the kitchen." She returned to the sink. "Yes?"

"I've been talking to Eddie about the Major."

"I know."

"His dead body was moved a few feet to save any awkward questions. On the second occasion, Doris Leveret's corpse was moved out of devilment." Ruby twitched her shoulders as if to shrug this off. "I don't know who killed her but I believe I know who fished her out of the Wuffen and put her in that marquee. It was a damn fool thing to do—I suppose the two of them panicked when I kicked up such a hullaballoo."

After a pause, Ruby said, "You wasn't supposed to find her."

"No. That was Miranda Kenny."

"You're not going to say anything?"

"No." The police could work it out for themselves. He had the slight advantage of knowing Wuffinge ways but they would reach the same conclusion from the forensic evidence.

"She never leaves us alone does Miranda Kenny. Thinks she's so superior. Always lecturing on what's best for the environment. As for Doris Winkle, she was a mean woman to work for. Hard and mean. When she came back here she treated us like dirt. I had to work for her, I needed the money."

"And Len found her in the river on Wednesday night."

"He'd gone poaching," Ruby said simply, "he was on his way home. He never heard a fight or anything, only Miranda Kenny shouting at her chap when he went past. She was chasing after the tall one at the vicarage. It was the other who must've jumped out at her that night, to frighten her off."

"You think so?"

"Who else could it have been? There's no one in the village fancied Mrs Kenny. She was very sniffy about us."

"What about Doris Leveret?"

"I never bad-wished her," Ruby said suddenly. "You got to believe that."

"Of course."

"When Len come back he got such a fright, finding her like that. Thought it was Mrs Kenny of course, because of the hat."

"You mean it was already on Mrs Leveret's head?" Ruby nodded.

"Len reached out to pull her into the bank, that's when he saw who it was. He run off and found Eddie waiting for the old vixen. Len asked him what he should do. They was so scared they helped themselves to whisky Eddie had in the van, otherwise they wouldn't have been so daft."

"To put Doris in the marquee, you mean."

"They were fed up with Mrs Kenny. She goes on at Eddie about his cottage. She was giving orders all the time by then, to do with the festival. They put Doris in Eddie's van and drove her down to Mrs Kenny's tent. Then they sat and watched, till it got light, to see what would happen. Afterwards we all swore Len had gone to play darts at Yoxford that night. Elsie said Eddie was due back from Milton Keynes Thursday morning. That was after you come along and mucked it all up."

"What did they do with the body?"

"Put it back in Eddie's van. They acted quick, before the police arrived. Eddie was supposed to be helping the craft people so nobody thought anything of seeing the van. He and Len put her in the allotment shed till they worked out what to do. Come nightfall, they put her back in the river where they found her. They didn't mean no harm. She was already dead. Someone else did that."

"Yes," sighed Mr Pringle. "Why did they tie her arms and legs?"

"She was big. Heavy. Kept flopping about."

"Yes." Rigor had obviously come and gone.

Ruby asked awkwardly, "You going to tell anyone?"

He shook his head. "I'm going back where I belong."

She chuckled. "You going to say bye-bye to Elsie?"

Why not? It was a challenge but he had Mavis with him, his shield and defence against any peril.

"I might," said G. D. H. Pringle boldly.

"Not a single piece matches the ligature?" DI Andrews was incredulous.

"Not so far. Give 'em a chance, they haven't finished testing yet. It'll be our luck it turns out to be the very last ball. They've established the bits round the arms and legs are from one source but the ligature is of a different weight and thickness. Those lab technicians are complaining of eye-strain, they've been up all night, staring at miles and miles of string."

"I wish they'd hurry up and finish . . ." Andrews wandered about. "I cannot believe the murderer came from outside this village, or that he bought twine especially for the purpose, it doesn't make sense. Yes?" An officer was at the open door.

"We've traced Simmons. He and Winstead drove to Felixstowe and boarded the Zeebrugge ferry at 2200 hours last night. They arrived on time this morning. According to the port authority who contacted the Dutch traffic police, the car is registered at an address above an art gallery in Rotterdam."

"I want them picked up and held. They're to be questioned separately on the attempted rape of Mrs Miranda Kenny. What news of her husband?"

"He's scarpered. Council office confirms they have no forwarding address."

"Right. Let's have a chat with his wife. Anything further from Leveret?"

"WDC Tyler's trying to wheedle information out of him. We're still waiting for the bank manager to co-operate. He wants to talk to Leveret's solicitor before he tells us anything. *He*'s due back in the office today after a week on his canal boat, which is why we weren't able to get in touch before."

"Haven't they heard of cell-phones on the canal?"

"Some people go boating for a bit of peace and quiet."

"I want to know what's in the Will, details of the marriage certificate, everything. Come on, let's pay Mrs Kenny another visit."

Miranda Kenny's humiliation was complete; she didn't know where her husband could be found and had to admit the fact to a male police officer. DI Andrews was no longer placatory.

"No one vanishes, Mrs Kenny. They always go somewhere they've been before. If you try hard enough, you'll remember a place you visited or that once appealed to your husband." He stopped short of suggesting another woman could be involved. She could discover that for herself. Outside, he said to Mather, "Let's see if Leveret is talking any sense."

"Sir, sir . . ." It was a summons from the caravan. An officer hurried across. "Information has just come through. Forensic have a match on the ligature. And the Leverets' solicitor has rung. Wants to tell you about Leveret's mental history."

"Mental?"

"That's where he and the victim met. She was a nurse at an asylum. Took responsibility for him. Removed him into her sole care and claimed they were married." DI Andrews had reached the caravan steps.

"First things first; whose roll of twine was it?"

"The hands and feet were tied with two lengths from the same hank owned by Leonard Runkle. The ligature matched twine which was used to tie up the decorations in the church. There were two balls; one came from the vicarage, the other was supplied by Mrs Felicity Brown of Woodbine Cottage."

169

DS Mather said slowly, "Felicity Brown is a big lady. Strong enough, at a guess."

"So's her husband." DI Andrews marshalled his thoughts. "Get hold of Tyler and tell her about the asylum. See if Cyril Leveret comes across with any more information as a result. I want to talk to the solicitor myself—and get on to that bank manager, John. He can't withhold information now."

"Right."

"I want a discreet watch kept on Mrs Brown. Do we know where Edward Leonard went to today?"

"Colchester. He's due back about eight thirty."

"Keep the pressure up on Mrs Kenny. I want to find that husband of hers. And bring in Leonard Runkle."

"We've tried that already. He's gone on an outing to Bury St Edmunds with the over-sixties. They're not due back till eight p.m." DI Andrews swore loud and long.

"Bloody geriatrics! They've no business going shopping. This is a murder investigation!"

The Allegro pulled up a short distance from Beggar's Row. "I've one more person to see, then we'll be off." Mavis was suspicious.

"It can't be Felicity, we've said goodbye to her."

"We have."

"And I've seen Guinevere. You're never going to visit that woman in number eight."

"Very briefly." His nerve was already beginning to fail.

"You're being silly." Sentimental perhaps, but not silly.

"I shan't be long."

"You better hadn't be." Mrs Bignell gave him an extremely old-fashioned look. "I know all about little Elsie Runkle. Felicity told me."

Elsie was waiting for him. He followed her inside, remembering to duck this time. He took Eddie's chair rather than submit to more scratching from the kittens.

"Tell Eddie I know most of what happened," Mr Pringle said. "When the police find out they may want to examine his van. These days, the most minute particle can reveal if a body was kept inside."

"They wrapped her in a bit of plastic sheeting left over from mending Len's shed," Elsie volunteered. "An' they got rid of that after."

170

"I still cannot understand how she came to be wearing Mrs Kenny's hat."

"Eddie said it was pulled on tight, nearly over her ears." Elsie used both hands to demonstrate. "It was woolly and stretched, like a bonnet."

"Yes." He'd seen for himself only too plainly.

"They didn't feel like taking it off."

"No."

"Chap who strangled her must've put it on. Did it for a bit of a laugh, mebbe." The suggestion was half-hearted. "Whoever did it didn't like Mrs Kenny, that's for certain," Elsie finished.

"You off then?"

Mr Pringle confirmed that he was.

"You're a widower now." He experienced slight alarm.

"I have a friend, Mrs Bignell."

"I've seen her. Red hair."

"Genuine," he replied automatically.

"Lively, is she?" Elsie demanded.

"She can be," he admitted.

She sniffed. "You needed that," she said, "a bit of life. Proper shy little sod you were. Always was."

And it all came back, as he half-feared it might. The scene in this very room, with Elsie on the sofa, one leg out-stretched supported on a stool and he kneeling, with a bowl of water, about to bathe and bandage a supposedly grazed knee.

"You lied to me!" After half a century it still rankled. She grinned.

"You was always boasting you did first aid in the scouts."

"You invited me inside . . . pretended your knee needed attention . . ." And there on the floor in front of her, he had become aware that little Elsie was no longer wearing her knickers.

There was a silence. He could hear the clock ticking, the sound of the cat's rough tongue licking a kitten's fur. Elsie was the first to speak.

"I never asked you for half-a-crown. I knew you only got two shillin' when your gran could afford it. I never even asked for sixpence."

"No," he said, and cleared his throat. Then, gently, "It was a very generous offer."

"Which you didn't accept. Toffee-nosed git!" After fifty years she was still resentful.

171

"I'm afraid I was an immature boy in those days, Elsie."

"You made up for it since?"

"I do my best." She snorted.

"Red-headed women are always the same. Sex mad."

Mr Pringle held out a hand. "Warn Eddie to be careful."

"He always is. Never got caught yet, Eddie hasn't." Mr Pringle hoped there wouldn't be a first time. He leaned forward to kiss the wrinkled, grubby cheek.

"It was a very generous offer," he said again.

"Well you can bugger off because you're a pensioner now and these days I charges five quid."

In the car he was foolishly sentimental. "Just imagine, Elsie's forefathers and mine may have lived in Wuffinge Parva from time immemorial."

"Yes," said Mavis caustically, "and we can guess how her great-great-great-granny earned her living, down in that cellar."

"Oh, I hardly think—" he began but she interrupted.

"Just a minute, that's Felicity coming out of the police caravan, with one of those lady officers. She looks dreadful!" Mavis was out of the car in an instant and hurried down the path towards her. "What's the matter?" she called. "You all right, dear?" Mr Pringle caught a glimpse of the terrified, tear-stained face. Patently, their hostess was extremely upset. He too, got out of the car.

Chapter Twelve

"So . . ." DI Andrews sat back, mug of coffee in hand. "Summarize it for John, would you. Tracy managed to persuade Leveret to talk." DS Mather prepared to listen.

"Cyril Leveret was committed to an asylum when he was eighteen. It was one of those cases where a family got rid of an unwanted child by claiming he was out of control. He'd had occasional hiccups with the law but his father was partly to blame. He was a violent man and took the strap to him once too often. On that occasion Cyril hit back, leaving him with concussion and a broken jaw. The family were wealthy. No charges were brought but they managed to get Cyril committed privately. It couldn't happen nowadays, thank God.

"Doris Winkle came on the scene several years later when she was employed as a nurse at the asylum. She discovered Cyril . . ."

"Discovered his money you mean," growled Andrews.

"His parents and sister were dead by then, he was the only survivor and the family money was in a trust. Once she'd taken Cyril out of care, Doris managed to get hold of some of that money. At a guess, the bank manager connived to break the trust. He certainly knew the two of them weren't married—"

"Did Leveret say why?" asked Mather. WDC Tyler shook her head.

"He wouldn't tell me any more than he would Mrs Brown. But it was one reason the bank manager needed to talk to the solicitor after you'd spoken to him." DS Mather nodded. "He sounded all of a do-dah when I told him what had happened."

"Doris spent the money on lavish entertaining when they first came here. They gave out that the guests were business colleagues from London but most were from the hospitals where she'd worked. According to Cyril she wanted to impress Wuffinge Parva. Revenge for being kicked in the teeth in the old days. They raised capital from the fund—that's where the bank must've helped—without the solicitor's knowledge. Once *he* found out, he immediately applied the brakes but by then there wasn't much left. Doris had to find a new source."

"Do we know where?"

"We think she went to ask the vicar."

"The vicar?" Mather's eyebrows went up.

"I know," Tracy Tyler sighed. "It sounds unlikely but Cyril was convinced that was who Doris was trying to meet last Wednesday. She referred to him as Leonard, his second name, although in the village he's generally known as Reg."

"But why him? Has he got money? Vicars aren't usually rich men."

Andrews drained the last of his coffee.

"Maybe she wanted a share of the dosh?" he suggested. "They must've taken a fair amount at the festival. We'll have a chat with the Rev Reg/Leonard later and find out what was discussed. I suppose he didn't tell us before because of the confessional aspect."

"That's high church," Tracy demurred. "I wouldn't have thought St Boniface's was in that league."

"Maybe our Doris only wanted advice. She couldn't ask Cyril. Sounds as though she didn't have many friends."

"True."

"Anything come to light on Oliver Kenny?" Mather opened his notebook.

"Yes, Mrs K's memory returned."

"Oh, good."

"Seems she met him at university. Before that he'd been friendly with another student, a bloke whose family had a business in Droitwich. They used to play rugby together but Miranda disapproved. Once she and Oliver were married, he had to keep in touch via Christmas cards. She thinks it possible Kenny might have gone to stay with him."

"Do we have an address?"

"We do. It's a repair depot for HGVs and buses."

"Right. I'm sick and tired of these four walls. Let's you and me go to Droitwich, John."

"I thought our money was on Simmons and Winstead?"

"Keep an open mind. What reason had they got to kill her?"

"What reason had Kenny?"

"Remember the hat. Suppose Doris found it and despite what people keep telling us, she put it on. She might have felt cold or something. It was dark. If Kenny did know about his wife—and his disappearance makes it more likely—he might have made a mistake in the dark."

Tracy Tyler said doubtfully, "He saw the hat and thought it was his wife, you mean?"

"It's happened before. Lucan mistook his nanny for his wife."

"But she was a similar build. Doris Leveret was years older as well as shorter and fatter."

"All cats are grey in the dark, Trace."

"What about the twine?"

"It was lying about in the church all Wednesday afternoon. Anyone could've snipped off a length—obviously one person did. See if you can coax the vicar to tell us what he knows. Doris must've been on her way to see him when it happened, or on her way home."

"It's odd the appointment was so late."

Andrews shrugged. "Probably because of the festival. Most of them were working round the clock last week." He called into the outer office. "Any progress from Rotterdam?"

"Not yet."

"Keep at it. What about the Leverets' solicitor?"

"Williams went over half an hour ago. It's an office in Sudbury. He's phoning the details through."

"Fine." Andrews was impatient. "I've got a sore bum from sitting too long. Let's be off."

They were once more in Woodbine Cottage. Mavis was making tea while Mr Pringle waited sympathetically for Felicity to recover. "You're sure you wouldn't like me to contact Ted?"

"Quite sure." The smile was watery but the tone resolute. "They were difficult clients he was visiting today, I don't want to add to his worries. Also . . ." She hesitated.

"Yes?"

"It's not the twine, although it's bad enough knowing the murderer used my ball." Mr Pringle agreed. Privately, he'd decided he must return to the vicarage and insist Terson tell the police the whole tale immediately. What did it matter now if the secret of the vault had to be revealed? Felicity was speaking again. "Cyril came out with such an extraordinary remark."

"Yes."

175

"About Ted. You remember the police wanted to know his whereabouts between five and seven p.m. on Wednesday?"

"Yes."

"Well Cyril said . . . this is going to sound completely ridiculous."

"Tell me."

"That Ted was already in Wuffinge. Cyril was sitting on the bench in the back garden, sipping a gin and tonic and claims he saw Ted and Len Runkle go past."

"Ted and Len?" Mr Pringle repeated stupidly.

"Yes." Felicity laughed awkwardly. "Isn't it silly. He must've been mistaken. Why would Ted be talking to Len anyway?"

Mr Pringle ignored the question. "Has Cyril told the police?"

"I don't think so. He's so grateful for his meals, he wouldn't want to upset me. But surely he must be mistaken?" She was begging him for reassurance, her former jolly features sagging with fear. It made him sad that she should age so much in less than a week. "Ted doesn't tell lies," she whispered.

"Of course he doesn't," Mr Pringle said loudly. All the same, he hadn't heard any mention that Cyril Leveret's eyesight was deficient. "I'd forget about it if I were you. Leveret has had a terrible shock. He may have seen them together on another occasion and muddled the date." She nodded but looked away. It was a relief when Mavis came in with the tea-tray.

The squat building of Wuffinge church still came as a surprise to Tracy Tyler. So many Suffolk churches stood tall and grand, this looked more like an old barn. She walked past it, up to the vicarage front door and rang the bell. No answer. She walked round the back. There was a car in the garage but no sign of life. After ringing the bell once more, she began reluctantly to walk away then changed her mind and went through the lych gate.

The door was unlocked. Reg Terson sat where DS Mather had left him, in one of the front pews. He didn't move. It was awkward—was the man at prayer? She coughed. He turned to face her; he looked ill.

"I'm sorry to disturb you."

"If it's about Robert Simmons, your colleague has already been to see me. I knew about his prison record, I've always known. I was the chaplain."

"It's about Mrs Leveret. Can I get you a glass of water?"

"Thank you, no. Fresh air, perhaps? Yes, that's what I need. Shall we go outside?" He took a deep breath and made an effort to shake off his mood. "That's better . . . I've been cooped up inside . . ." The tombstones were warm in the sun. Tracy settled herself comfortably.

"So've I. It seems like weeks since we first set up that caravan."

"You wanted to tell me something."

"I wanted to ask a question," she corrected. "You may feel unable to answer but it could be important. Did Mrs Leveret come to see you on the evening she was killed?" His expression was blank and daylight showed even more how tired he was. "We've reason to believe she may have wanted to consult you."

"She certainly returned here that afternoon, both she and her colleagues—I've told you that already. I wasn't there on that occasion. She and I had festival business to discuss but we finished our discussion before lunch. Pringle arrived during our conversation."

"Was anything said of a private nature?"

"I don't understand."

"We believe Mrs Leveret intended to ask your advice." When he didn't reply this time, WDC Tyler said, "We don't need to know the content, we realize it may be private—"

"No," the vicar was already shaking his head, "I didn't see Mrs Leveret again."

"That's a pity. If you had, she might still be alive. We think she came again later, intending to consult you and instead, met whoever it was who strangled her." He was shaken.

"I've no idea why you should imagine such a thing. She can't have been on her way to see me. We'd settled every outstanding matter, there was nothing which could not have waited until the following morning."

"No, no," Tracy Tyler interrupted, "it was personal. She needed to see you privately."

"You're mistaken, Miss . . . ?"

"Tyler."

"Had Mrs Leveret wished to speak to me, she would have telephoned first, as was her habit. That night, there was no call." A familiar looking two-tone blue car pulled up. The vicar recognized it. "What on earth does Pringle want now?"

Mavis refused to stay in the car. "I know you. You never notice the time once you start chatting. We need to start back soon, before the rush hour, otherwise you'll get fussed on the motorway."

"I never get fussed!"

"Yes you do. Besides . . ." He knew what was coming next: why the hell had he ever told her about that clinic! "It's bad for your cholesterol."

The young, blonde policewoman was a further complication. Her presence was an irritant to Mrs Bignell. She nodded to the vicar then said accusingly, "Shouldn't you be at work."

"Oh, I'm always on duty." Tracy Tyler gave an innocent smile.

"One of your lot upset my friend, Mrs Brown."

"Did we?"

"Just because it was her ball of string that was used to strangle Mrs Leveret."

"What!" Reg Terson was clearly shocked.

"Which anyone could have picked up," Mr Pringle interjected, "it was here with other items on Wednesday afternoon."

"But how can they be certain?"

"With magnification each strand can be matched."

"Which is very reassuring," Mavis announced firmly, "considering how often the police get things wrong. Anyway, now we've agreed Felicity had nothing to do with what happened, I hope you'll cross her off your list. The very idea!"

WDC Tyler continued to regard her pleasantly. Mollified, Mavis reclined on a memorial to a long dead Petrie Coombe-Hamilton. "Sorry if I scolded, dear, but Felicity's had a very nasty morning and as a student of human nature, I'd take my oath this business has nothing to do with her. You can't help studying people when you're pulling pints." She lowered her voice and confided, "A few of my customers have been inside, mostly for nicking stuff. One did a bank. Irish. Tried to take the security camera. Said he wanted to video his kids on holiday. There's another duffed up his auntie but not many are that violent." She shuddered. "Not like the country."

Behind her chatter the vicar asked, "Did you want to see me?"

"We came to make our farewells," Mr Pringle answered vaguely.

"And to ask you to call on Mrs Brown, vicar," Mavis added. "She really was very upset. Anyone would be, wouldn't they? If you had the time, I'm sure she'd appreciate it."

"Yes, of course."

Having done her duty, she was obviously ready to leave. Mr Pringle's mind froze. He had to convey his message, but how? For no apparent reason he pointed to the church.

"What a secretive building." All but Mrs Bignell stared at it. She looked at him in alarm.

"Just what I was thinking," Tracy Tyler agreed calmly. "Suffolk has so many great churches, this is in complete contrast."

"Secretive, withdrawn," Mr Pringle was incoherent. "Yet what do secrets matter when the graveyard is full of innocent souls."

"What are you saying?" demanded Mavis. He fell silent. "If you want my opinion, there's too much conservation. What you should do with that place, vicar, is pull it down and build a nice clean, modern church instead."

WDC Tyler giggled. "Sacrilege!"

"That's as maybe. Ready, dear?"

"Yes." Mr Pringle held out his hand.

"Goodbye."

WDC Tyler responded briskly, "We have a number where we can contact you?"

"You do." He could think of nothing more to say to Reg Terson.

"Bye-bye," called Mavis. "You won't forget to look in on Felicity." As the two of them walked back to their car, Tracy Tyler heard her add, "Not that he'll do her much good. He looks like a wet weekend, poor chap."

Mr Pringle switched on the ignition. The sun was lower now, reflecting the flints in the thick walls; shiny black patches against the dull creamy chalk. Mavis bestowed a final glance on the building.

"Spotted dick, that's what it reminds me of. It might make a pub but it's a rotten looking church."

In the small flat above a row of shops, Oliver Kenny was sullen. "My departure had nothing to do with what happened. I've left my wife, that's all." And I don't blame you, mate, thought DI Andrews.

"A few questions, Mr Kenny. We won't keep you long."

"Who gave you this address?"

"Mrs Kenny remembered your college friend. We called at his repair depot. They told us."

Disillusion was writ large on Oliver's face. Andrews came straight to the point.

"Mr Kenny, your wife was having an affair with one of the men staying at the vicarage, Robert Simmons. Were you aware of this?" Colour flooded his face. Obviously he was. "What happened on Wednesday night?"

For a few seconds, Oliver debated then he said quickly, "I followed Miranda. One of the villagers had hinted she was seeing someone . . . Her behaviour to me . . . She's been very off-hand lately. Her excuse was the festival, or those damn frogs, but I knew something was up. If she was seeing anyone from the village, it was likely to be one of them.

"I followed her via the towpath to the back of the vicarage. She started chucking stones at a window. That chap—Simmons—called at her to stop. He came down and Miranda began arguing with him." Oliver's embarrassment grew. "She was throwing herself at him, it was humiliating . . . It was plain to anyone he'd had enough. He took her arm and dragged her towards the river."

"Was he attacking her?"

"No. There was a light on in one of the other rooms so Reg was probably about. I reckon Simmons wanted somewhere more private to have a row."

"Did you follow?"

"A little way. It was awful. Miranda was making a fool of herself." Andrews shrugged.

"It happens. Then what?"

"He—Simmons—spelt it out. She'd been a 'diversion', nothing more. Miranda protested. It got pretty crude," Oliver muttered, "some of the details."

"But Simmons offered no violence."

"No. Miranda did, though. She hit him hard."

"How did Simmons react?" Oliver managed a ghost of a smile.

"He ran off." He corrected himself. "At least, not ran exactly. He pushed her away, called her names, then he went back fast to the vicarage and I heard the door slam." There was a pause.

"And . . . ? Come on, Mr Kenny, let's have the rest."

"I went home. I didn't want to hear any more."

"Did you see anything else before you left?"

After a pause, Oliver said awkwardly, "The other chap,

Winstead. He came out of the church as Simmons rushed off. He stood there, watching. It was dark in the porch. Miranda was making a racket by then, yelling, she didn't see him. He nipped across the graveyard and jumped on her."

"What did you do?"

Another pause.

"Nothing."

"What?" Mather didn't hide his surprise.

"I went home. I wanted to get back before she did."

"How could you be sure you wife would get back?" asked Andrews sarcastically. Oliver clenched his fists.

"If you must know, I wasn't sure if she wasn't actually enjoying it!" There was an awkward silence. "I was debating whether to call the police—"

"Oh, really?"

"I was, yes. I was standing there, wondering what to do when Miranda arrived. She was in a state, but I was fairly certain she hadn't been raped. Her story was that someone had tried to . . . she never claimed he'd succeeded."

"And you believe that man was Winstead?" Oliver nodded.

"It couldn't have been Simmons. I told you, I saw him go. And Winstead took a leap at her, as I said. There was no one else about. The point is Miranda would insist it was a *stranger* who'd tried to, but she knew perfectly well who it must be. I know it was dark but she recognized him all right. It was one more bloody lie."

Andrews let the pause ride for a second or two then he said, "Did your wife arrive much after you?"

"About ten minutes, that's all. She was crying. Told me she'd been attacked while guarding the frogs. I gave her every chance to tell the truth. It went on for hours and hours. Finally I told her I didn't believe her—she still didn't know I'd followed her—but that's when she phoned the police. She had to by then, to back up her story."

"Was she wearing her woolly hat when she returned?"

"I don't think so. Her clothes were torn. He'd had a real go at her."

"And you didn't see Doris Leveret?"

"No. But there are masses of trees up there, anyone could have been hidden and I wouldn't have seen them. I ran back down the lane and across the green, the quickest way. I think Miranda did, too. If Doris was about then, I never noticed."

181

"What time was all this?"

"Elevenish, half past. It was midnight when Miranda got back, I remember seeing the clock."

"And the only people you saw apart from your wife were Simmons and Winstead?"

"Yes." DI Andrews watched him intently. Oliver was aware of sweat breaking out.

"Are you going to give Miranda this address?" he asked.

"Not if that was the truth."

"It was, I swear it!"

"This chap, Winstead, you say he came out of the church?"

"He stood in the doorway a moment then came into the porch."

"You saw him clearly?"

"There was a light at the far end of the church, presumably where he was working, not near the door. I could only see his silhouette but I recognized him. The two of them have been in the village once or twice."

"And you saw no one else at all?"

"Only the light at the vicarage window."

"No one else in the lane or on the green?"

"I didn't pass anyone. There might have been someone on the green—it's a big area—but I didn't see them."

"And that's the whole truth?"

"I swear it," Oliver repeated. Andrews rose.

"We shall need a new statement."

"Are you going to tell Miranda?" Andrews didn't bother to reply.

As they weaved expertly through the stream of traffic, DS Mather said, "You believe him?"

"Yep."

"Thought you had him in mind as a possible?"

"He's a worm who turned but he's still a worm. A man who can leave his wife in that situation . . ."

"You'd have thought he'd have done *something*." Mather was disgusted.

"He was thinking about it," Andrews reminded him, "but as for attacking Doris Leveret, what reason could Kenny have?"

"Maybe it was she who told him about his wife and Simmons?"

Andrews considered briefly then shook his head.

182

"Strangled the messenger, you mean? Doesn't add up, not with Kenny. He might have played rugby once but that was a long time ago. All he'd have done nowadays was stamp his foot." He picked up the car phone and called the Incident Room. "What's new?"

"Rotterdam have just faxed a report through, sir. D'you want me to read it?"

"The details. Rotterdam," he said to Mather, turning up the volume. The voice from the Incident Room sounded excited.

"We've got it all now. Simmons agreed to talk. He and Winstead had a row. Simmons admits seeing the Kenny woman on Wednesday night. Says they'd been having an affair—"

"And?"

"Claims it was Winstead who attacked her. Winstead came to his room, boasted he'd scared Mrs Kenny off for good then went back to the church to finish what he was doing. Later that night, Winstead turned up again, in a lather this time. He told Simmons he'd stumbled over the deceased beyond the grave-yard wall."

"What!"

"According to Simmons, that's what he said. Winstead swore the body hadn't been there earlier. At the time Simmons believed him. Simmons now thinks Winstead must've been the killer, doesn't know why. Can't think of a single reason in fact."

"What does Winstead say?"

"Nothing. Refuses to talk except to confirm 'roughing up' Kenny, to scare her off. Won't admit anything else."

"Not even finding the body?"

"No. Simmons claims victim already dead. Says woolly hat was where Kenny had dropped it and Winstead put it on the body. Then they shoved her in the river."

"Why?"

"To make sure she wasn't found near the church and implicate them."

"Does he actually *accuse* Winstead?"

"Not exactly. Said he heard Winstead attack Kenny after he and she had parted but left them to it—"

"Another gentleman!"

"Went back to the vicarage. When Winstead turned up the second time he was in such a tizzy Simmons believed him."

"Really."

"Simmons now says Winstead must be lying. 'His conscience won't let him rest' unquote which is why he told us."

"Especially now there's a chance of a murder rap."

"According to Rotterdam Winstead has been told but he's still refusing to talk."

"OK, I'll read the rest when we get there." Andrews hung up. "Well, well, well . . ."

Mather was puzzled. "It's odd. Simmons has always steered clear of violence before. Winstead didn't have a record."

"Unusual with their background, I agree."

"What's the motive? Deceased wouldn't have gone to them for cash, would she?"

"That alias of Simmons—R. L. McCormack, wasn't it? What did the L stand for?"

"Dunno."

"We'll check. If he's another Leonard, I reckon it wasn't the vicar she went to after all." The glow from the instrument panel illuminated Mather's frown.

"I thought you were convinced this had to be a village affair?"

Andrews yawned.

"The business with the tent made it appear so."

"Winstead didn't seem violent," Mather insisted. "I interviewed him—colourless sort of guy. Interested in painting. Admires Simmons's work, says he's a genius. If he did attack Mrs Kenny, I'd say it was to rid his friend of a problem, that's all."

"Hmm."

"Winstead might do some of his dirty work but I can't see him agreeing to strangle for him."

"Look at it this way: suppose the victim had demanded a cut of the festival proceeds? She knew the vicar would be responsible for looking after the money, perhaps that's why she gave Leveret the impression she was going to see *him*. Suppose instead she asked Simmons for cash—and Winstead objected."

"It's weak. What grounds did she have? And anyway, why kill her on Wednesday, before the festival? The logical time would have been Sunday, when she came to collect. They could've fobbed her off somehow till then." Andrews agreed it didn't make sense.

"And why stick her in the river, fish her out and dump her in the tent? Why change your mind after granddad found her, hide her up somewhere and then stick her back in the river for us to find? Assuming we're not looking for a psychopath, was Winstead capable of that particular scenario?" he asked crossly.

"No, he wasn't," Mather was positive.

"OK. We'd better go and lean on him though, Simmons as well," Andrews sighed. "Which is the quickest route to Rotterdam?"

"Fly out of Norwich, I should think."

Mr Pringle parked in his accustomed spot outside his Edwardian semi. "We've arrived." Mavis came to with a start.

"Goodness, so we have!" She gazed about in contentment. "Isn't it *nice* to be home! Oh, goodness . . ."

"What's the matter?"

"Did you leave the cloakroom window open?"

"Of course not!" His heart began to pound, he couldn't get out of the car fast enough. The front door yielded to the touch, it didn't need a key. Mr Pringle ignored the mess in the hall and raced upstairs, far too fast. Inside his study he surveyed the walls rapidly. Thank God! Oh, thank the Lord indeed. Downstairs Mavis sent up a wail. "You've been burgled!"

"It's all right," he panted, "it doesn't matter. They haven't touched the pictures." The small collection, lovingly built up over a lifetime. Late Victorian, some Edwardian, one or two pre-war, all of them northern landscapes of the Manchester school. He knew every line, each nuance of colour. His special favourite was as usual on the easel by the desk. Mr Pringle ran his finger round the rough edge of the sketching block, "It doesn't matter," he murmured again.

Downstairs, amid the wreckage in the living-room, Mavis Bignell muttered savagely, "Pictures!"

Inside the dark, squat building, moonlight was diffused by the thick glass. In the silence there came the sound of the flagstone being levered upwards. The crash as it fell backwards was muffled this time by a kneeler.

Outside, a wind made branches dip and brush against the roof. It almost concealed another noise that had begun under the thatch.

In the Incident Room caravan, Andrews and Mather collected papers and made phone calls. No one stared in at them.

185

The few street lights were out; most of Wuffinge Parva was asleep.

In the vault, a match was struck. The flame wavered then steadied as the man set down the lamp. Anxious for privacy, he tugged at the flagstone and all but closed it using the kneeler as a wedge. He could hear the thatch beginning to crackle above, but had allowed plenty of time for what he wanted to do; he set to work.

DI Andrews put down the phone. "That's everything fixed. Williams is taking over in the morning, he and Tyler will hold the fort here. We'll collect passports and overnight things and be on our way. I've warned everyone it could be an extradition job."

"Right."

"Let's go."

The straw smouldered until the fire took hold. Licks of flame snaked everywhere, consuming and spreading, heating the roof timbers until they were unable to resist and burst with a roar of cascading sparks.

Ancient oak pews had to succumb. Nothing could withstand the embrace of white-hot, all-consuming fire. The roar was deafening but the man worked on, determined to complete his task.

Two people lay wrapped around one another in supreme, satisfied contentment. "You were lively tonight," Mavis giggled. "You should have been feeling depressed."

"I was feeling deprived."

"Being in the country put me off," she admitted, "because of the animals."

"They do it as well."

"I know they do! They could've been watching, that's all."

"Mavis, we were in a bedroom on the first floor. Animals do not climb ladders."

"They might've been hiding in the thatch," she said with dignity. "Badgers peering in, all teeth and claws."

"Badgers live in setts in the ground."

"That's only what they show you on television. There could

be others that live in roofs, ones we don't know about. Up there, laughing at us."

"Badgers don't laugh."

"How do you know?" Then, to placate him, "I'm ever so sorry about the burglary . . . I'm glad you weren't too upset because of your cholesterol."

"Mavis, d'you think, just for once, we could ignore what they told me at the clinic." She sighed, mournfully.

"If you think you can afford to . . . You've not got a single piece of silver left."

"That doesn't matter. It'll mean less to pay for insurance."

"What about the television?"

"I very rarely watch."

"Fancy, fifteen burglaries in this area today, according to that policeman. Because of 'gentrification'."

"He must mean the skips blocking the pavements."

"I wonder how many robberies there used to be? Here . . ." a thought struck her. "This area must be looking up. Perhaps your house is worth more?"

"It doesn't matter, I shan't be leaving London."

"Good!" Mavis snuggled up in a most delightful way. "I could never have managed, not with all those moles and bats."

"I doubt if the moles would have been a problem, not in Wuffinge."

"No." She was complacent. "Guinevere thinks she's sold her house, did I tell you?"

"No."

"To a vegetarian author who wants to breed llamas. She's made a fortune out of a diet book. Funny, the things people pay money for." Mrs Bignell moved her shapely bulk over to her half of the bed. "Night-night . . . Got a lot of clearing up to do tomorrow." Which was enough to send Mr Pringle fast asleep.

The roaring filled his eardrums. The man had ripped off his clothes in agony at the heat. Stretched out on the mosaic pavement, he sucked in the last vestiges of oxygen. Dear God, let me lose consciousness. Let me not know what it is to be consumed! Flames came searching beneath the flagstone, greedy for more and found the great pile of dust.

"Thou knowest, Lord . . . Into thy hands . . ." It was too late for repentance; the purifying fire had taken hold.

Chapter Thirteen

"Hello, Mavis? Felicity Brown here."

"Good morning, dear. How are you? You're sounding much better."

"I am, which is surprising. I assume you've seen the news?"

"We haven't seen anything. Mr P's been burgled. They took the telly and God alone knows where the radio's got to. The place is a complete mess."

"Oh, my dear, what a home-coming!"

"So what's been happening?"

"Wuffinge Parva church burned down last night."

"Oh, goodness!" Mavis Bignell had a sudden vision of herself, sitting in the vault beside Mr Pringle, each with a candle in their hands. "Was it badly burnt?"

"It's completely destroyed. A lorry driver on the motorway raised the alarm but it was too late. The firemen are still there, sifting through the rubble. No one can find Reg. Presumably he's in London and hasn't heard."

Mavis suddenly remembered the vault.

"Oh my god!"

"Mavis? What's the matter?"

"Felicity, how far *down* is it burnt? To the ground, or what?"

"I'm not sure. After I've given Cyril his breakfast I'm off to see for myself. It'll be on the lunchtime news. Oh, you can't see that, can you."

"We'll nip round to the Bricklayers. They've got a set above the bar."

"It's incredible. The village is reeling. Attempted rape, then murder—now fire."

"Shocking," Mavis replied mechanically.

Mr Pringle had been wrongly accused of the first two but it was possible he and she were responsible for the third. She promised to ring Felicity back later and put down the phone.

In the bathroom her lover looked foolish at being caught in a sea of bubbles.

"I was taking my time this morning."

"Yes, well, you'd better hurry up. The police will be here shortly."

"What!"

"We'll both be charged this time. What's the penalty for arson?"

His heartbeat was still irregular as they sat in the bar. On screen, the commentator stood in front of smoking rubble.

"Although experts haven't yet had time to examine the site, traces of a mosaic pavement are clearly visible . . ."

There was a wobbly cut-in shot of the ash-strewn vault floor.

"No sign of Lord Wuffa's you-know-what," Mavis whispered.

"Evidence would appear to suggest a Roman bathhouse below the foundations of this ancient Saxon village . . ."

"A bathhouse!"

"Ssh!"

The picture reverted to the commentator, now wearing his serious face.

"Excitement was mixed with tragedy however for the inhabitants of Wuffinge Parva . . ."

The shot changed again: two men were carrying a covered stretcher towards an anonymous blue van.

"Charred remains were found in the wreckage, also containers of paint stripper. Enquiries are still being made for the rector of Wuffinge Parva."

In the aircraft, the stewardess recognized two passengers from the outbound flight. "Hello again. Your visit didn't take long, or did you forget something?"

"My toothbrush," said DI Andrews sourly.

Mavis's voice was unsteady as she asked, "You don't think we could have been responsible?"

"I fear it was a deliberate attempt, which went dreadfully wrong, to rid the church of the mural as well as the paintings."

"Poor man!"

"I agree . . ." Reg Terson might have been weak but surely no man deserved that fate.

"Hello, Felicity? It's Mavis. Yes, we've seen it now . . . Dreadful, yes. We're very sorry."

"It's been quite a shock."

"It must've been." But guilt had been lifted from her shoulders and Mrs Bignell was cheerful. "I forgot to ask why you were feeling better."

"It was Ted." Felicity's relief spilled out. "You remember Cyril thought he'd seen him and Len Runkle on Wednesday—well, he had. Ted knew I'd been wanting a gleditsia triacanthos for my birthday."

"Oh, yes."

"He'd asked Len to find one—Len's a gardener, you know. Ted had come back early to inspect it, but couldn't admit it without telling me the secret. By the way, there's an incredible rumour going about; the police are now saying that Doris Leveret was actually married to Reg."

The letter lay on the desk. DI Andrews contemplated the various pages.

"He married Doris Winkle in 1963. She was ten years older. It was a step up for her, of course, marrying a professional man. She hadn't worked out that vicars rarely get rich. When she came across Cyril, there wasn't a divorce. That could've prejudiced Terson's career and he still had hopes of preferment," Andrews broke off. "Any coffee left in that pot?"

"A drop," Mather tested the temperature, "not very warm."

"It'll do. Terson tried to dissuade her from returning here but she was determined. She was a village girl, in deep water by then over the trust money but probably still assumed she could count on his support. Judging by this . . ." he tapped the letter, "Terson didn't know what she'd been up to."

"She wanted a share of the festival money?"

"Terson says he was 'under pressure from all sides'. A bit further on, 'Doris insisted the paintings should be on permanent display. I knew they weren't genuine. I could not go on. They had to be destroyed.'"

"Does he say why he killed her?"

"'She came to the church late on Wednesday night and repeated her demands for money. We had a violent quarrel. I half strangled her in my anger. She lay unconscious. I wrapped the twine round her neck to stop her wickedness. I dragged her out of the church but couldn't think what to do next. I begged Winstead for help and promised him my share—'"

"Oh-ho! No wonder he wouldn't talk—he'd lied to Simmons. I don't suppose he mentioned the extra cash."

"Doesn't seem likely. 'I intend to expiate my guilt . . .' Terson rambles on a bit, something about more pictures. Seems to have had a fixation about those." DI Andrews indicated the inscription on the envelope: "'In *the event* of my death.' He half-hoped to get away with it, I reckon."

"What about the inquest?"

"The coroner doesn't intend to read all of this. Just the facts about Doris Leveret."

"There's all that business of the body disappearing from the tent."

"So?" DI Andrews was terse. "We know how she died, we've got a confession. If she went walkabout for a day, what concern is that of ours? Cyril Leveret doesn't care. We've got enough on file to keep Simmons and Winstead quiet. I shall make 'em contribute half their dosh to the Wuffinge church appeal—anonymously—to help keep their memories fresh."

"What about granddad?"

"Ah, I shall persuade him to forget. Just that brief period when he peeped in the marquee on Thursday morning. Provided he agrees, that just about wraps it up."

The theatre outing was a success but Ted Brown was edgy. In the restaurant afterwards, Mavis chivvied him about it.

"Didn't you enjoy it, dear?"

"It's not that." Felicity laid a sympathetic hand on her spouse's arm. "We're feeling fed-up because of Eddie Runkle."

"That blasted Miranda Kenny was responsible, and she doesn't even live in Wuffinge any more," Ted exploded. "She's sold up and gone to live in Droitwich, no one knows why."

"Who's bought her house?" asked Mr Pringle, mildly interested.

"Michelle Brazier." Of course. "And what's Eddie been up to?"

"See for yourself." Ted produced several photographs. "I took these for the public inquiry. Though how they'll force him to put it back the way it was, I do not know."

Number eight had been transformed. Not a trace of thatch; shiny red tiles now covered the roof. The windows had modern double-glazed PVC frames, the gutters were white plastic, the front garden had been concreted over and a painted number-plate hung from the yellow brick porch. "Bide-a-wee?" he read.

191

"That was little Elsie's contribution," Ted said savagely. Mavis couldn't fathom why he should be so upset.

"It looks much more modern. Bright."

"Very bright." His jaw was tense.

"Milton Keynes without the ambiance, perhaps?" Mr Pringle was saved by the arrival of a waiter.

"So nobody knows about that cellar," Mavis said when they were alone once more.

"All trace of it must have been destroyed. I'm sure that's what Terson intended. Everyone assumes it was the three forgeries but he wanted to obliterate Lord Wuffa's pictures as well, for all eternity."

"Quite right, too," she said piously. "No one will ever be exposed to them again. Felicity says the village is delighted with that piece of Roman pavement. They've put a shed over it and charge £1.50 a visit. They hope to build a new church out of the proceeds one day."

She asked with a slight change of tone, "D'you remember that *very* naughty bit of the mural? Over by the corner?"

"What about it?"

"I was just wondering if it was physically possible? I don't see how it could be, do you?" For one fleeting moment he thought it might have been, once, for little Elsie.

"You'd better ask if they have a manual at that shop in Tottenham Court Road."

Mrs Bignell drew herself up.

"Don't be ridiculous," she said with hauteur.